PRAISE FOR

a friend of dorothy's

"Nothing can have prepared you for the wit and insight, the eccentricity and inspiring optimism with which this consistently surprising young writer depicts a year at the heart of his generation's greatest calamity."

JOSEPH PINTAURO, author of *Cold Hands* and *Raft of the Medusa*

"There is a knowingness, a sense of timing, a compassion and forgiveness under all the action, character to character. What Richard Willett has—in abundance—is love for the people he is chronicling and, by recording, saving."

ALLAN GURGANUS, author of *The Practical Heart*, *Plays Well with Others*, and *Oldest Living Confederate Widow Tells All*

"The writing is poignant, realistic and fine; the reader is pierced and instantly seduced by the characters' appeal and immediacy."

HARLAN GREENE, author of *The German Officer's Boy*, *What the Dead Remember*, and *Why We Never Danced the Charleston*

a friend of dorothy's

a
friend
of
dorothy's

—

richard willett

THE
MAGIC
SHOW
PRESS

WEST HOLLYWOOD

First Magic Show Press edition, June 2025

The Magic Show Press
PO Box 69553
West Hollywood, CA 90069

For information on ordering, please visit magicshowpress.com.

Excerpts from *A Friend of Dorothy's* appeared in Christopher Street (That New Magazine, Inc., 1993) and *Permafrost: A Literary Journal* (University of Alaska, Fairbanks, 1994).

Library of Congress Control Number: 2025901852

ISBN 979-8-9923398-0-2 (hardcover)
ISBN 979-8-9923398-1-9 (paperback)
ISBN 979-8-9923398-2-6 (e-book)

Cover design by Laura Duffy
Book design by Karen Minster

Printed in the United States of America

For the man with red hair

foreword

I met Richard Willett, the author of the brave and deeply affecting *A Friend of Dorothy's*, online during the Covid lockdown when a handful of writers and theater people came together to discuss classic movies. It was a good tonic for the moment, and eventually Richard and I began talking about our writing. Richard is primarily a screenwriter and playwright, and I'm a prose writer who for a time wrote plays. I had written a novel, *Remember This*, that was very important to me. It had come close to publication with a major publishing house, but had fallen just short (it eventually found publication with University of Wisconsin Press), and Richard told me he'd had the same experience with his novel *A Friend of Dorothy's*. The longer you're exposed to the world of publishing the more you find this story repeating with others. I once thought if you wrote something terrific then it would find its way to a big publishing house, but I realize now that much of the very best writing may never even be seen. Because the best writing challenges the reader, and big publishing houses can only afford to take so many chances with daring work.

In talking about our novels, Richard and I found we were exploring a common time and place that had marked us both deeply, and that is New York City in the late eighties; his novel set in 1986–87, and mine in 1988. An aspect of the most meaningful times in one's life is often loss, and beneath the music in the air and the gritty beauty and thrill of that time and place was also fear, as well as a constant pulsating grief around the dead and the dying, and the disease most of them caught by way of desire.

Richard is gay, and I am straight, but there was no one marginally conscious in that city at the time who was not affected by AIDS. For one thing, though it was clearly more dangerous to be gay than straight, there was no way to know that it wasn't breaking into the straight community as well. Paranoia ran deep, and the lines of transmission blurred, especially in the arts where boundaries between people tend to be more permeable. You spent the vibrancy of your youth looking over your shoulder, questioning an encounter you had, avoiding another you might have had.

For me, as a young playwright, I watched theater heroes fall, and I flinched awaiting the next one to go. All this death broke down the infrastructure on Broadway because in art, people, more than anything, *are* its infrastructure. When they're gone they take that with them. There's no replacing a Michael Bennett, an Alvin Ailey, a Peter Allen.

I say all this as a straight male, but not a traditional straight male. In fact, I came to NYC to find my people, and more often than not I saw them on the streets, especially at Halloween. All the wild crazies, the creatives, who, like me, had never really fit in their hometown. But here, among this wild mix of people, I found my tribe and family, as well as my home.

Then they began dying. The disease shadowed everything. The examples were everywhere. And so the question became, *Then how will you love?* And *Will you love? Will you love at all?*

It was a crucible in which to test yourself. In my novel, a young man from Texas named John is in an affair with his married female supervisor, Alena, who is also a mother, while a gay coworker named Jeremy is her best friend and confidant. When John's not with her, he wanders the city at night trying to come to terms with what he is doing, the sin of it and his inability to leave it, and finds himself identifying with gays, who historically have slipped past danger and broken taboos because of how desire manifested itself in them, all so they might make contact with the beloved body. Because the heart wants what the heart wants, and whether to turn from that or not was the question of that time for all of us.

In Richard's novel, Eric, the protagonist, is in his late twenties and not fully realized as a sexually free and active gay man. There's baggage from his childhood in Canada, as well as introversion. Then there's that disease out there wiping out everyone. Again, how do you love in such a time? When Eric's flamboyant, socially successful, and sometimes abrasive friend Dale comes down with the disease, Dale keeps it a secret from his wide circle of friends but for some reason confides in Eric, who ends up taking care of him as he becomes sicker.

At this moment in time, there was not nearly enough help from the government to contain the disease (being seen as a "gay disease") or to take care of the sick and dying. An aspect of gay culture in that time that still staggers me is that in the absence of institutional support, gay men, these lovers of the body, these sexual outlaws, whom the straight protagonist in my novel found kinship with, turned from adoration of the body's perfect beauty and moved toward taking care of their dying brethren. There they willingly experienced the intimacy of the body's decay. Put another way, instead of running from death and fear, they turned toward it, like angels of mercy. Their ministrations of the body take my breath.

And so Eric goes on his journey, taking care of his friend Dale and seeing him through his disease and through his passing. Which interestingly, is never distressing or gloomy reading. It's matter-of-fact, and at times humorous when their friend Paul, who is just beginning to show symptoms, comes to help with the workload. Apparently, this is just something Paul does, even as he's getting sick himself.

And it is the generosity of this culture, presented so directly and matter-of-factly in the book, that for me is its first feat of magic. Their brothers, their friends and lovers, were dying, so they stepped up and took care of them when no one else would. I've not read anyone present this in the way Willett has.

And in the second feat of magic in the book, there's the personal journey of his protagonist, Eric, who, in his selfless ministrations with Dale, through his direct work with that body, emerges from his service, his trip through that underworld, finally complete, finally ready and able to follow the call of his heart.

I am so glad that Richard Willett did not give up on this book and that it found its way into print. I'll admit it is a little strange to find what is possibly the most critical time of my entire life relegated to a historical period, because for me it's still as present as yesterday. And yet, this time demanded so much of us who were there, broke so many, and tested and strengthened so many more. We should not forget its lessons any more than the lessons of any other war. *A Friend of Dorothy's* makes sure that we do not.

—STEVE ADAMS
Memphis, Tennessee, November 2024

———————

Steve Adams's short stories and essays have been widely published. His writing has won a Pushcart Prize and has been listed as a Notable Essay in *Best American Essays*. He's won *Glimmer Train's* Short Story Award for New Writers, been a guest artist at the University of Texas, and his plays have been produced in New York City. His debut novel, *Remember This*, was published in October 2022 by the University of Wisconsin Press.

One sees that beautiful and ultimate metaphysical truth, which has been stated by poets and physicians and metaphysicians in all ages—by Leibniz and Donne and Dante and Freud: that Eros is the oldest and strongest of the gods; that love is the *alpha* and *omega* of being; and that the work of healing, of rendering whole, is, first and last, the business of love.

—OLIVER SACKS,
Awakenings

———

Nothing unnerves me like a barroom full of fags.

—WILLIAM S. BURROUGHS,
in an interview in *The Advocate*

a
friend
of
dorothy's

chapter one

There are no women here.

This Eric thought as his eyes darted about Dale's living room and his face tightened with that glazed party look, that desperate nonchalance he faked whenever he stood alone in a room full of gay men.

He watched Dale move through the center of it all, strangely elegant in a purple Lacoste shirt and a pair of white sweatpants, the humble and dedicated host who simply hadn't had time to change into anything more complicated. He was shorter than Eric, four years older, thinner, and his close-cropped black hair had been receding for a while. But he was much better at playing the game.

He flitted merrily here and there, and wherever he landed, laughter went up, gaiety, more loud, artificial joy. What is he saying that's so goddamn witty? Eric wondered and downed half his drink. And why do I care? he thought and took another gulp.

He cared because he could never seem to become one of the laughers. And he wished to. The only thing Dale had said to him all night was his greeting at the door: "You look a little haggard. Did you walk down?"

The apartment was, as ever, in great shape. It was a small one-bedroom in a renovated tenement in the Village, an illegal sublet, but it gave the impression of something grander. The wood floors glowed, the stark white walls set off every object in the place, so that each chair, table, vase, even each piece of electronic equipment, appeared to have been chosen with exquisite care. It was an apartment in which you could crumple a piece of paper and toss it in the corner and it would seem to be a unique work of art. Eric's studio uptown gave the opposite impression: Things he believed he had chosen with great care somehow ended up resembling crumpled pieces of paper.

At the bookstore the other day, as he came up the stairs from his basement office, he noticed with pleasure that the two cashiers behind the front counter snapped to attention when they saw him. But then Dale called to him loudly from the middle of the Sixth Avenue side of the store: "Hey, Mavis! Look sharp!"

One of the cashiers hid a giggle behind her hand, and Eric turned to see Dale scurrying about one of the windows that lined that side of the store, a shiny pink tie swinging in front of him, settling now and then against the dark red paisley pattern of his shirt. Thwarting the company dress code was a personal challenge to Dale, whereas Eric had recently purchased several items to help him fulfill and go beyond the code: That day he wore his new blue suit and carried his new green trench coat, slung over his shiny burgundy briefcase, the first he'd ever owned.

"Isn't she devoon?" Dale asked as Eric approached him. He rested his chin on a copy of *Mayflower Madam*. "I'm trying to create a sort of call girl atmosphere in here." He played with a length of purple rayon. "You wouldn't happen to know any cheap tarts, would you? Present company excepted, of course."

Though it was 1986 and he was only thirty-one years old, Dale seemed determined sometimes to preserve the stereotypes of another era. Although unquestionably modern in much of his thought and behavior, he often spoke and acted like something out of *The Boys in the Band*. "Metahomo" he had called this. "I am not a stereotype. I am a comment on a stereotype."

"I'm having a party," he said now, and immediately Eric felt a thrumming in his stomach.

"You are?"

"Yes. Next weekend. And you're invited. An intimate gathering of about ninety-three people."

"What's the occasion?"

"Oh, I don't know. The leaves are changing color, how's that?"

Eric tried to smile.

"I was going to have a Halloween party," Dale went on, "but I want to go to the parade. Are you going?"

"No," Eric said.

"Why not?"

"I stay in on Halloween."

Dale stopped arranging the purple material and faced Eric for a moment. "I'll help you with your costume," he said. "You could go as something exotic—an interesting person, for example."

"Thanks."

"I'm trying to save you from yourself. At least come to my party."

"I'll see," Eric said and turned away. "I've got to go now."

"Where are you off to?"

"Oh, just home," Eric said, turning back but continuing to step away slowly.

"Do you want to come to the movies with Paul and me?"

"Um . . . no, thanks."

"Why not? What great plans do you have for the evening? Another heart-to-heart with the cat?"

"Ha, ha," Eric said flatly. "I'm just tired, OK? I just don't feel like going out."

"I don't know where you got your degree in faggotry, Loretta, but remind me to cut off their grant money."

"I'm gonna go," Eric said. "I don't know how I get into these conversations with you."

"Call me if you change your mind," Dale yelled after him.

He had tried to think of an excuse not to go to the party. But it was harder and harder to come up with them, since Dale knew his datebook was far from crowded.

And he guessed a part of him actually did want to be there, since he shuddered to think of spending another Saturday night home alone watching *The Golden Girls*. Lying on the bed in his studio apartment each weekend, chuckling with a beer in the flickering television light, he'd hear the clip-clop of busy feet, the animated night-out chatter passing his ground-floor window, as an almost taunting distraction, an acute reminder of his isolation from the rest of humanity.

His eyes moved anxiously now about Dale's living room. He tried to focus on individual men, but the crowd of about twenty kept congealing into a sea of heat and color and loudness. Why don't I just pick one of these little groupings, head over, and join in the conversation? I must have something in common with someone here.

But he knew that wasn't the problem. He wasn't standing alone in a corner, flushed and perspiring, because he had nothing in common with these men. If he'd had nothing in common with them, he'd have stayed home, not shown up and then stood there agitated like this. He was standing there in the corner because the thought of talking to any of these men meant risking . . . what? Something. Something that even for a moment completely terrified him.

If he even managed to make eye contact with any individual in the room, the other man would get a kind of alarmed expression on his face and look instantly away. What had he seen?

Eric was a little over six feet tall and at twenty-seven still had all his shaggy dark blond hair. He had been told he was good-looking often enough over the years that he could sometimes now almost believe it. And he had disciplined his body with free weights since he was seventeen and discovered that with a little willpower he could produce results that won him considerable approval. He had worked on himself physically, but at some level, despite gay men's preoccupation with surfaces, that didn't seem to be the problem. It was a more mysterious something he seemed to lack, at his core.

He began to recognize some of the faces in the room. Whenever he and Dale got together away from the store, Dale always invited at least one other person to join them, no matter what the circumstances, as if he couldn't stand to be alone with Eric for any length of time. "You don't mind if Ted comes along, do you?" he'd say. "Oh, I ran into Reg and I invited him to come with us. You don't mind, do you?"

In the warmth from another blast of vodka and tonic, Eric saw, there across the room, on Dale's giant white couch, his favorites: Jake and Tony. They'd been together for so many years he couldn't imagine Dale referring to one without the other. It was always Jake-and-Tony, Jake-and-Tony.

Tony was a beefy guy with a bushy dark mustache who, for Eric's money, was made all the more sexy by the horn-rimmed glasses he wore. Jake was much taller and thinner and blonder. The domesticity of Tony's hand on Jake's knee, a quietness about them, seemed to clash with the party atmosphere. They had been sitting there on the couch for over an hour. They didn't seek out conversation with anybody; they chatted amiably with whoever happened by.

What would it be like, Eric wondered in a near-swoon of envy, to be in an environment like this and know that whatever happened, you'd have each other?

He looked up, startled, to see that Dale's friend Ted Myer was standing next to him.

He hesitated a moment, then managed to shout, "Hi."

Ted nodded.

"How have you been?" Eric asked.

Ted may have said something then, but Eric couldn't tell. He looked away from Eric, his eyes moving about the room, his body bouncing in time to the deafening music.

Although old enough to have salt and pepper in his beard and a slight scowl between his eyes, Ted seemed ageless at the same time, in that way peculiar to gay men, in a white T-shirt, butt-hugging black jeans, and cowboy boots.

Eric prayed to think of something to say. He sensed that he was already losing Ted, that Ted was already glancing about the room for a better opportunity.

"What is it that you do?" he screamed. "I mean, for a living?"

"Huh?" Ted yelled back.

"Your job!"

Ted squinted at him. "Yeah. Right," he said and returned his gaze to the room.

Eric then tried to move a little to the music, too, but he succeeded only in splashing some of his drink on himself.

"Woops," he said in what he hoped was a carefree tone, but Ted hadn't even seen the spill.

Eric searched his mind frantically for another conversation starter. There was always Dale. He could ask Ted where he knew Dale from. Except he already knew that. They belonged to the same gay roller skating league.

"Warm night," he said finally, and turned to Ted. "On the way down here I—"

But Ted was smiling and nodding at someone on the other side of the room. "See ya," he said and bopped away.

Eric thought he might throw up. He figured he should get to the bathroom soon.

Once he got his feet going, he seemed to travel along fairly easily, even though the upper part of his body seemed to be moving at a slightly different pace and angle from the lower part. Off a stocky, dark-skinned man he nudged by, he caught a wave of cologne that lifted him suddenly, added to his slight drunkenness, the scent of longing, it seemed, the Ghost of Christmas Past.

In the bathroom at the end of the hall, he took a private breath finally. He faced the mirror and thought that he looked haggard.

If he consciously relaxed his face, it formed a more satisfying impression, but masklike, failing utterly to reflect his inner life.

He stayed as long as he could in the bathroom, but then someone pounded loudly on the door and he was returned to earth with a start.

Outside again he waded quickly into another drink, and then saw Dale closing the apartment door behind someone. And Jake towering over dark, stocky Tony, as they said their good nights. Eric got so apprehensive before going to these affairs of Dale's that he inevitably arrived quite late, and right about now, when the Absolut was beginning to free him ever so slightly, things would start to wind down.

He stood behind the group saying good night to Jake and Tony and sent them his own silent wishes. He sank down in the warmth they had left on the huge couch.

Then someone changed Dale's dance tape to Judy Garland's Carnegie Hall album, and Eric leaned his head back and let that unmistakable, heartbreaking voice wash over him.

"My God," Dale had exclaimed when he caught Eric looking for the umpteenth time at one of the many books on Garland they carried at the store, "you're a closet Judy queen!"

Judy Garland had also had scoliosis, a lateral, S-shaped curvature of the spine for which Eric had been operated on when he was fifteen. Judy's case had been less severe, but Eric's had significantly deformed his adolescent body, from side to side and back to front, and the year of treatment, involving major surgery and several months totally bedridden and in a body cast, had been designed literally to straighten him out. Which it hadn't quite done. Eric's curve was so extreme the surgeon had been unable to get a complete correction.

Other people seldom seemed to notice the problem: in the back one shoulder blade stuck out farther than the other, and in the front the opposite side of his rib cage did the same thing, as if someone had taken hold of him near his heart and twisted. Even the scars often escaped notice: a neat line hidden in the crevice between the muscles of his back, and a broader, rougher mark above one side of his butt, where hip bone had been taken to create a spinal fusion. If people noticed anything, it was how the fusion and the steel rod implanted with it often made Eric appear to be standing or sitting very stiffly. "Relax!" he was frequently told.

He opened his eyes and saw that the crowd in the room had thinned considerably.

Judy was winding down, too.

Had he fallen asleep? He leaned forward to finish his drink and realized that his head was spinning. On the massive white coffee table in front of him was a half-empty bottle of wine, and he refilled his glass from it.

"Someday I'll wish upon a star and wake up where the clouds are far behind me . . ."

It must have been well past midnight by now. At the door Dale was talking to someone Eric couldn't see. ". . . a friend of Dorothy's from way back . . . ," he said, apparently referring to Eric on the couch. "He's gonna stay all night," Dale slurred. "He's gonna sing 'em all!"

Eric's eyes drifted shut. But a moment later Dale flopped down with a whoosh next to him on the sofa.

"Well, it's over," he said with a sigh.

"Congratulations," Eric said. He lifted his empty glass in a toast.

"I'm glad you came," Dale said, and Eric almost laughed. "You're much more down to earth than the rest of my friends," Dale continued, "and I appreciate that."

"Thanks," Eric said, and passed out against Dale's shoulder.

chapter two

At the bookstore, Eric began to notice Dale closing his eyes and slumping against a bookcase or a doorjamb as if it were a bed. Or he would find him asleep on one of the hard gray-and-white slatted park benches that had been dragged in from somewhere to furnish the "staff lounge," a tiny, mouse-infested area partitioned off downstairs next to the men's room. He would happen by an hour or so later and Dale would still be lying there, sometimes asleep, sometimes with his eyes open but strangely unresponsive. He'd try to get up, but the effort would seem to exhaust him.

"Are you OK?" Eric asked a few times and then stopped, because Dale's answers were so odd, so oddly fierce and defensive. "I'm *fine*," he'd say, as if Eric were asking for the thousandth time. Or, pulling himself into a livelier stance, he'd reply, "It's nothing," when Eric hadn't suggested that it *was* anything in particular. "Oh, Wilma Worrier," Dale scolded.

He'd get a funny look on his face if he saw that Eric had been watching him—a mixture of irritation and shame that seemed contagious, because Eric would often feel ashamed for watching, for noticing.

Occasionally, on his way home from the subway on East Eighty-sixth Street, Eric passed a table where money was solicited for an AIDS organization, the name of which he never got. "Money for AIDS," a man with a clipboard would call as Eric passed. Eric had been walking by this table for a while now, and having the same response each time: a tight-lipped, eyes-averted resentment of the man with the clipboard—for bothering him with this, for assuming it had anything to do with him.

He had first heard about AIDS not in New York but in Vancouver, on vacation five years ago, in the summer of 1981, in the living room of the house in North Van where he grew up. The tiny item buried deep inside *The Province* that June morning was headlined "Gay Cancer Found in New York."

Eric had dismissed the item. The idea of extrapolating from a handful of cases a phenomenon as large as a "gay cancer" seemed undeniably the product of conservative minds bent on blaming homosexuals for everything.

As the numbers grew, so had Eric's explanations. It must be connected somehow with the bar life. It was inconceivable that just any old homosexual was susceptible. It was somehow related to lifestyle. Or as this idea formed itself in Eric's mind on more than one occasion: I must have been right all along.

Dale was out sick for three days, and when he returned to work, he at first seemed much better.

"Let it be known," he was saying as Eric came through the front door, "that I have now played Camille this season and do not expect to be asked to do it again." He dashed past Eric carrying a stack of books. "The truth is I wasn't even sick," he said. "I was just all torn up over who's going to get Baby M."

He set down the stack and Eric followed him to the Sixth Avenue side of the store, which was fronted by giant windows, at the base of which ran a narrow, defunct radiator, the only surface Dale had to work on.

Dale knelt on the floor, his feet splayed out behind him as he sorted through the books spread in front of him on the ratty orange-colored carpet. "Look," he said with a gasp and held up a copy of *Women Who Love Too Much*. "Someone has finally told your story."

"You're hilarious," Eric said, still in his overcoat and scarf, carrying a brown bag from Frank's, the deli next door.

Then he saw a small purple spot on Dale's face, a little bigger than a pimple, on his cheek, just above the bone.

"Did you get me a coffee?" Dale asked, and turned to face Eric, a fiery look in his eyes.

"I . . . uh . . . I didn't know you were going to be here."

"Well," Dale said in a persnickety tone and turned back to the books, "next time I think you really ought to check."

"What's this window anyway?"

Without turning, Dale held up a copy of the new hardcover *Men Who Hate Women and the Women Who Love Them*. "It's a 'Women Who' window."

"Well . . . ," Eric started. He wanted to say "I'm glad you're back," but he stopped. Why can't I tell him how happy I am to see him? he wondered, not for the first time. But today his reluctance had a focus. "I'll see you around," he said and headed for the stairs.

Later, in his office behind a partition at the back of the basement remainder floor, he thought, I don't think it was as purple as I'm imagining it was.

He stared at the giant squares of his calendar blotter, which had been almost entirely empty since his promotion five months ago from manager to the somewhat figurative position of district supervisor. At present, the only store in Eric's "district" was the one he was in.

After all, if the spot were red, or even a reddish purple, or a red that only looked purple in certain lighting, it was fairly easy to find another explanation for it. But purple was damning. It was hard to get around purple.

At his break time, Dale breezed through the door to Eric's office and plopped himself down in the chair across from Eric's desk, a *Vanity Fair* in his lap and his hand digging in a Frank's bag and pulling out a sandwich.

"So . . . ," he said, still looking at the magazine as he unwrapped and started in on the sandwich, "fill me in on what's been happening in your exciting life. Did the cat finally catch the ball of string?"

Eric smiled, but it seemed dark in the office all of a sudden, so much so that he actually looked up to see if another of the buzzing fluorescent tubes had flickered out.

Dale glanced up from his magazine and their eyes met for just an instant, an accident, but Eric saw for certain that despite Dale's having taken three days off, something essential hadn't healed. There was an expression in his eyes new to recent weeks, a reluctance to look at Eric, a fear, a darkness that made Eric unfriendly.

"Oh, honey," Dale remarked enigmatically to someone in the magazine. "See you at Betty Ford's, dear. I mean, *really*."

At the end of the day, Eric waited until about twenty minutes after five before he headed upstairs. Only to find Dale still there, at the top of the stairs, bundled up to leave but talking to someone on the phone behind the front counter. He clearly motioned for Eric to wait, or at least afterward, in the guilt that trailed him out the door, Eric was certain that he had. A slight raising of his hand and eyebrows. Obviously he had wanted Eric to wait. And obviously Eric hadn't. He had waved, as if he thought Dale were only signaling farewell, and more or less bolted out the door. Walking east on Forty-eighth Street, past the window behind the cash desk, he felt Dale's eyes heating up the back of his head, but he couldn't stop.

The darkness that had hung over him all day seemed now to engulf the city. He took the subway uptown in a thick mental fog that made his ears ring. At home he barely acknowledged Simone, his silver-gray tabby, and ate nothing. Still dressed, on his unmade bed, he fell into a sleep that seemed drugged, and did not wake until late the following morning.

At first he couldn't remember what had sent him to bed under such a cloud. He was preoccupied with getting to work on time. But everything had gone gray. There were too many people on the street, and Eric seemed to have allowed himself to live disastrously alienated from them all.

It suddenly seemed, as Eric stood compressed in a subway car, physically as close as it was possible to be to another human being, that you could get sick and die in New York like an insect, of no consequence. Why did I come here? he asked himself with an edge of panic as the train rattled through what seemed to be one dilapidated station after another, even the recent renovations failing to disguise the city's essential ruin. He barely knew why he was going to work or what he would do when he got there, but he made his way into the store and started down the stairs anyway.

And felt someone looking at him from over the balustrade above. Not a friendly feeling at all. He stopped and glanced up. Their eyes met, almost expressionlessly, and then Dale walked away.

Dale's lunch break came and went, and he didn't appear in Eric's office. And Eric found himself putting off his own lunch just to avoid going up on the floor. When he finally couldn't wait any longer, he put on his coat to head out, and stopped at the men's room on the way.

And there was Dale inside, turning abruptly away from the mirror as if he'd been caught at something.

"Break time?" Eric finally said.

"No," Dale replied. He reached for a piece of paper towel and wiped his dry face. "Already had my break," he said and dropped the towel into the trash can.

Eric turned to a urinal. "Did you see *Designing Women*—" he started but stopped when he heard the men's room door swing open and then shut behind Dale.

That night it rained. And, as ever, Eric found himself ill-equipped and had to stop and buy an umbrella on the street outside the store. It promptly blew apart and had to be ditched in a garbage can, so that he ended up running to the subway with his briefcase over his head. He did the same thing uptown, and as he ran, all along Eighty-sixth Street, he kept passing the same *New York Post* headline—AIDS COUPLE IN DEATH LEAP—flickering out at him from newsstand after newsstand along the crowded, rain-slicked sidewalk.

At home, he drank a couple of beers and ate a peanut butter sandwich and half a bag of potato chips. He fell asleep and dreamt of a photograph he'd seen in the newspaper as a child, a famous photograph, of a woman and her baby falling to their deaths from the collapsing balcony of a burning building. Only in Eric's dream, two men fell, arms out as if to ward off the ground, hands nearly touching in midair.

The next morning at work, as he tried to hang up his new raincoat so that the loose hook on his battered wooden clothes tree wouldn't dump it onto the floor, Grace, who had replaced him in the spring as store manager, came to the doorway of his office.

She was a heavyset woman, forty years old, who lived with her younger, thinner, blonder lover, Suzette, in the East Village. Dale and Eric had gone over there for dinner about a year ago and ended up in a fierce argument over pornography, which Dale ended by starting a food fight.

"He called in sick again," Grace said.

As she stood in the doorway, her arms stiff at her sides, Eric scanned her for any indication that she, too, was wondering about Dale's illness. But her normal military expression only cracked suddenly with raised eyebrows and the grin of a silly face, the kind you make to get out of saying something.

That was another gray day. Eric had no appetite at lunchtime, so he just went for a walk, but he felt such a terrible loneliness on the crowded street that he ducked into Frank's anyway. It was busy in there, too, fast-moving lines at both cashiers and the deli counter, and Eric scanned the shelves with a sense of wonder that he had ever been able to decide something as simple as what to have for lunch. He bought a carton of chocolate milk and went back to his office.

Off and on throughout the day, he thought of calling Dale but didn't. He told himself that the fear, the grayness, stalking him wouldn't do Dale any good; he was probably just out for a couple of days with a head cold.

But when he got home that night, there was a message from Dale on his answering machine.

"Hi," it said. "Could you possibly come down here for a bit? I can't get ahold of anybody and I'm really sick."

Can't get ahold of anybody? How was it possible that *Dale* couldn't get ahold of anybody?

Eric tried calling him back, but he just got his machine. He stood there in his raincoat, scarf, and one glove, listening to the no-frills outgoing message Dale had made months before.

"This is Dale Corcoran," it said. "You know what to do."

chapter three

On his way to Toronto the following week, Eric noticed again how much better he was treated on airplanes when he wore a suit and carried a briefcase, even though the company never paid for business class.

When had he first begun to enjoy so much, to *need*, moments like this, when for an instant he managed to win even dubious favor in the world?

At home, the night before, on his third beer, the TV commercials had begun to seem particularly strange. When had businesspeople become appropriate subjects for their own commercials? So many products these days seemed to be sold by the president of the company, looking fairly boring and businesslike, photographed with a hand-held camera and flickering for some reason between color and black-and-white. Or else a group of people Eric's age, also photographed hand-held and flickering, and speaking in a manner Eric called "casualeze," a pretentious tone apparently intended to sound lifelike but in fact gratingly artificial, would go on about their new wine or their car or their latest charge card.

Who were these people? Did they exist, outside of some advertising executive's imagination? Were they the people Eric saw every day on the subway? Each morning he watched his contemporaries crowd the train, dashing from their early morning gym routines, cramming on the *Wall Street Journal* as they hung competently from the subway straps, briefcases nestled between their calves, seething with an apparent faith in their own indestructibility, pursuing their careers with an intensity that suggested this could keep mortality at bay. How, Eric wondered, had he managed to evolve so differently, to arrive at the same age with drastically different furniture, little knowledge of wine, and no idea who or what Drexel-Burnham was?

He knew these people, yuppies, were supposed to be obnoxious, easily dismissed, but he envied the clarity of their delusions. The bookstore was hardly on a par with the insider trading set, but it was the only status Eric had been offered.

From Lester B. Pearson Airport in Toronto, he took a cab directly to the Colophon Bookshops Head Office in Agincourt, an industrial suburb just outside the city.

The squat, aluminum-sided building that housed the head office and abutted the company's main warehouse was interchangeable with the other bland buildings spread out around it. A cloudy sky cast a dull light over the whole area, and enveloped everything in an unearthly silence. Eric paid the driver, remembering to scale down his tip to a Canadian level, and made his way up the walk, past the drab shrubbery to the glassed-in entrance.

At Head Office he dealt mostly with a woman slightly older than him named Jane Frost, whose official title was vice president in charge of sales. She was an energetic sort who strode through life as if she were always just coming from a brisk run, dressed in corporate styles that seemed barely to hold her in, even though she was not at all overweight.

Eric knew that because of his Canadian background Jane was more comfortable with him than with any of the other New York employees. But he had to be careful not to suggest this around her, or any of the other Head Office people. Just as he had to be careful not to go on about how *clean* Toronto was, how *safe* he felt in the subways, how *nice* the people were. Torontonians did not wish to be thought of this way. They might have trouble admitting it, but most aspired to New York standards—the dirty, hard edge of a *real* city—an aspiration Eric had once understood completely.

He and Jane generally went for lunch at a local restaurant that reminded Eric of places back home in Vancouver: bright and shiny new, with ferns hanging everywhere and a menu that included a French dip sandwich. The waiters were friendly and spoke with that unmistakable Canadian inflection, the sound of an almost peculiar politeness, which Eric noticed increasingly the longer he lived outside the country. Jane spoke that way, too, and this, plus a couple of glasses of wine, would make Eric surrender to her more than he'd planned to.

No one at Head Office ever listened to him anyway. All they wanted to hear about was the results of his store reports, which they orchestrated from the get-go to satisfy their own peculiar concerns. Was there a sale banner on the top book of each stack of remainders? Were books displayed in symmetrical pyramids as demonstrated in the manual? Was every employee wearing a name badge?

As he entered the vast reception area at Head Office and took his first breath of that familiar canned air, Eric recalled that when he'd last checked, Dale was wearing a name badge, but his read "Neely O'Hara."

It was early evening by the time he got into the city, and as he walked under the cover of Yonge Street's neon, he noticed again what an eerie quiet the nighttime streets of Toronto had about them, as if the city were in a perpetual state of abandonment, its inhabitants never quite inspired to come out and make full use of it.

Not unlike how Eric felt about his own life.

But had he always felt this way?

Checked into his hotel, he put three bottles of Labatt's Blue in cold water in the bathroom sink, opened one, and leaned against the window.

He had first seen Toronto on his way from Vancouver to New York in 1978. When he was eighteen and starting college, he had moved from suburban North Vancouver to the West End, the chicest, gayest part of the city, but he had yearned then for even more of the itch and spark of genuine city life. If you're stuck in Canada, he'd thought restlessly, in this forever frustrating, half-baked imitation of Britain and the United States, the only possible place to be is Toronto. But then, with his American birth certificate, he wasn't stuck in Canada, and so didn't need Toronto.

He swung away from the window and fell back on the bouncy bed, a little drunk already. He had left Canada at the age of nineteen, and he thought maybe it was this, this reminder of being that age again, that had made the Canadian men at the airport that day, especially the men around nineteen, seem so incredibly sexy. He'd noticed them as soon as he was off the plane, the boys in their ski clothes and their fresh-faced Canadian reserve, and been filled with such yearning he'd ended up in a men's room stall, not sure whether to jerk off or weep.

The whole country seemed suddenly to have become his hometown. The place he had fled in such a hurry eight years ago now seemed so much cleaner, newer, more stable than the life he'd found. Even the Colophon Bookshops were part of this, and there was one you practically walked right into when you got off the plane, so incredibly shiny and bright compared to that dank, deteriorating wreck of a place in the middle of the Manhattan jungle.

When he'd first moved to New York, he'd prided himself on learning to deal with the extremes of the city. But recently he'd found himself experiencing the little Colophon touches in the store—the logo letter C on everything; the French on all the Head Office-generated forms; the section sign that read "Humour"—as encoded messages from the free, sane world to agents deep in the abyss.

Climbing out of the Christopher Street subway station on the way to Dale's apartment the week before, he had recalled sitting on the same corner of Sheridan Square late one night in 1979 with a tall, athletic schoolteacher from New Jersey he'd met at Ty's.

They'd been headed to Eric's apartment uptown, but Eric was too drunk to walk and asked that they sit a bit on the curb, watch the crowd go by. Then, later, a little steadier, in the subway station, he'd said one of those foolish things he was always saying in situations like that. The schoolteacher had mentioned something about having to be at work early the next day, that Eric's apartment was sort of out of the way but he figured it would be worth the trip, and Eric said, without even thinking, that he would make sure he got him up on time in the morning. The schoolteacher laughed then and, in a deep voice dripping with condescension, said that he would not be staying the night, as if it were the height of ludicrous sentimentality that Eric had thought this could be anything but a trick.

It seemed that it had also been Ty's where Eric met another tall man, a bearded photographer who took pictures for Broadway shows.

He asked Eric to have dinner with him when they left the bar. He said he didn't like the idea of just tricking. He wanted them to spend some time getting to know each other. They ate at Pennyfeather's and spent most of the time talking about how disenchanted they were with the bar scene and with trying to meet people that way. Then they went back to the photographer's apartment, a luxurious converted loft in Soho. There were giant copies of some of his photographs on the walls of the spacious living room, which also had large windows, and a view downtown from the tenth floor.

There had been many other men. Eric remembered these two at random. He could have spun the dial and another couple would have popped up.

He fucked the tall, bearded photographer on his enormous bed. The man ran his hands over Eric's chest and arms and said, "I love your body," but when he reached to turn on the light, Eric stopped him and said, "I like it better this way."

He could fuck the man but he couldn't come. He could bring the other man to orgasm, but not himself, unless he used his own hand.

He had had this problem for so long, he hardly thought of it as a problem anymore. He enjoyed the companionship of sex, and he assumed that one day he would get into a steady relationship and learn to relax more.

But a coldness had set in slowly, and he had now been completely celibate for four years.

So when he looked at those nineteen-year-old Canadian boys in the airport, what he longed for was not so much something he had ever known, but a time in his life when he still hoped to find it, when he had not yet begun to give up.

When Dale opened the door to his apartment, he had looked like a ghost. "I keep—" he started and then put a hand to his mouth and ran down the hall to the bathroom.

Eric shut the door and followed him. Dale knelt on the tile floor with his head resting against the rim of the toilet. "I'm sorry," he said.

"Don't do that," Eric said and got down to guide his head back from the toilet, but Dale began to vomit again.

Eric knelt beside him but then wasn't sure what to do. He had never heard anyone make sounds like the ones Dale was making. And he found himself fiercely preoccupied by what seemed inappropriate: protecting his new raincoat, for example, which rustled down onto the bathroom floor with him.

Then, kneeling there, as Dale convulsed and brought nothing up, Eric couldn't believe what he noticed; this whole day had moved by so much like a nightmare: There, at the back of Dale's neck, just below the hairline, riding up and down behind the collar of his pink polo shirt, was another purple spot.

When Dale seemed to have finished, Eric helped him to his feet. He looked around for a washcloth and found one hanging by the sink. Holding Dale upright with one arm around his back, Eric tried with his other hand to moisten the cloth with warm water and then wipe Dale's face. As he did so, water dripped down the front of his coat and onto the shiny shoes he'd worn the first time only a week ago, so proudly he'd believed they could solve life problems.

He walked Dale slowly across the hall to the bedroom. The bed wasn't turned down, so Eric guided him to lie on it and then asked where he kept blankets. Dale pointed weakly to a closet in the hall. Eric opened it and took a dark blue wool blanket down off a neat stack on the top shelf. He covered Dale with it.

"What happened?" he asked. "You weren't this sick the other day."

"Chemo," Dale mumbled. "This is normal."

"Oh."

"They found it inside."

"What?"

"I have lesions inside me."

A bad smell hung in the air.

"You can go now," Dale said, drifting near sleep.

"I'll wait a bit longer," Eric said.

In the bathroom, he flushed the toilet and rinsed out the washcloth. Soaping up his hands in the sink, he stopped and looked into the mirror, lit from above by a row of bright movie-star bulbs. Watermarks splotched his trench coat. "You'll never be rid of it now," a voice seemed to say.

He went back to the bedroom. Dale had thrown off the blanket and lay asleep on his side, his mouth open, his hand curled against his chest.

Eric brought the blanket up over his shoulders.

He let go of it and stood back. He almost reached to brush the hair back from Dale's forehead but he stopped.

He could not believe he was being asked to take care of another person this way. He couldn't even manage to take care of himself.

Dale had so many friends to choose from. Whereas he himself was practically Eric's only friend, and their association had always seemed more or less accidental. Some combination of Dale's personality and the fact of their working together every day had allowed him to penetrate Eric's shield. But how did that qualify Eric for this kind of care, this kind of intimacy, he who sometimes had trouble leaving his apartment in the morning?

Dale would just have to find someone else, Eric had thought, standing there at the side of the bed watching him breathe. That was all there was to it.

chapter four

"Excuse me," Eric said, but the grim, middle-aged woman didn't seem to hear him. He pushed the glass partition open a little farther, and she shot him a look. "Sorry," he said. He motioned to Dale. "He has to go to the Oncology Department," Eric said. "He was there last week, but he can't remember how he got there."

The woman pointed upward with her index finger. "Third floor," she barked and went back to work.

The building was old and smelled everywhere of cleaning fluid. "What is Oncology anyway?" Eric asked as they walked toward the elevator.

"Cancer," Dale said.

When they got upstairs, they turned the wrong way and ended up almost colliding with an orderly pushing a cartload of bedpans. He had no idea where the Oncology Department was, but they began to assume it must be the other way and turned around.

When they finally found it, the nurse motioned for Eric to sit in a small waiting area and then walked Dale down a hallway.

Eric figured the nurse assumed he was Dale's lover, and he found that this irritated him in a strange way. In the drab waiting room, lit by the same fluorescent fixtures that cast an uneven, dirty light on the entire hospital, he sensed panic bubbling up inside him, like the feeling he used to get late at night in the bars, when he'd given in and hooked himself up with someone less than perfectly desirable and then discovered, just as he was about to leave, that some really hot guy was giving him the eye.

"It's the same regimen," Dale said as they took the elevator back down. "But if I'm lucky, I won't have any problems this time."

Within a few seconds of entering the apartment, however, he was at the toilet again. Eric followed him down the hall, but Dale waved him away. Eric paced then, listening to the incredible noise Dale was making and walking in circles, through the living room, the kitchen, the dining area. Finally he heard the toilet flush and experienced a peculiar rush of relief at the sound.

Dale staggered across the hall to the bedroom. "I'm just going to lie down for a bit," he said and seemed to fall face-first onto the bed.

Eric went to the closet again for the blue blanket and draped it over Dale. "This seems worse than the . . . ," he started.

"I know, I know," Dale said. "But if it helps . . ."

Eric stood for a moment at the side of the bed, and then when it seemed that Dale was going to sleep, he turned to go.

"Oh no," Dale said.

"What?"

"I have to shit now, too."

He shuffled back across the hall, and Eric heard him moaning and cursing on the john. Finally, he flushed the toilet and came out.

"Diarrhea," he mumbled as he moved back across the hall to the bed. "They get ya comin' and goin'."

For about an hour, he went back and forth to the bathroom, staggering a bit more each time, declining any assistance Eric offered. Eventually he stopped bringing anything up or out and just went through the body-wracking motions of each symptom with no real result. "All talk, no action," he muttered as he headed back to bed. Finally, this, too, subsided, and Eric heard no sound from that end of the hall.

A flash of fear went through him then, and he headed for the bedroom, feeling perversely like a parent with a newborn baby. Dale was asleep.

Back in the living room, Eric leaned against the window and looked down on Christopher Street, his shirtsleeves rolled up, his tie loosened, his hands in the pockets of his dark suit pants.

He remembered nights years ago when this street had resembled something out of a Bacchanalian dream. Now a young woman in a business suit and sneakers and socks over stockings hailed a cab with a briefcase, and four adolescent black men chased each other the opposite way, laughing raucously, their open down jackets bobbing behind them.

Eric turned from the window and sat, then lay back on Dale's couch. He closed his eyes and heard a man's voice calling from Christopher.

"Bert!" the man cried, as if to a disobedient dog, but with the sadness, the panic, of a deeper loss. "Bert... Bert..."

"It must have been Jay," Dale said. They were standing under the flags of the world above the skating rink in Rockefeller Center, tinny Christmas music echoing about them, and Dale bounced a little, holding his red mittened hands against the railing. "I've been practicing safe sex since it was invented," he said. "I'm the queen of safe sex."

"Then how could Jay have given it to you?" Eric asked.

Dale sighed. "He's just more likely to have come in contact with it, that's all."

"Did you tell him about it?"

"Of course I did. What kind of a person do you think I am? You have to tell everybody. From the sublime to the ridiculous."

But how far back do you have to go? Eric thought but didn't say.

"Has Jay been tested?" he asked.

"He claims he's negative," Dale said. "But he'd say anything to get into that boy's pants. People are very selective about this thing, I find. What they tell. What they remember."

For a moment they watched the skaters. Then Dale glanced at Eric, who continued to watch. "You should have that coat altered," he said.

"Huh?"

"It doesn't hang right on you."

Eric blanched. A familiar whirlwind of discouragement passed through him. He looked askance at Dale, as if he might explain how or why he could so skillfully make Eric feel this way.

But Dale had returned to a topic he'd brought up earlier. "The chemicals do not actually affect the digestion in any way," he said. "They just trigger something in the brain that says 'poison,' and the body reacts accordingly."

The disease itself is like a memory, Eric thought the next morning as he stared into the lukewarm residue at the bottom of his coffee cup.

Jane Frost had resumed her Canadian mission near the front of the store, bobbing up and down behind the New Release sections, the store so empty at that hour that Eric could actually hear the squeak of her slippers and the swish of her slacks all the way at the back. He couldn't hear the comments she was making into her hand-held tape recorder, but he figured that was just as well.

He looked down and saw fanned out on the counter before him the replacement section signs Jane had brought down from Toronto. As ever, Head Office had failed to include certain sections, such as Black Studies, but had managed to send signs for others that had never existed in the New York store, such as Back to the Land. "What the hell *is* the Back to the Land section?" Grace had asked when the signs kept appearing.

"I'm just going to go to the washroom," Jane said and headed toward the stairs. She looked downright rustic this trip in a bulky green cable knit and black slacks, her tiny black ballet slippers having replaced knee-high fleece-trimmed suede boots left downstairs in Eric's office.

Eric watched the growing light on the pin-striped towers of Rockefeller Center across the street. He remembered looking up from dusting a bottom shelf his first year in the city and feeling oddly anchored despite the dizziness the towers produced, anchored in the Canadian domesticity of the bookstore, focused on a dust bunny while a god the size of Exxon hovered overhead. Now the towers were such a familiar background Eric barely saw them.

A harsh memory. The disease was like a recollection of something that made you wince.

Eric didn't associate it with his life in Vancouver, even the two years he had lived on his own in the West End. It had grown in New York, it seemed, in the late seventies; it had incubated in the filth that had so amazed him when he first came to the city. Even bars that were considered "nice" by New York standards were dingy former speakeasies with sawdust on the floor, and the men who went there might also frequent darker places, like the Mineshaft or the Anvil, where the dirt wasn't incidental, it was the whole show.

Eric had buried memories for so long that as they bubbled back into consciousness, they shocked him, chilled him sometimes, and then just as suddenly filled him with the nostalgia of an old man. Watching Jane circle a pyramid with a critical eye at the front of the store, he wanted suddenly, desperately, to know how this gulf had come to separate him from her, how he had come to be the American, clawing for life in the infested city.

chapter five

The first man Eric slept with was from Moose Jaw, Saskatchewan. His name was Ken Dawson, and he did volunteer work for SEARCH, one of Vancouver's first gay organizations, the acronym standing for the Society for Education, Action, Research, and Counseling on Homosexuality.

Eric was eighteen and it was 1977. He had just begun his first year of university and was living on his own in an L-shaped bachelor suite in a postwar low-rise called, for some reason, the Garth. The building was on Barclay Street in the West End, a neighborhood of tree-lined streets couched between Stanley Park and English Bay. Eric's parents had lived in the West End, on Haro Street, in the forties, when they were first married, but by the late seventies the area had become known for its gay residents and the building they'd lived in was part of a landmark preservation project.

It was not the first time Eric had called SEARCH. In the past, though, late at night in the basement rec room of the family home in North Van, in a surge of inspiration, having just watched Geraldo Rivera go "live to an actual gay bar!" or listened yet again to Rod Stewart's groundbreaking ballad "The Killing of Georgie" or spotted the tiny SEARCH ad in the pages of the underground *Georgia Straight* newspaper his brother Jerry bought regularly, he'd always hung up if anyone answered. Often, he'd gotten a machine, and called back to listen to the taped greeting over and over again, in amazement that this was a gay voice he was hearing, that somehow, somewhere, at the other end of the line there existed a world where a man openly avowing these feelings could sit before a telephone answering machine and speak.

His parents had not resisted his decision to move to an apartment downtown. They did not resist much that Eric did. He had not told them that he was gay, but he suspected that it would not be a big problem for them if and when he did.

He had been born in Los Angeles, but his family had moved from there when he was two years old. His father had worked for years as a journalist in Hollywood, interviewing the likes of Marilyn Monroe and Elizabeth Taylor and Marlon Brando, but a number of his steady magazine markets had dried up around the time of Eric's birth, and he and Eric's mother had decided to move the family back to Canada, where they had both been born and raised. Eric's father went to work for scenic *Beautiful B.C.* magazine and eventually became head of their Vancouver office, a job he had retired from just two years ago.

Once back in Canada, Eric's parents seemed to work overtime to try to convince him and everybody else that the move north had been for the best all round. They sang the praises of their home country to such an extent, in fact, especially to friends from down south, that Eric often wondered how they had managed to survive their twelve years in La La Land.

As the youngest of three children, he was the only one with no memory of California, of this time when it seemed obvious to him that his father had done this terribly exciting thing: toiled day after day in an office in the garage off the house in Mar Vista, pounding out movie star profiles, between trips to the studios, the stars' homes, world premieres! And as a child Eric had never understood why anyone would give up such a thing, trade it in for the anonymity of green Vancouver. But "Smell that air!" his parents cried.

And yet the stories his father most loved to tell were the stories about Hollywood. And he told them often, the same ones over and over again, even if, as had become more and more common in recent years, he was begged to stop. He told these stories compulsively, with the gleam of showmanship in his eyes, lost to the story, unaware of anything else in the world. The house could have caught fire, it might have taken a moment to convince Eric's father he had to stop. And newcomers to the household were generally enthralled. It wasn't everybody in North Vancouver who had been told by Marilyn Monroe he was the kind of man she ought to have married, who'd feuded with Natalie Wood, or held Jeanne Crain while she wept against his shoulder.

He had saved Eric's mother's life, or so the story went. She had come of age under the unbalanced thumb of Eric's grandmother, who had herself been viciously abused by her mother. Eric's mother was the only child of her mother's second marriage, to the Danish immigrant farmer for whom she had been a housekeeper following the death of her first husband. Several years separated Eric's mother from her stepsisters, and it was she, Lara, who was expected to care for her parents, particularly her mother, in old age.

Lara's genes, however, had other plans. By the time she was eighteen, the blond good looks she had inherited from her father's side of the family had blossomed, enough to catch the eye of a hotshot Vancouver radio announcer destined for Hollywood.

Eric's father introduced her to sex prior to their marriage, and this, and the love it represented, pulled her away from her mother, freed her, but also made her give up thoughts of a nursing career and marry before she was twenty. She had been sheltered, hidden from the world in many ways, and despite her beauty, was vastly inexperienced, naïve, and insecure. Two years into marriage and pregnant with her first child, she was not entirely sure where the baby had come from or how she would give birth to it, and was too shy to ask.

Though Eric's grandmother lost the battle, in many ways she won the war, for she and her husband proceeded to follow Eric's parents about, buying or renting a home a few blocks away from them whenever they moved, even taking out American citizenship and trailing them to Los Angeles. And his grandmother's mental stability grew more fragile as the years went by. He had many fond memories of her from his early childhood, but by the time he was ten or eleven, things were winding down in a spiral that would color all their lives until her death: phone calls in the middle of the night to say she was dressed and ready to go grocery shopping, where was everybody; more hostile calls in which she threatened to jump off her balcony, or go "stick her head in the river" (there was no river); bizarre accusations that reduced Eric's mother to a hand-shaking, tight-mouthed anxiety that would bring on a mild stroke before she was fifty.

The thing that had saved her from living at even closer quarters to this was love, or more specifically sex, since her mother would have claimed to love her. So sex was always spoken of highly in the Summerfield home, along with the idea of giving children their freedom.

When he was still a small child, Eric's mother and father, in their late forties then, were very much impacted by the 1960s, an experience that so infiltrated the family life—from the intense, somewhat arbitrary rebellion of Eric's two older brothers, to the sexually explicit literature dotting the living room bookshelves and the "anything goes" tolerance Eric's parents had for mood-altering substances—that it was years before he realized how temporary in a wider cultural sense the whole thing had actually been.

He sought to set himself apart from all of it. The vicissitudes of the sixties only further undermined his hope that the Summerfields would one day blossom into the kind of family he wanted them to be—the kind of upper middle-class family the children he went to school with had.

At the age of nine he had been put in a special program called Major Works, which was supposedly for children of above-average intelligence, but which had recruited a disproportionate number of kids from the neighborhoods north of Queens Road, where money not brains was the major influence. These classmates of Eric's had homes with living rooms like museums, which they were never allowed into, and mothers who wore a different outfit every time you saw them and enrolled their children in a seemingly endless parade of healthy activities. The program itself was located at the same school Eric had been attending all along in his middle-class neighborhood, but he was one of only a handful of Major Work kids who lived nearby.

"My only regret about the program," one of the other mothers remarked to Mrs. Summerfield once, as the children boarded the bus for a field trip to Victoria, "is that Alistair may be associating a bit too much, you know, with children from around here."

"Well," Eric's mother replied acerbically, "that's not a big concern for me with Eric, you see, because we live around here."

The crucial difference between Eric and his mother, his father, his whole family, was that he would not have said this to Alistair's mother; he might even have said, "Oh, I know. I worry about that, too."

He watched his brothers, Ralph, the eldest, and Jerry, three years older than Eric, weather the storms of adolescent drinking, dating, drugs. Ralph was almost kicked out of high school for refusing to shave off a beard and spent long summer months wandering the U.S. and Canada with a backpack and no money; Jerry stole liquor from their parents and threw parties in the basement with music so loud Eric's mother and father had to scream at each other across the living room upstairs. ("You want another glass of wine?!!" "What?!!")

By the time Eric turned thirteen, his parents themselves seemed lost in a second adolescence. Following the death of Eric's grand-mother, Eric's mother blossomed in a way that made her often seem girlish, and that seemed undeniably connected with the knocking of the headboard Eric heard against the wall of his bedroom on a regular basis now, the mattress straining, the panting that built to a crescendo and then a lull, followed by his father trundling to the bathroom.

This chaos Eric perceived engulfing his family would not be his way, he vowed; he would build a different sort of life for himself.

But he seemed to lack the skills to pull it off. And no one in his family seemed aware of what he needed or to have any clue how to provide it. His first year in the Major Work program he withdrew so far into himself that no one knew what to make of him—the kids or the teacher, who told his parents she didn't want him in the pro-gram. In a toggle-buttoned duffel coat done up to his chin, his hands clasped behind his back, he paced the schoolyard in a hypnotic cir-cuit, imagining himself to be a small train, headed somewhere.

Later, when he looked back on the first two years of high school, it would seem to him that he had moved through them in a drugged state. He refused to respond to any of it, which later did not seem to have been the best strategy. He felt even then that the hatred was beneath him, and that to fight back would be to dignify it in some way. And he was also very disoriented by it and fearful of further humiliating himself if he engaged with it in any way.

Boys, girls—it spread through his whole grade and beyond; even the walls seemed to whisper: "Fag."

He came home one day after having been attacked on the way from school and sat in a kind of trance making tapes of songs off the radio on the stereo system his parents had just acquired. He didn't hear any songs he particularly wanted copies of, but he pretended he had, taped them anyway, and said to himself, "Yes, I have found something I want. This is exciting. I am happy."

In the cafeteria, as he began to eat the cheeseburger he had just purchased, a boy a couple grades above him suddenly jumped from his seat, pointed a finger at him, and roared with laughter, so loud and exaggerated that everyone turned to look.

A girl threw a large rock at him as he left the school, just missing his blond head. "Hey, you," she called as her girlfriends giggled next to her. "You're ugly, did you know that?"

He evolved a theory that the reason they made fun of him was that he washed his hair too often, and so he stopped washing it altogether. The only thing he ate in any quantity was chocolate chip cookies, and he lost a lot of weight. His arms were sticks and his eyes bore a haunted look, but even years later, looking at photographs, no one in his family seemed able to notice this.

Or that one shoulder was dropping down, and the rib cage pushing forward, a hip tilting, silently.

chapter six

The first night Dale spent in the hospital, Eric couldn't sleep. It was one of the first warm nights of spring, and he took a long walk by the East River, back and forth along the promenade behind Carl Schurz Park and then farther south, next to the FDR Drive, where only a few feet separated him from the dark water on one side and the oncoming rush of traffic on the other.

In bed again he felt a vague sexual energy hovering about but no will to do anything about it. He closed his eyes and wrapped his arms around a pillow. He's so thin, he thought. He was so much smaller than me to begin with, but now he's so thin.

In the morning, when he arrived at the hospital, he was surprised to see a tall green tank next to Dale's bed and a mask strapped to his face. He was unconscious.

Eric went back to the nurse's station to ask someone what was going on, but there was no one there. He was finally able to stop a nurse around the corner in the hallway.

"I understood that this was a fairly simple procedure," he said.

"Are you a relative?" she asked.

"No," Eric said. "Dr. Morris said I could come."

"Because regular visiting hours aren't until two o'clock, and only—"

"That's not the point. I want to know why there's an oxygen tank next to his bed."

"Well, it's normal for there to be a certain amount of trouble breathing after a procedure of this nature."

But Dale seemed to be having quite a bit of trouble breathing. And the nurse had the distracted air of a sales clerk fudging answers about a product she wasn't familiar with.

Even though he was still asleep, Dale kept coughing and pressing a hand against the mask to breathe. Dr. Morris was supposed to be coming by soon, so Eric squeaked a green Leatherette chair over to Dale's corner and sat to wait. There were three other beds in the room, all occupied; when Eric first got there, he had almost walked past Dale next to the door. He's already surrendering his identity to this place, Eric thought, blending with the sheets.

He had finally completed the chemotherapy; his lesions, only one of which, on his cheek, was visible, had been officially declared "stable," and he had managed to make it through the whole process without losing his hair, when this trouble with his lungs started.

When she arrived, Eric was prepared to confront Dr. Morris as to why the bronchoscopy had been so falsely advertised, but the doctor's words soon eclipsed his plans.

"Your friend has pneumocystis," she said.

During the chemotherapy, Dale had given Eric a set of keys to the apartment, but it still felt odd for him to be there without Dale. He had never used the keys before; they were just in case of emergency.

Walking a deserted Christopher Street under a dull afternoon sky, letting himself into Dale's building and trudging up four creaking flights of the narrow staircase and around the corner onto the landing, Eric tried to imagine that he lived there, in the zany Village, tamed now in daytime, and what his life would be like if he did. But he kept coming to the same raw conclusion: He'd be sick.

Dr. Morris had said she would keep Dale in the hospital for at least a week, possibly longer. They were going to intravenously give him a drug called pentamidine, which she said was used a lot, and successfully, in treating PCP.

Eric hesitated inside the apartment. Why, he wondered, are places you don't think you belong in always quieter than others? And what is that unique scent each home creates about itself?

He found a small overnight bag in the bedroom closet and took it into the bathroom. He was not really sure what Dale would need for this longer stay.

There were a number of cologne and aftershave bottles behind the sliding mirrored doors of the medicine cabinet and arranged on the back of the toilet with a bowl of little round soaps and a couple of sprigs of something in a tiny ceramic vase. There were many prescription pill bottles in the cabinet, some dating back several years, for ailments with unfamiliar Latin names, problems Eric hadn't even known Dale had had.

He always found it odd to see different brands of the commonplace things; he got so used to seeing the same familiar packaging every morning, every evening, he figured everybody's soap or toothpaste looked like that. Standing there before the neatly packed, narrow glass shelves of Dale's medicine cabinet, he was reminded of the feeling he used to get tricking in a stranger's apartment, that unpredictable, arbitrary glimpse into the way another person lived.

He threw shaving cream and disposable razors into the bag, one of the cologne bottles, and some extra deodorant, then turned and found himself face-to-face with a naked man pinned to the wall behind him, smiling coyly above a massive chest.

He pulled some clothes from the bedroom closet to put in a duffel bag he'd opened on the bed, which was still unmade, Dale's blue blanket strewn across it.

He had no idea what clothes to bring either. It didn't look like Dale was going to be posing for any magazine covers for a while. Eric found himself staring at a large closet full of the clothes he'd envied Dale for, because Dale had always known what to wear.

On one of the shelves along the side wall of the closet there was a blue glazed bowl that Dale had filled with buttons he'd collected over the years—"How Dare You Presume I'm Straight," "So Many Men, So Little Time," "We Are Your Children."

Eric added what seemed like too much underwear to the duffel bag and then went back to the living room, where his eye was caught by the collection of magazines fanned out expertly on Dale's giant white coffee table—*Christopher Street* and *Advocate Men*—alongside a big gift book on movie poster art. He realized then that the feeling of discovery came not just from a glimpse into another person's life, but specifically a glimpse into another gay man's life. He had a flash of remembering the miracle of it: someone like me.

But no. Never really.

For days, under the influence of pentamidine, Dale slept. After work Eric sat next to the bed, in what Dale had often called his "office drag," his raincoat folded in his lap and his briefcase on the floor beside him.

"You're so loyal," a woman visiting the man across the room said. But Eric believed he got too much credit for things other people were just too busy to do.

Dale perspired heavily and struggled sometimes with the sheets and covers, twisting back and forth without waking. His skin was stretched tighter on his bones now and had turned a grayish color, accentuated by beard stubble; his breathing was wheezy and ragged, broken by coughing fits. His free hand curled around the oxygen mask, which was no longer strapped to his face but rested now on his chest when he wasn't using it.

Eric tried speaking to him, even though Dr. Morris had said he should be allowed to sleep. But if he managed even to rouse Dale to consciousness, he'd just mutter some gibberish, with his eyes still closed, maybe reach for the oxygen mask, and then go off again.

How did I get into this? Eric kept thinking, because it seemed like just yesterday that he had been resisting the whole concept.

He thought of calling some of Dale's other friends, but not only did he not know any of their phone numbers, he also knew that Dale wouldn't want him to call anybody. He had been compartmentalizing people recently—those he wanted around him when he was well, and those he wanted around him when he was sick (or the one he wanted around him)—and Eric felt a need to respect that. Besides, the thought of talking to any of Dale's friends, let alone filling the room with them, unnerved Eric more than what he was doing now.

Why me, though? he thought, and didn't know whether to be flattered or pissed off. Mostly what he felt was fear. He was afraid not only for Dale but for himself. He feared the censure of those people, those friends of Dale's who hadn't been consulted, and he feared Dale's censure—the same way he did at his parties. Surely none of them would have just sat there and let this happen.

Dr. Morris had asked twice now about Dale's family, and Eric had no immediate idea how to get in touch with them. He also knew that Dale had not wanted them to know about his illness either, but he didn't tell the doctor that. He said he would see what he could do.

He got to know the other patients in the room and their visitors mostly by sight. He spoke only if spoken to, but day by day he felt himself becoming a citizen of a tiny country separated off from the rest of the world and marked by a certain rawness. There was something undeniably bracing about seeing a friend or relative diminished in this way, amid the anonymous institutionality of the hospital. Even eye contact was more loaded here; a simple hello communicated something more profound than it ever could outside: I, too, am through the looking glass.

The loneliest Eric could ever remember being was the night before he went to the hospital for his back surgery. His parents had gone to bed hours before; his older brothers had left home by then. He couldn't sleep, so he watched *The Tonight Show*, and the guest was Charo.

After that, he stood in his bedroom, wearing only his walking body cast, next to the hospital bed that had already been rented so that he could get used to it, and jerked off, not knowing when he would be able to do it next. He didn't feel particularly inspired, but some instinct sought the erotic anyway.

Total nudity was now an impossibility, but he could still feel the thrill of exposure, his chest sticking sweatily at the top of each breath to the plaster and the plastic tape that lined the rim of it, the weight somehow freeing the naked rest of him, the undamaged part, and making it especially vulnerable: his long, skinny legs and his round bottom.

The next morning, on the drive with his parents overtown to the hospital, under a rainy October sky, he watched his surroundings move past in a disconnected state, as if he were surrendering his image, temporarily donating his teenage body to science. The radio, he remembered, played Elton John singing "Don't Let the Sun Go Down on Me."

It took forever to be admitted to the hospital, waiting alongside all the other sad faces and slumped bodies with their suitcases and their nervous relatives. A middle-aged woman with a gray bouffant hairdo and a crisp polyester uniform eventually motioned Eric and his mother into her office and began very mechanically to ask a number of personal questions.

Eric's mother answered what he couldn't or wouldn't. She approached the surgery with a determination that Eric thought reflected an undue faith in the power of medical science. She had been thrown into a quagmire of guilt and fear by the condition: Where had she been while her child's spine curved seventy degrees out of shape? Eric's father, too, had seized upon the surgery as justification for the blustery optimism he had brought to the situation long before it was appropriate. Only Eric seemed to wonder if the operation could truly fix anything.

He was escorted deep into the bowels of the place, to a cold and empty cement room where he was asked to strip to his underpants and pose for photographs that might one day appear in a medical textbook. He stood all the way at the end of this drafty space, what seemed to be miles from the man behind the camera, who gave instructions like "OK, now, bend at the waist" to be sure the camera caught the extremes of Eric's deformity.

Years later, he opened a textbook in Barnes & Noble at Eighteenth and Fifth in New York and under "Scoliosis" saw a photograph he was certain was of him. Taken from behind, it displayed a familiar frail teenage body swerving in an S, one shoulder blade drooping outlandishly, one hip weirdly hitched up. But then as he explored the book further Eric realized that all the pictures reminded him of himself, even the ones of teenage girls, and that it was unlikely an American publisher would have obtained photographs from a Canadian hospital. But still it would be forever impossible to tell: the subjects were all pictured either facing away from the camera or with an anonymous black rectangle over their eyes.

Eric had played hide-and-seek with these memories for a long time. He thought of himself as deformed, but seldom of the actual events surrounding it. He had come through the surgery fine, his back no longer bothered him physically—enough said. But now, in a hospital environment for the first time since then, he found that his mind would flood unexpectedly with detail, and he would be caught.

chapter seven

When his mother first discovered the curvature of Eric's spine, she was applying suntan lotion to his back. They were on vacation, his mother, his father, and Eric, on the Canadian prairie, a nostalgic trip for his parents back to the places where they had been born and raised in the twenties and thirties, his mother in Alberta, his father in Saskatchewan. They were staying at the Dinosaur Motel in Drumheller, Alberta, and were on their way to the swimming pool, and none of them could figure out what was wrong.

"Stand up straight," Eric's mother said, but it didn't make any difference. "Jack, come here and look at this."

Once it had been noticed, it became impossible to miss. Eric looked in the bathroom mirror and was stunned to discover how lopsided he had become without knowing. The condition had developed quickly, but it was more than that. He had been asleep.

Drumheller is the site of a famous archaeological dig in the Alberta badlands. Everything in the small prairie town seemed to have been named after something related to the dinosaur bones and other finds in the area: the Tyrannosaurus Inn, the Prehistoric Pharmacy, that kind of thing. But it was a sleepy town, despite the hype.

One of the attractions there, which Eric's mother remembered from her youth, was a group of rock formations in the hills nearby called the Hoodoos. These were table rocks, giant flat stones balanced on uprights in arrangements that were quite striking, especially if the light hit them just so. The rocks were big enough to climb on, and Eric's father took a picture of him sitting on top of one of the perpendiculars, which only highlighted Eric's lack of symmetry.

Eric's father took a lot of pictures, then and now. He poured an enormous amount of vitality and creativity into everything he did. Whereas Eric, at fifteen, felt suffocated by the prairie air, by the presence of his parents on this trip; his very body seemed to be pulling him into the earth, to bury him before he bloomed.

The Hoodoos were hard to find. Driving through the dusty, deserted streets of Drumheller, Eric's father insisted he knew where they were going, but as they seemed to be driving in circles, his mother kept suggesting they stop the next person they saw and ask for directions.

When Eric's father finally relented, the person they spotted was a heavy, older, somewhat bedraggled woman in a billowing housedress, walking with two children by the unpaved side of the road. Eric's father slowed the car and his mother rolled down the window.

Eric's window was already down, and almost immediately the taller of the two children, a dark-haired beanpole of a girl in shorts and a halter top, began to climb through it into the car. This distracted Eric's mother only a moment. She returned her determined attention to the woman, who, Eric suddenly realized, was a ragamuffin version of younger photographs of his grandmother, who had tyrannized his mother for so many years, and whose death had freed her to live a new life, including taking this trip into her past. His mother didn't seem to notice the resemblance.

"Excuse me," she said in her voice of controlled, professional friendliness, under which hostility always lit the flame, "can you tell us how to get to the Hoodoos?"

A moment's pause followed, and then the woman went into a kind of spasm, apparently attempting to form words with her mouth but unable to emit anything but slurred gibberish. The smaller, towheaded child at this point started to climb in Eric's mother's window. In the back, Eric was wondering what to do if the girl flopped any farther forward and tumbled down beside him.

Eric's mother began to quickly roll up her window. "Jack," she said, a different sort of edge to her voice now, "for Christ's sake hit the gas."

And they lurched away, sending the two children to the ground, and leaving the heavy woman with a hand raised, still trying to articulate her billowing, dust-swept message.

The sunsets on the prairie were gorgeous. From motel after motel across the expansive, flat land, they watched the fire spread out on the horizon, darken, and disappear.

Eric's father's determined optimism had prevailed, and they did not plan to see a doctor about Eric's back until the vacation was over and they returned to North Vancouver.

Eric lay in bed in a motel room in Calgary late one night and began to believe that the curvature of his spine must be linked somehow to the sense of imbalance he felt in his whole life. Maybe this is the explanation, he thought, for my not being a proper man, for my not having the right feelings. And this gave him an odd sense of hope, for he was thinking anatomically; he was thinking that pressure was being put on some organ or other, that there was perhaps a cure.

From the other bedroom he heard only intense murmured conversation and silence. The discovery of this physical problem of Eric's had succeeded where none of his psychological woes had: It had pulled his parents' focus away from each other and back to him, the child they still had left to raise.

Back home, they tried to get an appointment with the family GP, but he was on vacation, so Eric ended up seeing one of his partners, Dr. Rutledge, a tall, folksy fellow he had never quite trusted, who smoked a pipe and was most famous for recommending, no matter what the problem, that patients "get out in a deck chair."

He did not recommend this to Eric. He was quite aghast when he saw Eric's back, couldn't for the life of him figure out what the problem was, had never seen anything like it. The look on his face suggested that this was a condition bordering on the catastrophic, that the best Eric could hope for was maybe a couple months, during which he'd probably go blind or insane and lose all muscle control.

They whisked him to the emergency room at Lions Gate Hospital and apparently decided that since they didn't know what the problem was, they would test him for every disease known to man. "Has he ever had polio?" Dr. Rutledge asked, as if this were something you might forget.

He sat in the cold X-ray room, wearing only a hospital gown, waiting for the doctors and nurses, who had disappeared somewhere for a confab, and thought that he was going to die, literally began to prepare for this and to find that at the age of fifteen it didn't upset him very much.

His mother, he would later learn, waited outside in tears, while his father went to get sandwiches. "What did I do wrong?" she sobbed to a volunteer in the waiting room. "I just can't understand what I did wrong."

Finally, when every test had been run and no conclusion had been come to and Dr. Rutledge was still wandering about saying helpful things like "What a case! Never seen anything like it!" a quiet older man with a calm face approached the foot of Eric's bed, curtained off in one of the emergency wards. He listened to Dr. Rutledge's near-hysterical précis of the afternoon's events, looked Eric over briefly, and told all the grim and perplexed people ringed about him that Eric had scoliosis.

"It's quite common," he said, and Dr. Rutledge nodded his head and creased his forehead knowledgeably.

With Eric's mother leaning in behind him, the older doctor then placed a hand on Eric's shoulder and uttered the first compassionate words any of the professionals had spoken to him that afternoon. "Don't you worry about this," he said. "This can be corrected."

They kept mistaking him for a girl. For some unknown reason, scoliosis is much more common in teenage girls than boys, so this set them up to make the mistake. And then there was the general loss of identity that went with any stay in the hospital, especially if you were encased in plaster.

Lying in the plaster room, waiting for his post-op cast, Eric heard one of the attending nurses say, "How old is she? How bad is her curve?" Then one of the others nudged her, made a face, and whispered something in her ear. "Oh," the first woman responded, "well, he's such a handsome boy, it's hard to tell."

On his first trip to the hospital, months earlier, for the first of two walking casts he would wear for several weeks prior to the surgery, an unshaven, shaggy-haired young intern in green scrubs had come sleepily into his room and watched while Eric took off his hospital bathrobe and gown. "Best slip off your underpants, too," he said.

Apparently he needed to examine how the curvature of Eric's spine was affecting his musculature, and after Eric had pulled his underpants down and off and lain shyly on the bed, the young doctor, whose eyes were a hypnotic blue color, asked him to tense different parts of his body so that he could see Eric's muscles.

"OK now, tighten your buttocks," he said with husky professionalism, and ran his hands down Eric's back to trace the latissimus dorsi.

"All righty," he said when he was done. "You can cover yourself back up now." And he waited by the curtain until Eric was dressed again.

The anesthetist sat by Eric's bed and talked with him the night before the operation, reassuring him that this surgery had been performed successfully countless times and that Eric needn't be afraid that he was going to die. The only possible complication was that his body would reject the steel rod that would hold the fusion in place while it set, and that was neither particularly serious nor likely. He told Eric exactly what procedures would be followed in the morning to put him to sleep, where he would wake up, how long he would be in the recovery room, and so on. Eric had the most wonderful feeling that if he'd kept coming up with questions, this man would have sat there till morning.

The boyfriend of a neighbor was an intern at the hospital and had asked permission to observe Eric's operation. He came and talked to him a few days afterward as he lay immobile on a device called a Foster Frame, a metal structure on which a piece of canvas was stretched for the patient to lie on and which became the bottom half of a sort of sandwich when another frame was strapped on top and the whole thing flipped, ostensibly every four hours, so that the patient lay faceup for four hours and facedown for the next four, without ever actually turning or shifting from side to side.

His neighbor's boyfriend told Eric how impressed he'd been with Eric's doctor and how well the operation had gone. And then he surprised Eric by reaching his hand out and gently brushing the hair off Eric's face, with a tenderness that seemed shocking and desperately needed coming from a young man.

He was the oldest patient in the children's ward, and to the nurses, who were used to dealing with four-year-olds, he seemed to be something of a novelty.

When flipping him on the Foster Frame, some of them would "accidentally" expose his genitals and then giggle as if it was the funniest thing in the world. A nurse got so involved one night in applying lotion to his feet and legs that she continued on up and spent several minutes massaging his backside.

He was being given so much morphine for the pain he could sometimes be remarkably easygoing, but the drug also lent the events of this time a heightened quality, a bizarre clarity.

In the plaster room, they needed to know he was a boy before they put the cast on, because the first thing they always did was take an X-ray, and boys and girls were given different lead shields, to cover the parts of their bodies considered most vulnerable.

Then they lifted him onto a table built especially for this procedure, on which the middle of his torso was supported by only a thin strip of cold metal, which could be withdrawn once the plaster-covered gauze had been wrapped around and around him.

Dr. Hodges had devoted his life to perfecting this treatment. He was nearing seventy at the time, and was said to have an invalid wife and to have had open heart surgery himself the year before, but still he pressed on. In fact, he told Eric's parents at their first meeting that his assistant was well trained in the procedure, so that he could take over should the doctor expire during the operation, which would take more than five hours.

Dr. Hodges was pleasant, but also always professional and quite intense. Despite his heart condition, on office visits Eric and his parents frequently caught him stubbing out a cigarette when they entered. And his hands sometimes made contact with Eric's body as if spring-loaded.

He kept getting Eric's name wrong, which wasn't exactly reassuring. The night before the surgery, he came to visit him, which was nice, but then signed off by saying, "We'll see you in the morning, Ernie."

He applied the casts like a master craftsman. First, a body stocking made of rough burlaplike material was popped over Eric's head and upraised arms and unrolled down to his waist. Then Dr. Hodges took tight rolls of warm, plaster-covered gauze from a steel bowl on a side table and unfurled them dexterously in circles around Eric's body, smoothing out more and more and applying more just plain plaster as he neared completion of the work.

For the walking casts Eric wore prior to the operation, which were supposed to increase the flexibility of his spine, the assisting nurses would pull and prod his body to get him as straight as possible before Dr. Hodges began. And as he worked, the doctor would bark out orders at them if Eric seemed to be slipping back to his original shape. "Straighten him out. Straighten him out. Pull! Pull!"

Eric became very familiar with the smell and feel of being encased in heavy, warm, wet plaster. It took a good twenty-four hours to dry. He was instructed each time to keep the covers on his bed rolled all the way down to the bottom of the cast and to make sure he turned often enough to air both sides. He had been taught how to turn over in a body cast—one arm across the chest, the other above the head, and turn—and how to roll in and out of a shirt.

The nurses would put their hands on the cast to check its progress whenever they were in the room. "A little while longer yet, Eric," they'd say. Toward the end, they'd knock on the cast and say, "Sounds good."

They knew that he was not allowed to go home until the cast had dried enough for a nurse to bend pieces of rubberlike tape all along the top and bottom edges, which were too rough to leave raw.

And it was a given that everybody in the hospital wanted, more than anything, to go home.

chapter eight

"Am I going to die?" Dale asked.

"Not right now," Eric said.

"I feel a little like I'm dying," Dale croaked and took a hit of oxygen.

"Actually you seem to be getting better."

"And I'm not suitably gowned."

Eric thought of all the things he'd wanted to talk to Dale about in the past two weeks. He had no idea how long this opportunity was going to last, so despite a bad feeling he had about it, he said, "I was wondering . . . Do you want to get in touch with your family . . . at all? Or anyone else for that matter."

"I must be dying," Dale said.

"No. It just seemed like something that maybe you would want to do, I don't know."

"It's the worst aspect of AIDS." Eric leaned forward to catch what Dale was saying in his rasping voice. "The opportunistic infection they don't tell you about . . ."

"I didn't know . . ."

"Turns your life into a TV movie."

His voice was so physically garbled, it was a shock to hear how lucid his thoughts were. "Here come the relatives. Having tortured you for thirty-one years, they wouldn't want to miss out on this."

"I wasn't sure . . ."

"You get along with your family."

"Well, I don't know that I . . ."

"This puts you in a distinct minority. You don't think the same way as other people about things." Dale pulled a deep breath through his oxygen mask.

"Maybe you shouldn't talk so much."

"Just try and stop me."

Eric shifted in the chair. "Does your family even know you're gay?" he asked.

"Please."

"It was just a question."

"Have you ever been to Kansas?"

"No."

"Well then," Dale said conclusively and took another breath through the mask. "I grew up on a farm," he added.

"I know," Eric said and smiled. "It's a little hard to imagine."

Dale let the mask fall loosely against his chest. "It was harder to do," he said.

Approaching the hospital from the street, Eric breathed in the vitality of the world around it, anticipating summer, and couldn't believe that it was just on the other side of those walls that the other world, the country of the unwell, resided.

For a while, he had kept expecting Dale to have more visitors. On his way to see him after work, he'd feel the familiar queasiness he'd always experienced socializing with Dale, who always brought someone else along.

This neighborhood was full of such memories. Eric recalled standing near where the old Stonewall Inn had been, at Christopher and Seventh, looking for Dale the first time he went to the Gay Pride parade, six years ago, in 1981.

Eric wandered in gym shorts and a muscle shirt, nervously squinting in the sun, oblivious to anyone giving him the eye, convinced that the bare-chested men with mustaches and deep tans and hand-kerchiefs stuffed in the back pockets of their torn, tight Levi's were the real catches there, the ones in the know. They danced as if they'd been born to the thunder of disco music and passed vials of amyl nitrate competently among themselves in the crowd.

It had seemed to take forever to find Dale, standing with several other friends, all tanned and wearing baggy khaki shorts and Lacoste shirts, making Eric think yet again that he had gotten the look wrong. None of these friends of Dale's were still around in his life it seemed. Then, Eric had been too shy to speak to any of them.

He remembered the exhilaration of the day, though, a younger self, twenty-two, marching up Fifth Avenue in the sunshine with thousands of other gay men and women, feeling the power in the cheers that bombarded the avenue. But later, when he tried to explain to Dale how important the experience had been for him, to thank him for talking him into going, he felt as if exteriors would forever betray him, because Dale said, "My friends didn't think you were having a good time. You didn't say anything."

Eric had only been to Fire Island once, with Dale and some friends of his Eric could hardly remember. He did remember sitting on the beach, on a coarse wool red-and-black blanket, in the incred-ibly white sun, looking about at a sea of gay men and experiencing that familiar sense of amazement at how out of place he felt. Where had these men learned to be so good at it, this business of being gay? How had they all managed to get the same even tan, to buy the same style of bathing suit, the same sunglasses, to develop the same muscle groups? Even the ones who were basically out of shape looked better than he did, Eric thought, because they possessed that magical some-thing he didn't, that mysterious password he'd never been given.

Bathing suits of any kind were optional on this beach. "Why don't you take your clothes off?" Dale said cheerily when he and his friends had disrobed.

Eric passed. In fact, he was still wearing a T-shirt, because, he said, he was sun sensitive, although he was really sensitive about his uneven back and the scar running in a straight line down the center of it.

They went to a "tea dance" that afternoon, at the Monster in Cherry Grove. The same men they'd seen on the beach were there, or carbon copies of them, seemingly hundreds of them, jumping to the beat of that disco hit Michael Jackson had before he became what he became. Eric got drunk and then upset because Dale didn't want to leave at the time they had agreed upon. If they waited much longer, they'd miss the last boat to the mainland, and they had nowhere to stay.

Eric got drunker, and more bored and irritable, and then couldn't find Dale anywhere. He circled the dance floor several times; he ran into Dale's friends, who either couldn't understand what he was asking or were deliberately misleading him.

Finally, after dark, he left the disco and headed to the water, where he was stunned to discover that there was no one about, no one to witness the beautiful star-filled sky, the serenity of the waves washing in and back, what must be the most soothing sound in the world. He could still hear the palpitations of the Monster, and almost instinctively, he began to walk away from them.

He ended up walking back and forth along the empty beach for hours, slowly calming himself but still sad and spent and pissed to the gills. Finally a tall, soft-spoken black man met him walking the other way and said hello. He'd seen Eric earlier at the disco but been too shy to approach him. They jerked off all over each other, naked on the moonlit sand, and then walked to the man's place in the Pines, where they slept together and where Eric was bought breakfast the next morning, feeling all the while an emotion that seemed not unrelated to the tricking phenomenon in general: revenge.

———

As several days went by and no one else appeared at the hospital, Eric came to the conclusion that in this he was finally alone, and he felt a peculiar relief, a kind of possessiveness, as if he had always wanted Dale to himself.

"As usual, you have exquisite taste," Dale said sarcastically as Eric arranged some gladiolus in a tumbler one of the nurses had found for him. He had agonized a long time selecting the flowers; now, in the hospital room, they looked way too big.

"I did my best."

Dale flipped through the magazines on his bed. "Yes, you did."

Eric sat then and experienced the familiar awkwardness of starting conversation under these circumstances.

The man in the next bed, Bill, a loud, heavyset gay man whose plumpness made it hard to believe he had AIDS, was seldom in the room. He flounced about the halls in a tattered chartreuse bathrobe, barking orders at nurses, cruising orderlies, and chatting with everyone else. He seemed to be one of those people who instantly claim any space as their own, maybe because no place has ever really been home.

Bill's family came to visit one night from Florida: his mother and father and one sister. His parents wanted to bring him back to Tampa, or at least his mother did, and she claimed to speak for both of them. His father looked bewildered the whole time they were there, and much older than his mother, with an odd recent sense about his aging, as if he'd become elderly, suddenly, in the last few days.

Bill was not interested in being moved anywhere. "Good God, Mother," he shouted on the other said of the ugly beige curtain Dale had asked Eric to pull between their beds, "have you already picked out an urn and made space on the mantel?" His mother sobbed. "Good God," Bill said.

Bertram, in the bed directly across from Dale, was a young black man with a sparse mustache who looked somehow as if he'd always been this thin. He was apparently a straight drug addict, AIDS having a way of instantly categorizing people whether they liked it or not. And everyone in the four-bed ward had AIDS.

Bertram's girlfriend, Janice, had visited a couple of times while Eric was there, shuffling in in thin shoes and wild hair and staying for about a half an hour, at the end of which she was always yelling at him.

The man in the bed diagonally across from Dale, by the window, whose name no one ever mentioned, looked to be almost a hundred years old, but Eric had heard a nurse say he was thirty-two. There were so many tubes and machines stuck in or taped to his emaciated body, Eric had given up trying to figure out what they were all for.

"So tell me more about your family," he said to Dale.

"Y-e-e-e-ch."

"I'm interested. You're the youngest?"

"Yes."

"Me, too. I—"

"I was an afterthought," Dale said. "Or, as I heard it described more that once, 'a mistake.' When I was born, my youngest sibling, Valerie, was already nine; my brothers, Walt and Gene, were teenagers. I felt about as connected to them as I did to Kansas. I even look different; my siblings are all tall and blond."

"Do you have pictures?"

"In my wallet, I carry only a photo of my ex-boyfriend Mickey. And of course one of Edith Head."

"No, I mean at home."

"My mother writes frequently. I don't even open the letters anymore, but I'm sure some of them contain photos."

Dale continued to speak hoarsely, but he seemed possessed by a fierce need to use his voice.

"Apparently Walt works on the farm now, which was recently sold to a corporation. Leading my father to more or less retire. From the farm. He retired from my life somewhat earlier.

"My father's a drunk. Basically. He isn't one of those romantic American farmer types they keep writing about. He's an asshole. A bigot and a drunk, who practically drove the family into bankruptcy because he wouldn't admit that the days of 'owning his own land' were over."

Dale hitched himself up in the bed. "You know," he said, "they make such a big deal out of how all these farmers had to give up their land, give up the family farm and all that BS; they even romanticize the ones who go into town with a shotgun and blow the banker away. But I'm here to tell you, most of them are just grade-A American ass-holes, macho shitheads who can't take no for an answer. I mean, if the bottom fell out of the bookselling market tomorrow, would you expect the government to support you for the rest of your life because selling books is romantic? No! You'd get another job!"

Dale reached for the turquoise plastic water pitcher on his bed-side table and poured himself a cup. "The farm hadn't even been in the family a long time. My grandfather, my *mother's* father, bought it more or less on a whim with some money he made in the stock market. It wasn't a big place; it *isn't* a big place, and the only possibil-ity of survival was to sell it and go on farming the land as tenants, which my mother and her brother worked out a way to do. But it took them two and a half years to convince my father—or rather to figure out that after a certain hour in the evening, he'd sign anything they put in front of him."

He downed the last of his water. "Getting a little more than you bargained for?" he asked.

"No, it's—"

"My sister I remember mostly as a baby-sitter, which is more of a relationship than I had with my brothers. Valerie lives in Wichita now, but I've long suspected she harbors some of the same itch I did, to get away. She shelved it, though, when she married... *Ron*, after becoming pregnant at the age of eighteen. She's the only one I've thought of maybe telling I was gay. Mostly because I think she already knows.

"It seems rather obvious in retrospect. How many heterosexual five-year-olds when told by their sandbox playmates that 'Mary Poppins won an Academy' correct them by saying the award is an Oscar and Mary Poppins didn't win it, Julie Andrews did.

"Another girl was very proud of herself for having figured out that Batman was actually Bruce Wayne. Remember that? And I completely confounded her with the information that *in point of fact* they were both Adam West. I just don't think straight boys are concerned about these things.

"I mean, from an early age I loved to dress up in costumes, including clothes of the opposite sex. Did you do that? You probably didn't, did you? I'll bet you're one of those oddballs who made it all the way to puberty without putting on a dress.

"Once, when I was about four, I remember, the little girl who lived on the next farm, Mary Alice Spender, and I were playing in the yard behind my house with a box of her family's old clothes and I got myself into this little red crinoline number of Mary Alice's and couldn't get out. The zipper at the back was stuck and I couldn't reach it, and Mary Alice either couldn't or wouldn't undo it for me and she began to giggle, being, as she was, a first-class bitch. And I remember panicking then, I remember panicking with a feeling I still remember that she was never going to stop laughing and that her laughter would eventually kill me.

"The only person I could think of who could maybe help me was my mother, so I ran from Mary Alice, that ball-busting Midwest cunt, back to the house. But on the porch I heard the voices of Mary Alice's visiting parents and realized I didn't want to go in there after all. I turned to run away, but too late. My mother had seen me in my little red dress, and she, too, thought the whole thing was very funny.

"'It's stuck,' I remember crying as though I were really saying, 'It's on fire!' And Mother's sensitive and thought-out response was to pull me inside and get a laugh out of the half-crocked Spenders. 'You look so pretty,' she said, and naturally Mr. and Mrs. Spender, clinky highballs in hand, thought I was just about the funniest darn thing they'd ever seen."

He paused then and a look crossed his face, for an instant, of vulnerability, as if he'd waded in too deep.

"But what I most remember," he said, "is the look on my father's face. His lined, sunburned man's face. He didn't laugh. He mumbled something shitty under his breath, something that shut the Spenders the fuck up and made my mother drag me from the room. What had Daddy said? I wondered—and knew enough not to ask. What had Daddy said as he downed the last of his drink with a giant hand and went quick for another one?

"'Queer'? 'Faggot'? 'Sissy'? Maybe he only said a swear word or two. Maybe he said something much more unrelated to the situation at hand than I thought." He flung a hand back in the air. "It's irrelevant, you see, because the look on his face that day, in my mind, came to symbolize his whole attitude toward me, and the specific words no longer really mattered."

He reached for his oxygen mask and breathed in slowly and deeply. His eyes watched Eric.

"What's your earliest memory?" he asked when he was done.

"I don't know."

"You must. Everybody has a first thing they remember."

"What's yours?"

"I asked you first."

Eric thought for a moment. "I remember a lot of things from . . . about age three, I guess, four."

"In L.A.?"

"No, no. I don't remember any of that. I've heard about things from down there so many times it's as if I remember them, but no, these things are from Vancouver."

"What?"

"I remember . . . sitting in the corner of the kitchen while my mother did . . . something, washed the dishes? No, I think she was cooking, preparing something . . . and the shirt I was wearing, which she had dressed me in just a few minutes before, was made of this rough, prickly sort of material, wool I guess, a gray-colored material, and for some reason that morning I just couldn't stand the feel of it against my skin. But I felt . . . powerless to do anything about it, powerless to communicate to her, to my mother, how much I didn't want to wear that shirt. I felt there was no way she would understand how important it was to me to wear something different. It was a feeling of real helplessness, and I started to cry, very quietly; it took a while for my mother to notice me. And then she was very concerned, and completely surprised when I told her what it was I was crying about, because it seemed like the simplest thing in the world to her: We'd just change the shirt. And we did."

Dale was staring at him. "So this fashion victim thing started early then?"

"You asked," Eric said.

"That's all you remember?"

Eric thought a second and was about to say no, when he flashed on something else. "A vacation," he said, "of some kind. We were on a trip somewhere, on Vancouver Island I think, and we went to the supermarket, for groceries, and I got sick, I threw up right in front of the entrance. They had to mop it up, and it left a wet mark. And for days afterward, as my parents tried to entertain me with other aspects of the trip, all I kept asking to do was drive by the supermarket again, so I could see the spot where I'd thrown up."

Again Dale was staring at him. "These are very odd early memories you have."

"And standing in the backyard, this is maybe my earliest memory, I don't even remember what I was doing exactly, but when I think of this moment I'm always standing alone in the backyard, in twilight, looking up at the house, where everyone else is inside, behind the lighted windows, and I remember thinking that there was something different about me, there was something that would separate me from other people, forever." He stopped and looked at Dale, who continued to watch him. "I was three," he said.

"What's *your* earliest memory?" Eric asked.

"I remember," Dale began immediately, "the smell and feel of a dress my grandmother wore as she rocked me on the porch of our house, under a starlit summer sky, reading me stories. They're the thing I most remember, the stories—bedtime stories . . . fairy stories.

"You know, that whole area out there, around Russell, is quite visually striking. I mean, people have done entire books of photographs. Antique farmhouses against a cobalt sky; a grain silo the only obstacle on a limitless horizon—I hated it.

"In that same sandbox, at the church kindergarten I attended, I composed my first Academy Award acceptance speech, and delivered it to the other children, who stopped, amazed, in the midst of their mundane bucket-and-shovel play.

"Even then, even in my earliest memory, I preferred those stories my grandmother read me out of a book to running around and doing all those things the other children did, all those outdoor things they do. From the earliest age I prayed for a cyclone."

Dale brought his palms flat together above his chest, and his IV tubing swung with them. The he dropped his hands and turned to look diagonally across the room to the window and the clear sky.

"Who did you thank?" Eric asked.

"What?" Dale turned back from the window.

"In your speech. Who did you thank?"

Dale looked off again. "No one," he said.

Dr. Morris wanted to get Dale up and walking. It was a shock for Eric to see how he had deteriorated. When he was sitting up in bed, a swank bathrobe wrapped over his hospital gown and the covers hiding half his body, it was not as obvious that he had lost a lot of weight since coming there, and his difficulty breathing also became more pronounced as soon as he tried to move around.

Eric would walk him down to the sunroom at the end of the hall, and the progress was painfully slow, accompanied by the squeak of the IV pole Dale wheeled at his side and the flash of sudden scenes in the rooms along the way. "I can't do anything right," a man's high-pitched voice cried from behind a curtain one day. "I don't even know how to die."

"Slow down" was the thing Dale said most on these trips, and though it was a step forward for him to be out of bed, Eric believed it must depress him to find himself so weakened. Although it was hard to tell, since he almost never spoke of his illness.

"I never went to college," he said as they sat in the sunroom on a bright afternoon. "Sometimes I wonder why."

Dale was always relieved to find the room empty, which surprised Eric, who expected his own relief. Dale had also failed to make much of an acquaintance with any of the other men in his room, even Bill, who seemed to be friends with everybody. Dale made bitchy comments about him behind his back, but to his face he adopted an austere politeness, something Eric had never seen him do before, and which chilled him.

Around the doctors, too, Eric was surprised at how docile Dale became. He would have expected him to be more of a fighter, full of complaints and questions, one of those guerrilla patients the surveys kept saying had better survival chances. Instead, whenever Eric observed him in the company of the experts, he was shocked to see an intimidated civility come over Dale, an almost childlike desire to please, to move these people out of the room as smoothly as possible.

The nurses were another story. Before one of Eric's trips to Dale's apartment, Dale had requested that he bring him his Polaroid camera. Eric asked him what he planned to use it for, but Dale was coy and refused to say. Then one day when Eric was visiting, a heavy-set nurse named Deanna, whom Eric liked actually, and had found to be one of the more compassionate and prompt of the lot, came into the room to take Dale's temperature and check his blood pressure. As she released the cuff around his arm, Dale reached behind her and slid a magazine off his bedside table and onto the floor. Eric went to pick it up, but Dale shook his head quickly and looked up at Deanna, who bent to get the magazine. Just then, Dale whipped his camera out from under the covers of his bed and snapped a picture of Deanna from behind.

"What are you about there, Mr. Corcoran?" she asked as she stood, huffing slightly, and handed him back the magazine.

Eric agonized as they all stood there waiting for the picture to develop. Slowly it seemed to dawn on Deanna what exactly Dale had taken a picture of. She stood rooted to the spot, her face conflicted by humiliation and an effort to mask it, an urge to leave the room and a desire to know exactly what it was Dale had gotten on her.

With a grin, he turned the photograph toward her and Eric, and there she was, in full Polaroid glory, bent over, her short skirt hiked up to reveal a broad expanse of flesh, barely contained by a pair of support hose.

Dale, of course, thought the whole thing was clever and hilarious. But Eric recognized the look on Deanna's face: beneath the embarrassment and the attempt to laugh it off was the sinking realization that she was hated.

"Why do you do things like that?" Eric asked when she had gone.

And Dale looked at him with an expression on his face Eric had seen before, under similar circumstances: it was a look of triumph, and a look that said triumph was all that counted, no matter how cheaply attained.

"You went, didn't you?" Dale asked now in the sunroom.

"Hmn?

"College."

"For a year. Yeah."

"Why'd you quit?"

"I don't know. I think—"

"I moved to Kansas City instead. Missouri. It was the nearest almost big city." He leaned back comfortably to take the sun, his sunglasses reflecting bits of the skyline outside. "I'd first discovered the gay life there on a high school field trip when I was fifteen. We'd gone to the county museum, but I met this man. Everyone thought I'd just somehow gotten separated from the group. Apparently the police were called, my family was notified, the whole town was in a panic.

"This is one of the less charming features of small town life: You can't get away with anything. But somehow that just hadn't occurred to me when this tall, handsome man came up to me in the museum, whilst I lollygagged among the half-naked stuffed Indian braves, and said, 'You in a hurry to get someplace?' I most certainly was. I mean the answer I wanted to give him was 'Yes. Anyplace. Where ya headed?'

"His name was Dean. Are they all named Dean, or was it just me? He was almost twenty-seven years old, which at the time made me think he practically belonged in the museum himself.

"He took me back to his apartment, just a few blocks away. It only seems risky in retrospect. That's true I find of so many things from back then. Because what's missing when you tell the story now is that need, that need that was like a craziness it had built up for so many years. It wasn't just a question of sex, it was a question of identity. I remember lying in the tangle of sheets in that man's bed, my head resting on his chest, and thinking very clearly, I can die now. I am no longer afraid to die.

"Later I made up some story about having gotten lost and making my way back to Russell on my own, and I was believed. By everyone that is except my father. He knew. He always knew."

Dale clasped his hands on his chest and closed his eyes.

"Did you see Dean again?"

"No, he didn't last. But there were many others, many more trips across the state line." He sat up again. "I sometimes think our generation was the last to make that discovery—of the secret society. I miss the adventure of it—a whole other world no one had told you about, a language you could learn to speak. I remember the first *Advocate* I brought back to the farm as the most delicious contraband, like tickets to the moon stashed under my mattress. It was a newspaper then, remember? Crude and wonderful. Now it's just another silly old magazine."

His voice was still gravelly, but he seemed to put into it all the energy he couldn't use walking, creating a passage through time instead of space.

"Eventually I invented a friend in Kansas City I was supposedly visiting," he said and sat back, "and then I moved there almost immediately after graduating from high school and stayed for two years. I was involved with several men, two in particular with whom I lived, all older men. I worked part-time at a record store for a while, but mostly I allowed myself to be supported.

"And then I had too much of that finally. It hit me like a ton of bricks, on a trip back to my parents' place, at a time when I was thinking, yet again, of maybe going to college after all. I was rummaging around in the attic, looking for my high school transcript, when I came across this photograph of a very handsome young man. I remember picking it up and giving the guy the once-over, you know, thinking 'he's hot' in that way you just get in the habit of doing, and then realizing, too late, that I was looking at a picture of my father.

"I was becoming, you see, a gay version of my mother, who had so completely squelched her own identity in the face of my father's idiocy. In an odd way, this is even more noticeable now that she's taken a job to help them make ends meet, because she's constantly apologizing, overtly or otherwise, for the independence she knows it gives her.

"The last time I visited, which was in the early Mesozoic Era, she'd sit with me over coffee in the kitchen and talk about her job in the hair salon, and it was as if I was talking to someone new, someone who'd hidden inside my mother all these years. The job seemed to hold her in a kind of thrall, especially when she was able to solve some major problem or other all by herself.

"But then my father would come into the kitchen, roused apparently from his liquor-induced sleep, and docility would sweep over my mother's features and the spark would go out of her eyes. When she'd been talking about her job, I'd had the feeling I could almost be friends with her, you know, but when she changed the subject as soon as *he* came into the room, scaled back her excitement, I hated her.

"He never even let her do the books. A lot of the farm wives do that, you know, take care of the accounting, but my father wanted total subservience. So for years my mother went over his work and made corrections without telling him. She saved his ass on numerous occasions."

He adjusted his position in the chair. "So then I wanted to meet someone my own age," he said. "I suddenly felt as if everyone were condescending toward me. And I was supposed to be becoming an 'actor' at some point; I mean that had always been the life plan, right? And here I was prancing around Kansas City, Missouri, being Miss Congeniality.

"So I moved to New York. I mean, what else are you going to do? But the funny thing is... You know, I'm trying to remember what my plans were, at that moment, as the Greyhound rolled away from that all too familiar bus station, what it was I was going to do when I got here, and I remember, I remember feeling a tremendous excitement about the future, about what I was going to accomplish here, but it wasn't built around the idea of career—it was more of that secret world I wanted. I mean, I didn't see myself going to auditions or taking classes or anything industrious like that. I saw myself dancing at two in the morning with a cigarette and a drink.

"I had been to bed with so many supposedly straight men, men who passed in their day-to-day lives; the closet is very big in the Midwest. And I remember the most powerful sense on that bus trip here of having knowledge other people didn't have: that it was all bunk, that the lives people led on the surface were lies. And that was the most amazing thing to know; it overwhelmed everything else.

"I myself had been a lie for years; I was a lie finally come to light, and I couldn't get enough of it."

He paused a moment and took a conclusive, if ragged, breath. "I came to New York to have sex," he said.

chapter nine

In a paisley-covered wicker basket chair he'd inherited from home, Eric would sit at the window of his apartment in the Garth, looking out through the crisscross of telephone wires that marred his third-floor view of downtown and, beyond, Burrard Inlet and the mountains of the North Shore. Or he'd slump against the broken-down console stereo his parents had given him, listening to sad Dan Hill records, coughing as he tried to embrace the cigarette habit with a red-and-white pack of Craven A's, and crying because he had no idea how to begin being this new person he knew he had to be.

When Ken answered the phone at SEARCH, Eric said, "I'm gay and I don't know what to do."

It was late. It had taken Eric until ten-thirty, and a pack of Craven A's, two beers, and one Dan Hill record to find the courage to call. So Ken suggested that he drop by the following evening.

The SEARCH office was a tiny cubicle in a low modern building wedged into Pender Street, in an area just north of the downtown core and less up-to-the-minute, with office buildings that exuded a musty 1940s feel, about as old as anything in Vancouver. SEARCH's tacky boxlike building also housed, in the basement, BJ's, one of the oldest bars in town.

Ken pulled open the door and motioned Eric inside while he talked on the phone cradled against his shoulder. He turned out to be affable and intelligent, in his late twenties, nice looking—not the man of Eric's dreams, but a man, a gay man.

He had begun to have such dreams, to in fact feel a new push in his romantic feelings, as if his need to excel, to somehow move beyond his family, his country, his self, were now being channeled into the quest for romance.

He had dressed that night in what seemed as if it might be an attractive manner: wide-legged blue jeans and platform shoes, and a belted sweater his mother had bought for him. Since his graduation from high school, he had begun to sense a change in the way the world perceived him, but barely, and with no certainty. He flirted his way from the SEARCH office to Ken's apartment, on Harwood in the West End, but it came upon him in the moment, intuitively, that he had the power to do this.

Sex was a problem. From the start it was a ritual Eric felt outside of. The kissing was remarkable, transporting, but in bed the thread was dropped somehow, and an awful clumsiness took its place.

"Are you going to come or just do *that* all night?" Ken asked.

Eric kept thinking he had to pee. He kept leaving to run to the bathroom.

"It hurts," he said when Ken entered him, but Ken didn't stop.

Afterward he gasped, "I'm sorry," and rolled off of Eric.

Eric never entirely willingly let anyone do that to him again. Sometimes, out of a strange politeness that would possess him during sex, he'd consent, but always with regret. Years later, when this was identified as the major transmission route for HIV, he felt lucky, but it was a bitter luck. He seemed to have been protected only by being excluded.

That morning, however, walking away from Ken's apartment, up the hill from English Bay, a crisp winter sea scent on the wind, Eric felt mostly the pleasure of being no longer a virgin. This odd experience had given him a great, sweet gift, it seemed; it had made him a citizen of the adult world.

And standing in the lobby a few nights later at a play the campus gay club had brought from San Francisco, Eric looked up and saw Thomas Stroud for the first time, wide-shouldered and stocky in a sports jacket and tie, dashing into the theater with a briefcase under his arm, sweeping his black hair back off his broad forehead as he ducked to buy a ticket, all the while nodding hello to other members of the club.

Eric could still remember the narcotic power of that first sight-ing, the tremendous possibility it seemed to represent—to spot the proverbial stranger across a crowded room, to say this one instead of that. It was a power of choice that would be dulled by the years ahead, but in those initial moments, days, weeks, it created a drunken pleasure, the answer to every question there, suddenly, in the move-ment of another boy through the room, the turn of his head, the way his clothes fit.

Thomas Stroud chaired the next meeting of Gay People of UBC, which Eric went to, his first. From the front of the meeting room on the ground floor of the Student Union Building, Thomas asked with his dry English accent how everyone's weekend had gone, and a sex-edged tittering traveled through the group, made up as ever of young men. The club tried to encourage female members, but lesbi-ans tended to join the campus women's groups instead.

Thomas was eighteen, but he looked older than the others. He was on the short side, about five-eight, and thickset without being especially well-built, but he had full, sensual features; he was English and Jewish and a year older than Eric, and he exuded the intensity of identity a taller, thinner, paler Eric craved. Eric looked too young even to get into the bars downtown, for which you had to be nineteen.

"What's your major?" Thomas asked wryly after the meeting, when a group of them had commandeered a central table in the nearby cafeteria.

"English Lit."

"Oh, well. You can study me then." Eric smiled. "You see that's much more the sort of thing I ought to be majoring in, because it's what really interests me."

"What is your major?"

"Urban planning," Thomas said with some distaste. "It's more practical, don't you think? I mean, what if hard times come?"

He poured tea from a tin pot.

"I haven't seen you around in the bars much," he said. "Which ones do you go to?"

"Oh . . . well . . . I don't actually go that often," Eric said.

"Oh."

"I prefer to meet people other ways," he continued sanctimoniously, a lie; he'd been unable to find many other ways.

"I'm rather fond of the bars," Thomas Stroud said. "The Gandydancer," he added with raised eyebrows, naming the men's bar so popular and so closed to the underage it had taken on mythic proportions in Eric's mind.

They left the cafeteria to loiter outside the SUB, the campus still beautiful, so vast and open and green, even under the gray January sky. A couple of men from the club were going into town to shop—a thin, fey Japanese with the unlikely name of Murray, who was supposedly Thomas Stroud's chief bar-hopping companion, and Roy, also quite flamboyant but from Calgary. They invited Thomas to join them, and since Eric was standing next to him, he ended up being included also.

Pacific Centre was then one of only two malls under downtown Vancouver, which came to be riddled with them. Eric had his first job with Colophon there, and he loved working in the mall, *the* place to shop, far from provincial North Van, full of trendy clothing stores throbbing with disco music and mobs of people streaming in and out, filling the matchbox bookstore where he clerked nights and weekends.

He stood with Thomas Stroud in the bookstore that day, as he thumbed through a remainder about England and said, "I'll show you where I'm from."

"Where?"

"Well, I doubt the precise place of my birth is in here," he said. "It's called Gravesend, which I'm sure you've never heard of, in Kent, which is rapidly becoming suburban London. But *this*," he said and smiled slyly as he pointed to a picture of Piccadilly Circus, "is where I lived much of the time."

When Eric looked puzzled, Thomas added, "I went cruising there. With my homework."

"With your homework?"

"Yes. That way I tended to attract a smarter sort of gentleman, you see, standing there with my books. Rather clever of me, don't you think?'

He pointed to the center of the picture. "Do you see the figure flying over the fountain?" he asked. "It's quite funny. The inscription underneath reads 'Eros . . . the God of Love,' but that's a mistake: the figure is supposed to be something else; it's supposed to be the Angel of Christian Charity."

In the Elephant and Castle pub on the upper level of the mall, Roy became involved in some animated story he was acting out for Murray, who looked only mildly interested.

"Do your parents know you're gay?" Thomas asked.

"Yes," Eric said. He had finally gotten around to telling them, over after-dinner drinks in North Van on a night when just he had gone over there, instead of the customary gang of brothers, wives, and children. As he had expected, outwardly his parents accepted his sexuality with liberal aplomb. Although his mother did believe that he couldn't possibly know yet what he was, sexually speaking. As she had told him more than once, she herself had not even known where babies came from until she met his father. And although Eric was sure of his orientation, her comment did make him wonder momentarily, given what his mother had suffered and his parents' generally progressive views about such things, how he had managed to arrive at adulthood with so little knowledge of how sex actually worked, how one went about mining this life-changing pleasure.

One way or another, however, as with everything else, his parents accepted his choice in the matter of sexual orientation. And then never mentioned it again.

"Do yours?" he asked Thomas.

"Yes" was his dry reply. "Unfortunately."

"Why do you say that?"

"They found out accidentally," he said, "and are not happy about it. We're Jewish," he said. "As far as they're concerned I'm as good as dead. But . . . screw them, right?"

"How did they find out?"

Thomas looked up and then away for a moment, and just then Murray drained his rye and ginger and plunked the glass down impatiently.

"Time to go?" Thomas asked.

Eric was working that evening, so he stayed downtown and said good night to everyone outside the bookstore. Nothing he could think of to say seemed adequate as he parted from Thomas, who only shook his hand again and said, "I'm glad we had a chance to chat."

That whole night at the store Eric breathed the memory of him like fuel, worked twice as hard as usual and with a smile.

He looked for Thomas Stroud on campus for days after that but didn't see him. He saw other people from the club and engaged them in conversation to try to find out if they'd seen Thomas, but apparently no one had. When Eric asked Murray, he behaved as if he never knew where Thomas was and didn't know why on earth Eric was asking him.

Eric looked forward to the next club meeting with a vengeance, but Thomas didn't show. He kept glancing toward the door through the whole meeting and barely heard anything that was said. The sense of loss was keen; a kind of panic bubbled under it—to have come this close to the thing so long desired and then somehow let it slip away.

Eric bought that remainder on England with his staff discount. For days on end he wore his Britannia blue jeans on campus, with the Union Jack label on the backside. He read a biography of the Queen and a book on English Jewry called *Troubled Eden*.

Then one night, when he'd almost given up on ever seeing Thomas again, or more accurately, when the frustration had simply begun to exhaust itself, he was studying late at the library and left early when a dense fog began to settle on the mall outside the window. On his way to the loop to catch a bus back into the city, he got turned around and ended up walking toward the pool building, a glassed-in structure that loomed ahead of him suddenly, lit up in the haze like something unnatural, the secret landing site for a UFO.

He couldn't see a foot in front of him, but he did see that outside the pool, silhouetted in the darkness, an English flat cap on his head and his hands shoved in the pockets of his long overcoat, a stout figure stood, facing away from the road and watching the late-night swimmers through the plate glass.

Thomas Stroud seemed startled when Eric approached and then embarrassed. He immediately began to walk away.

"Aren't you in the club anymore?" Eric called after him.

But Thomas had disappeared in the mist.

chapter ten

"Where were you the night the Saint opened?" Dale asked.

"Is that like the gay version of the Kennedy assassination?"

"No. That would be 'Where were you when Harvey Milk was shot?'"

"Oh."

"Where *were* you when Harvey Milk was shot?"

"We knew each other then."

"That's right. We were probably both shelving."

"We were. I remember you going on and on about how little response there was in New York compared to the West Coast."

"I really wanted to be in on that riot." Dale reached for his oxygen mask and took a breath. His ID bracelet slipped down his arm. "You haven't answered my question," he said.

"I have no idea where I was when the Saint opened," Eric said. "If I hadn't known you, I don't think I would have even known what the Saint was. For years I didn't know where it was. I just knew that everybody went there."

"It was in the old Filmore East."

"That's supposed to mean something to me?"

Dale just looked at him.

"Where were you?" Eric asked.

"I was at the Saint. Where the hell else would I be?"

"I see."

"Every self-respecting homosexual was there. You, of course, had a *Pigskin Parade* revival to catch."

"Very funny."

Faint street sounds snuck in the window Eric had cracked open earlier, and mixed with the familiar echo of hospital noise from the hallway: the padding of rubber soles, the clang and clink of unidentified equipment, distant female voices and cries of distress.

"So what was it like?" Eric asked.

"What?"

"The Saint."

"Oh." He raised his eyebrows slightly and turned profile, a little as if the queen had been asked about royal secrets. "The Saint."

"Yes. What was it like that first night?"

"Well, it was... Well, the first night it was like standing in line on Second Avenue for three hours. And by the time we got in, we were recontouring our drugs for the third time and everything was getting a little hazy. But still, it was worth it. I mean, we knew right away that the place was going to be special when they charged us twenty bucks and checked our coats on this computerized contraption that moved like dry cleaning. Everyone had said that disco was dead and here we were, more than a thousand healthy, pumped, and gorgeous gay men, proving them wrong, in the flash of a strobe light, under a universe of artificial stars."

Eric noticed Dale's deterioration more when he caught him unawares. Arriving near dinnertime one evening he stopped in the hallway when he saw a little man perched on the side of Dale's bed, his scrawny legs dangling down to paper slippers, his hand, still pinned to a pentamidine drip, shaking a little as he moved peas onto a fork and struggled to lift them to his mouth. This was Dale, but it took Eric a moment to realize.

There was very little, it seemed, that the doctors could do for him. They bustled into the ward periodically, Dr. Morris and several other specialists, like visiting royalty, everyone who was still articulate hovering about them trying to get a zillion questions answered in the ten minutes provided.

The pentamidine was very, very slowly clearing up Dale's pneumonia, much slower than Dr. Morris had anticipated. His body had already been ravaged by cancer and chemotherapy, and he was developing a host of other, more minor infections as well. In May 1987, they were doing everything they could, and it wasn't having much effect.

Around Eric, Dale would mention how he was feeling from day to day, but never discuss the treatment at any length, or what any of his symptoms might mean. With Eric, he behaved as if this were an unpleasant and boring subject not worth going into.

"You know," he said early one evening, and turned, a look on his face a little as if he were about to give a speech to the UN, "the men at the St. Mark's were almost too good-looking, I always thought." He glanced at Eric. "Didn't you think so?"

Eric looked down.

"You went *there*, didn't you?"

Eric shook his head. "Nope."

"No? Did you go to the baths at all?"

"No. I told you that. We've talked about this."

"Oh, yes, right. Achilles was afraid to show his heel."

Eric felt sweat down the center of his back and stared at the cracked linoleum at his feet.

"It's always so embarrassing to go to the gay beaches with you," Dale continued. "The moment you get your shirt off, they cry 'Judy!' and come running."

"But you told me you didn't think it was that noticeable. You've said that."

"Of course the pathetic thing is your insistence on stumbling through an entire chorus of 'Get Happy.'"

He took another hit of oxygen.

"You're addicted to that stuff," Eric said.

"It's air. How bad can it be for you?"

"But do you really need it anymore?"

"Please. It's my one vice."

The late May sun slanted more intensely moment by moment, making shadow play with Dale's erector-set television rig, his IV setup, his call button and tank of air.

"Tell me about the St. Mark's," Eric said. "I was always curious. I used to walk by that big black door and wonder."

Eric looked at him for a moment in a double take. "You used to walk . . . ?" he started and then stopped as if what Eric had said were simply beyond him. "Well, the place was fabulous," he said, and hoisted himself up a little in bed.

"Do you want . . . ?" Eric asked and reached for the control pad.

"No. Please. Last time you practically folded me up in the damn thing." He settled into position and spread his hands flat and neat across the covers.

Eric waited for him to start in, but he remained sphinxlike, in his flashy Noel Coward dressing gown, as if waiting for his cue.

"So tell me about it," Eric said. "I never went to the baths. Tell me what you did there."

Dale raised his eyebrows and cocked his head slightly.

"I *mean*," Eric said, "like, did you get a room or what?"

"It depended on the night. And whether or not I felt like waiting in line. You could wait in line for hours on a weekend."

"So . . . Did you wear a towel? Everyone just wore towels, right?"

"Oh, my. This is Tubs 101, isn't it? Yes. Everyone wore towels. In various ways. The butch ones always seemed to know how to wrap it just so. Some of the queenier types would get playful and create something more sarong-like, with a knot on the side, say. Others slung it over a shoulder or did without. Unfortunately," he added with a genuinely puzzled look, "they were usually the ones who had no good reason to do this."

"And did you wander around? Or wait in your room? How did it work? What were the rooms like anyway?"

"Please. Contain yourself, Ms. Walters. One question at a time." Dale sat back and again smoothed the beige hospital-issue bedspread with a flat palm, his wrist extending loosely from his flashy robe. "The rooms were very small," he continued, "and the walls didn't go all the way to the ceiling, and there was always music playing, and the sound of people fucking."

"What was in the rooms?"

"A bed. Of sorts. A single bed, and if you wanted you could stay in your room and leave the door open and check out whoever passed by. If you liked someone, you'd smile or maybe play with yourself, and if you were lucky he'd join you. Some types, of course, just lay facedown on the bed and took whatever came along. And there were others who were terminally unavailable; they were just there, I think, to look pretty and torture everyone else.

"Or you could wander. And there were communal rooms, too. Everything was so wonderfully up front, so simple and democratic. Everybody was there for one reason; there were fewer games.

"I mean it's as if there's a level in all of us, a kind of mad religious place where all we really want is cock—up the ass or over the tongue—consuming the body of man. And at the baths you'd see people *there*, at that place, living for a whole night in delirious honesty. Men who by day perhaps had good clean-cut jobs and never broke the rules or spoke above a whisper would get down on their knees and howl for it, park their butts in the air and admit, ecstatically, that in the final analysis, little else had *ever* mattered."

A nurse bustled through the door then, carrying a tray, from which she took a tiny white paper cup and handed it to Dale.

"Isn't it a little early for my sleeping potion?" he asked.

"I'll leave it here, how's that?" she said and set it next to his water pitcher. Then she moved on to the next bed.

"I have them wrapped around my little finger," Dale said.

Once again, Bill was missing.

"That woman spends so little time in her bed," Dale said, "I don't know why she bothers to pay for it."

"When he comes back," the nurse said on the way out, "you tell him to take that pill."

"No prob," Dale said and winked at her.

"I always thought the baths were a clean place," he continued. "Sounds funny now, I suppose, but I mean there were showers, and some even had gyms, and it was almost like a health club. I mean compared to getting drunk in some smoke-filled back-room bar. The St. Mark's even had a pool."

"And an orgy room, right?"

"Yes, Virginia, there was an orgy room."

"Did you go there?"

"Nah. You know me—the shy type. Of course I went there." He stopped and looked off a ways, vaguely confused by something. "One tended to have the damndest experiences in the orgy room. The funniest people can feel very good when the lights are out and you don't know who they are. I used to run into people I knew. You'd realize too late you were being fucked by your friend Sam."

"You're kidding."

"Had I known you better at the time I'd have dragged you there. I *loved* the St. Mark's. I had better luck at Man's Country, but it wasn't the same."

"*Come* to Man's Country."

"You got it."

"That was right after I moved here, this giant billboard over Sheridan Square that said, 'Come!'"

"Those were the days. 'Loose joints, loose joints' and that lady singing opera with her cassette player outside the cigar store."

"It never occurred to me," Eric said as the sun shot one final blaze against the back wall of the room, "in all the time I toyed with the idea of going to the baths, got after myself for not going, for being inhibited, whatever, it *never* occurred to me that one day those places wouldn't be there, that I would no longer have the option."

"And now you're old," Dale said with a sigh, and the sun died quickly, leaving the room in an orange and then a gray darkness.

"Yes," Eric replied without thinking. "Now I'm old."

chapter eleven

Thomas Stroud, it turned out, was often spotted outside the pool building late at night, and his trips there turned out to be somewhat legendary.

"His nocturnal missions," Murray called them.

"Is he sleepwalking?" Eric asked.

"He can't swim," Roy said. "If he stops moving, he sinks. At least that's what I heard."

"Have you taken a look at some of those guys?" Murray asked. "In those sweet little Speedo bikinis? Some of them shave their entire bodies, I'm told. Very butch, very professional, very sportsmanlike and all that—I can't stand it! So what's the big mystery if Tom likes to ogle the boys?"

"So how come he won't talk to anybody?" Roy asked. "If they see him there? If they even pass by him on the way? He walks right by as if he doesn't know you."

"He's busy," Murray said.

Someone had passed him bolting through a dead winter's night with his hand covering a tearstained face. Someone else claimed to have seen him on his knees praying outside the glassed-in structure. He was a second-year student, so the stories predated Eric's arrival. Late one evening last spring one boy apparently came upon him with his shoes, socks, and shirt off, curled in the fetal position on the cement walkway, the pool light crossing him with quivering water shadows, deep, raucous voices echoing from inside, as if trapped behind the glass.

It poured rain the night of his first real date with Thomas.

Murray and Roy picked Eric up downtown, in Murray's red Honda civic, and the three of them headed out to the campus, where Thomas lived in residence. On the way, Murray said a couple things about Eric and Thomas that gave Eric the feeling that he was being had, that Murray was not playing matchmaker here, although this foursome had been his idea.

"So what do you think of the idea of a Valentine's dance?" he asked and then turned slightly toward Eric in the backseat. "Of course you and Tom would be there for sure," he added and made a kiss with his lips. "First in line."

He was the only one who ever called Thomas Tom, and around Eric he seemed to do it incessantly. He was Thomas's bar buddy, and it was as if he had to prove he understood his friend more cynically than anyone else: They were a pair of fallen women with no time for romantic pipe dreams.

As the car slipped along the Main Mall, Eric spotted Thomas ahead, through the whining swipe of the windshield wipers, standing by the side of the road in his long green coat, his tweed flat cap on his head. When he ducked into the backseat, he filled the car with the scent of his rain-beaded hair and skin, and Eric was flooded again with amazement to be near such an embodiment of all he thought a young man should be. Thomas was solid and dark, his face covered in dense stubble. Eric could go days without shaving and not produce the same effect.

The bouncer at the Gandy, an enormous man perched on a tall white stool, held an arm out in front of Eric and spoke the words that had begun to haunt his dreams: "You got ID?"

Murray and Roy had gone ahead into the throbbing cavern of the place, and Thomas had to call them back, expressions on all three of their faces suggesting this had *never* happened to them.

They piled back into Murray's Honda and headed over to BJ's, since it was known to have a slightly looser policy. Eric would just as soon have been dropped back at his place. He didn't relish the possibility of being carded again, and when he glanced at Thomas next to him in the backseat, it now seemed as if they might all be in on it together, Murray and Roy and Thomas, having themselves a great smirky laugh at his expense.

But then as they walked along Pender Street, Thomas took off his cap and plopped it on Eric's head. "There." He skipped backward in front of him, a reassuring smile on his face. "It makes you look older."

Maybe it did. Since the woman on the other side of the window downstairs at BJ's let all four of them pay the cover and check their coats, and the bouncer across the way seemed to follow her lead.

BJ's was a humble, low-ceilinged basement room, with a bar along one wall and circular tables scattered down to a postage-stamp dance floor, behind which a glittery curtain fronted a tiny stage.

"It's dead," Murray said flatly as they looked around the near-empty room. "No wonder they let him in."

Thomas reached back and held Eric's hand. "Relax," he whispered and shook it up and down.

They took a table near the front and ordered drinks, and the place slowly began to fill, with the usual BJ's mix: plenty of gay men, of all ages, as well as several drag queens and a couple of tables of women, several of them among the butchest Eric had seen. One crew-cut red-head in a motorcycle jacket, with a spray of freckles showing through the holes in her torn T-shirt, threw back shots by herself at the bar and topped every one with a grimace, a shake of the head, and the dry pronouncement, "For the luv-a-Mike." Next to her a thin young drag queen in a loose lamé gown and a wedge-shaped hairdo that might have been her own sipped a martini and smoked a More cigarette, her eyes darting weirdly about the room, the only part of her not possessed of a supernatural stillness.

Eric asked Thomas to dance and he resisted but finally allowed himself to be cajoled onto the floor, as Grace Jones sang "I Need a Man." The song was fast and funny enough to allow their movements on the half-filled dance floor to seem less awkward. Eric danced like someone who'd never done it before, and except for a cousin's wedding a few years back, he hadn't. But Thomas jumped and shimmied like a pro; with his English sophistication and his swank clothes, he seemed the least likely candidate for disco, but he took to the dance floor, bouncing and bopping and hunkering down to beat his fists in the air between his bent knees, as if on a tom-tom.

When the music changed, Eric instinctively tugged him close to slow dance to Dorothy Moore singing "Misty Blue" as a mirror ball spun shards of light about the room.

The top of Thomas's head came only to Eric's shoulder, and their movement about the dance floor was not exactly graceful, but there must have been something of grace in it, because Eric remembered the moment vividly years afterward, the last time, it seemed, he had absolutely known what he wanted.

When the song ended and he followed Thomas almost dutifully off the floor, he again began to detect an undercurrent of cynicism in the setup, as Thomas squeezed his hand proprietarily and said, "I'm not letting you out of my sight." He pulled Eric to the back of the room. "Do you realize how many men have stared daggers at me tonight?"

Near the entranceway again, he pushed Eric up against the wall and attacked him, his tongue plunging between Eric's teeth. Then he leaned back and looked sideways, as if for a reaction from bystanders. Over Thomas's shoulder, Eric saw Murray raise his eyebrows and beat a hasty retreat back to their table.

Thomas left to go to the men's room, and Eric felt so at sea with the etiquette of the whole situation he thought for a moment he should follow him in, that they would somehow have sex in there. But just then they announced that it was "showtime at BJ's," Thomas came back out, and the two of them made their way to the front to sit cross-legged on the dance floor for the show.

One of the performers was Sally St. Claire, a smoky, buxom blonde who had visited the university a few weeks before for a drag show the gay club had sponsored in a classroom in one of the Arts buildings. During her opening number she recognized Eric and Thomas. She ran a hand through Eric's hair and smiled at the two of them, and Eric felt the strongest sense of family then, as he sat there on the BJ's dance floor, stronger than he'd felt for years around his biological relatives. He and Thomas Stroud were the children, and the grownups, be they lesbian bikers or male torch singers, would parent them into this offbeat community, where years of hurt and alienation would fall away.

With another smirk, Murray dropped the two of them outside the Garth and tooted the horn as he and Roy waved good night.

Inside the apartment, Eric turned from locking the door, and Thomas stood on tiptoes to reach his mouth. Eric couldn't get over the taste of him, how he hungered for it. He opened Thomas's shirt to see his hairy chest, which he ran his hands across. He undid Thomas's pants and pulled them to his knees, so that his white undershorts seemed to glow in the dark.

"Let's go to the bed," Eric suggested, and Thomas waddled comically over there, his pants still bunched around his ankles.

But naked, in bed finally with the man of his dreams, Eric was stunned to come face-to-face with the same inhibition and awkwardness, and a drugged desire to just curl against his dream and sleep.

Thomas didn't seem particularly to care, and that seemed connected somehow: that Eric felt this intensity of helpless desire for someone apparently so far away.

As they drifted into sleep, though, in the peg-legged single bed Eric had brought from home, Thomas reached behind him and took Eric's hand, carried it forward and placed it in front of him, to cup his balls.

"There," he said.

In the night, he cried out, something Eric couldn't decipher that sounded like "Muh! Muh! Muh!"

"What?" Eric mumbled groggily, and Thomas stopped.

He turned to face Eric and then wrapped his arms around him. He brought his knees up so that his legs entwined with Eric's, and he pressed his rough, bearded face against Eric's smooth chest.

"Don't let go," he whispered.

chapter twelve

"What about Mickey?" Eric asked.

"Huh?" Dale said and looked a little slack in the face suddenly.

"When you were spending all these nights at the baths, weren't you still with Mickey?"

"No," he said with an attempt at finality. "I had broken up with him." Then, after a moment, looking off, he added, "I was faithful to Mickey."

"Really?"

Dale sighed.

"No," he admitted and turned back to look at the bedspread. "I was never faithful to anyone."

"Isn't that a slight exaggeration?"

"Hmn. I wonder. It just seems funny to remember having faith enough in the future to walk away from something so good. Right now, I'd give anything to be back in that apartment on Eighth Street. All the door frames were crooked, and nothing kept the thieves out—they even stole our dirty laundry."

"Why did you break up?"

"Oh, who the hell knows? Something that seemed very important at the time, I'm sure. You've never been in a relationship. You don't understand."

"Well, I like to think I have some capacity—"

"Miss Lonelyhearts. Do you even remember *how* to have sex?"

"Yes," Eric said angrily, in fact wondering if he had ever known.

"Mickey was four years older than me. Mickey *liked* relationships. I was always comparison shopping. That's what I remember from that time, as if there were almost too much choice. No matter who you were with, you were always thinking that tonight at the baths, or tomorrow at the bar, or next week at so-and-so's party, you might meet someone better.

"Our hours conflicted. Mickey worked during the day at a copy shop; I was a waiter nights at a Tex Mex restaurant. And after work, I'd be hyper. I'd come home to Eighth Street, up three flights of stairs and down that narrow, tilting hallway, and find him waiting up for me, painting sometimes, other times just waiting, in this sleepy domestic mood that made me feel as if I was suffocating.

"I started going out after work with some of the people from the restaurant, and when I got home, I'd find Mickey asleep, but in the middle of some attempt to stay up—a half-filled cup of coffee in his hand, the TV on, once with his head actually leaning against a canvas, pink paint fanning out in his curly black hair."

"How did you meet?"

"In a bar. Of all places."

"What attracted you to him?"

"He was an older man—twenty-five, ha! I met him in the Ninth Circle, and he seemed even older. He didn't fit into the bar scene—he was too serious and his look was too sixties, and that attracted me at first. I mean, he was different. I don't know. He was from Baltimore, but he'd lived in New York for two and a half years, and he took me under his wing in a way that seemed a great relief at the time. I imagined that we'd conquer the city. We'd become famous together, the artist and the actor: Broadway openings, profiles in *Interview* magazine, trips to Hollywood for the Academy Awards. But Mickey had much . . . calmer ambitions. And I wasn't even going to auditions."

Dale curled sideways and down in the bed. His talking today had less energy in it, although his voice was improving. "His hands always smelled of turpentine," he said and traced a lazy finger across the bottom sheet.

"I left him," he said, "after two years, crying in the crooked doorway of that tenement apartment, after a horrible fight in which our remaining possessions were thrown, so that red and green and orange paint covered everything."

He sat up a bit. "I drifted into the snack bar at the St. Mark's a few nights later and found him waiting for me. I still wanted to fight, but Mickey was quiet; he just wanted me to come home."

He turned to look out the window on the other side of the room, where the sky was gray and noncommittal.

"Did you go?" Eric asked.

"Hmn?"

"Home."

"No," Dale said and turned back.

"Why not?

"Because I'd had sex that night with three of the most beautiful men you've ever seen, that's why. I still remember them—one after another, like ticking off dreams come true. And Mickey couldn't compete with that."

Eric strained into one final chin-up, not even a full movement but enough to fatigue the muscles completely, and dropped to the floor of his apartment.

In the midst of Dale's recent treatment, Eric's twenty-eighth birthday had come and gone. He had been happy to let it go pretty much unnoticed. He'd never been a birthday person; the day itself he almost had to be reminded about. But the age would slowly dawn on him, and this one had been dawning for a while.

The late twenties seemed such a toxic time. Maybe it was the first real glimpse of thirty. There were so many things Eric had expected to have done by the time he was thirty: places he had planned to travel; money he had hoped to be making; personality problems he had figured would be resolved. Most of all he had thought that by thirty he would have a lover.

His workout completed, he rolled his weights into a corner and headed for the shower. Afterward, he fell down on the bed and closed his eyes. He slept almost immediately.

He dreamt of a white light over Astor Place. It's the most beautiful light I've ever seen, he thought.

Ahead of him was a crowd of some kind, and as he drew closer he saw that the crowd was all men, and apparently gay men, the kind of sunny, good-looking group Eric hadn't seen in years. In the dream, he was falling in love with everyone there.

"Did you hear?" a man Eric's age, with curly hair and a big smile, asked.

"What?"

"It's reopened," the man said. "Get in line."

And up ahead Eric could see the black door with the sign that read "The New Saint Mark's Baths," freshly painted; the whole building seemed to glow. And joining the line, he felt swept up in the celebration. He could have sworn someone had his arms around him from behind and someone else was snuggling a shoulder.

I get to go after all, he thought, with the rush of ecstasy he had felt before in dreams of going back to high school, university, dreams of returning and doing everything right.

chapter thirteen

The only way to reach Thomas was through a pay phone at the end of the hall in the Gage residence, a collection of concrete buildings where he lived on campus. Eric had the number, but whenever he called, he either got no answer or some butch dormmate of Thomas's who might or might not have sensed the fever behind Eric's voice. Whoever answered would leave the phone for a long while, then inevitably return with the message "He's not here." Whoever this guy was, Eric envied him his proximity to Thomas. "Please tell him Eric called," he'd say.

Thomas missed more club meetings, and the scuttlebutt was that he had come down with mononucleosis, the "kissing disease." Murray got a cryptic look on his face when Eric questioned him, as if he'd been asked not to divulge information.

"But if he's sick . . . ," Eric said.

"Yes. We're all very worried," Murray said flatly and then dashed from sight.

Finally, on a cooler night, when he'd again been studying late at the library, Eric made his way toward the swimming pool.

From a distance, he saw a figure he was sure was Thomas, standing as he had before, in his cap and overcoat, hands in his pockets, watching the swimmers through the glass in a kind of trance. But as he approached, the figure turned and bolted away. By the time Eric was in front of the glass himself, it seemed to have been only a shadow.

———

The Dogwood Monarchists Society, the oldest gay organization in Vancouver and one of a network of similar "courts" throughout Canada and the U.S., particularly in the West, was holding their annual Coronation Ball, where the empress, a transvestite, and the emperor, a gay man not in drag, would be elected from votes cast in the bars.

The ball was held every spring in the heart of downtown, on Granville Mall, at the Commodore Ballroom, where Eric's parents had gone dancing in the forties, before they moved south. There was a picture of the two of them in one of the family albums, taken at the Commodore on New Year's Eve by one of those roving night-club photographers. They look romantic and glamorous in evening attire: his pretty petite blond mother and his dashing dark-haired father. Right after that, the pictures in the album shifted locale, to the fantastic parched black-and-white landscape against which every-one shed layers of clothing and darkened.

Outside the Commodore that March night in 1977, Eric was greeted with jeers from a group who assembled annually on Granville to heckle the drag queens, although he himself was dressed only a little more flamboyantly than usual in honor of the occasion, in a denim vest, a white shirt open to the navel, and a blue checkered bandanna. He was still waiting for his sea legs in this world where he was somehow or other considered attractive. He kept trying to find the look that would settle on him and give him a firm identity; he grasped at compliments and errant shifts of the eye not as boosts to his ego but as clues to his very being.

Inside, the Commodore had been transformed into a fantasyland, filled with every imaginable gay persona. Ken was there, and Sally St. Claire from BJ's, filling out a chic skintight black satin number cut in a diagonal slash at the knee and capped by a swath of material wound around her blond hair, and the two of them and Eric ended up dancing between a bewigged male couple in eighteenth-century French costume, one a man, the other a woman, and a stout bearded fellow in broad, boozy genderfuck, a string of pearls swinging across the hairy chest he revealed in a low-cut black slip. They all ended up as part of a long chain that bopped in wandering zigzags across the spring-loaded dance floor while Tavares sang "Heaven Must Be Missing an Angel."

Everyone on the floor sat down for the guest appearance of drag queen/comedian Charles Pierce, who sashayed out in classy blond curls and a sequined gown, took one look around, and said, "Wouldn't Anita Bryant just shit if she knew how much fun we were having?"

The reigning empress, Miss Bernie, by day an accountant named Bernard Weinstock, was done up in a simple but elegant white evening gown, her hair in a black bun that made her resemble no one so much as Eydie Gormé. She stood energetically alongside her emperor, handsome, mustachioed Farley, who wore a wide-lapeled blue tuxedo with flared trousers and a ruffled shirt, and together they bid farewell to their subjects with a lip-synched version of "United We Stand," which they got everyone to join in on, so that by the end Eric found himself surrounded by hundreds of gay men and women with joined hands thrust in the air, singing, "If our backs should ever be against the wall, we'll be together, together you and I."

A cousin of his contacted Eric's mother to say she was singing with the North Vancouver Light Opera in *The Student Prince*, and would they all like to come see the show. Everyone else in the family quickly thought of an excuse, but when he finally managed to connect with Thomas on the pay phone at the end of his hall at Gage, Eric suggested the two of them go.

Thomas often spoke about opera, and the fine arts, things of which Eric felt woefully ignorant. Inadequate as this invitation to operetta in the burbs seemed, it was part of a plan, which Eric participated in without quite realizing it, to reshape his personality, to meld with this other, to please.

Thomas was not enthusiastic about the proposition. He said that he had an enormous amount of homework to do and couldn't possibly go, but eventually Eric wore him down. There was a single-minded determination in him now, but also something that must have seemed flattering, must have seemed like love.

Thomas was late meeting Eric on campus that afternoon. He stood at the loop for fifteen minutes while two buses left for downtown. When Thomas finally showed up, he told Eric he had met someone outside the library.

"An older man, who claimed to be a student."

"So what do you mean?" Eric asked somewhat testily.

"Well, he tried to pick me up," Thomas said, as if stating the obvious.

"Oh. I thought that's what you meant."

"Yes," Thomas continued as they boarded a bus. "He called me over and asked for the time, which is a little tired don't you think, but it does tend to work well enough, doesn't it? And then he started asking me all sorts of questions about what I was studying and so on, very interested of course, and all the while looking me over."

"I see."

"He asked me if I'd like to come back into the city with him for a drink. And I said I couldn't. I was meeting someone."

"Sorry to have interfered with your plans."

"Now, don't get huffy," Thomas said and patted Eric's knee with a hand.

"Would you have gone with him otherwise?"

"Hmn. Well, I might have. He wasn't bad looking, if that's what you mean. But I don't really do that sort of thing anymore."

"I thought you went to the bars a lot."

"Well, I do. But I don't go home with anybody anymore. I find I've grown rather bored with the whole thing."

Thomas had dressed for their date: dark pants, a herringbone jacket, white shirt, and a broad striped tie. As ever, these clothes made him appear elegant to Eric, older, of another world somehow. "You must get offers like that a lot," he said.

"Not really, no, I don't think any more than the average person. And when I do, I find increasingly that it doesn't mean much to me now. It just means that someone's decided this type will do, you know, this type will do for tonight."

Eric wondered what type Thomas was exactly, since it must have been his preferred type. This fascinated him at the time, this electric connection that could be established with someone based immediately on physical appearance. What caused certain features to read this way?

The men Eric was attracted to always had mustaches, they were always dark, and fairly heavyset, and though he wasn't necessarily aware of this as an attracting factor at first, they were also always difficult in some way: Communication was never a breeze; Eric perked up around dissonance, the opposite of the connection he thought he craved.

They went for dinner at the White Spot across from the Centennial Theatre on Lonsdale in North Van. There was something sublime for Eric about bringing dark, problematic Thomas to this place deep in the heart of his suburban past; he paced through this date as if on eggshells, breathing rarefied air. His brother Jerry had hung out in the White Spot during high school; Eric had eaten here with his parents the night his grandmother finally died.

"I don't think you'll like me very much when you get to know me," Thomas said suddenly, when they had ordered.

"Why do you say that?"

"Well, because I'm really a very strange person. I have various physical and psychological problems which are very unappealing." He folded his hands in front of him and looked out the window.

"Like what?" Eric asked.

"Well, for example, I've been known to throw fits of intense rage, in which I break things, things of value. I have thoroughly destroyed my room in residence more than once."

"You're exaggerating."

"I'm not. Although I seem to have stopped doing that this year," he added with a puzzled look. "Which is actually depressing in a sense because I think it only means the anger has gone inward. I just don't bother expressing it anymore."

"What are you so angry about?"

"Oh, various things, everything. My parents for one."

"For not accepting that you're gay?"

"Yes, and for torturing me the whole time I was growing up."

"Torturing you?"

"I was a hyperactive child. My memories of that time are hit-and-miss, but it's as if I were wired wrong. I just seem to have had an incredible amount of energy and nowhere to go with it. And Mummy's solution, when she wasn't chasing me with a wooden spoon or tying me to a chair, was to give me a sedative every time she thought she couldn't take it anymore, which was more and more of the time, despite the pills she was popping herself. It's amazing I'm not a major addict."

The waitress brought their food, two Legendary Hamburger Platters, and Thomas picked at his unenthusiastically. "I should have had professional help," he said, "but she thought she could knock it out of me. And my father went along for the ride."

"This . . . anger you feel," Eric ventured gingerly and took a bite of his burger. He swallowed and continued. "Does it have something to do with your trips to the swimming pool?"

"Oh, you've heard about that, have you?"

"Heard about it? You practically walked right by me the other night without saying a word."

"What is there to say?"

"Why do you do it?"

"We all need a secret, don't we? Don't we all need a secret?"

"Do you swim?"

"No, I watch. I will always be the one who watches."

"But why? Night after night. I heard—"

"I don't wish to discuss it."

He took a bite of his burger then and the filling ran out between his fingers. He looked up at Eric, a gleam in his eye, which faded when his eyes met Eric's.

"What's wrong?" Eric asked.

"I've failed, haven't I?"

"What?"

"I was trying to dissuade you," he said and set the burger back on his plate, then lifted his handsome head. "I was trying to make you see how unappealing I am."

The operetta seemed too long, and Thomas kept making dry comments about the inferior production. On the bus back to the city, Eric asked him if he wanted to spend the night with him in the West End, and Thomas said he couldn't. He had mononucleosis and a great deal of homework to do.

"You always have homework," Eric said.

Thomas had to transfer to the 10 UBC bus downtown anyway, so he agreed to get off with Eric at Bute Street. Then when he'd

done that, he agreed that all right, he would walk him to his apartment, all the while saying, "You really seem much more interested
in this than I am, and I just don't think it's fair to you. I'm generally
attracted to much older men, you see, and right now I don't find that
I'm attracted to anybody at all."

But at the apartment, he accepted Eric's invitation to come up for
a beer, and inside they sat drinking for a few moments, until Eric
couldn't stand it anymore, crossed the room, and sat in Thomas's lap
to kiss him.

He loved this newly discovered thing: that each man had a distinct flavor.

He still had no idea where sex would lead once started. He felt
hopelessly in the dark about it, out of synch with the whole world.
But at that age desire could obliterate all other concerns, even the
fear of failure.

Thomas lifted Eric from the chair to a standing position and
began to unbutton his shirt. He kissed him more and more vigor-
ously as he did this, and Eric kissed back, running his hands through
Thomas's thick black hair and under the collar of his jacket, knead-
ing the muscles beneath his thin dress shirt as Thomas leaned him
over and yanked his jeans down to his ankles.

Thomas opened his own pants and pushed against Eric so
hard he backed him into a standing lamp and sent it rocking. His
mouth locked on Eric's, Thomas just kept pumping, so that Eric
forgot about his own response entirely and felt only the pressure
of Thomas against him, the roughness of his hairy body, the feel of
his cock against his leg, his stomach. Finally Thomas jerked upward
with a cry and a burst of heat, and collapsed against Eric's shoulder.

They stood weaving in this lopsided embrace for a while, Thomas
breathing deeply, Eric more alert, reality moving back into the room
piece by piece.

Then Thomas leaned away from Eric and smiled—the biggest smile Eric had ever seen on his face. And he kissed Eric in a sloppy, friendly way on the lips.

"That," he said and pulled back to look at Eric again, "was the nicest thing I've ever done with anybody."

chapter fourteen

"Tell me about Jay," Eric said.

Dale didn't respond.

"Dale?"

"Hmn?" he mumbled, on his side in the bed, turned away.

"Tell me about Jay."

"Who?" Dale brought his knees up into a fetal position.

"Your other lover."

"Oh."

"Tell me—"

"You knew me when I was with Jay."

"Huh?"

"You knew me when I was with Jay," he almost shouted and then started to cough.

"Yeah, but there was still so much we never talked about. I don't know why. What were we doing instead?"

"I think we were at the movies," Dale said and turned onto his back. "Which may have been wise."

"Where did you meet Jay?"

"Oh, what's the point? What's the point?" Dale's eyes looked everywhere but at Eric.

"Uh . . ."

"I thought I was going to . . . I really thought . . ."

"What?"

Dale still looked away, toward a stack of magazines on the table swung to the other side of his bed. The new fellow in the bed across the way, Charles, had an extremely eclectic and seemingly endless supply of magazines, which he lent soundlessly to Dale and Eric, whether they asked or not. Bertram had been discharged a few days ago, escorted by Janice, who stopped yelling and cried as she wheeled his hunched figure out the door, going home but apparently not getting better.

Charles was another gay man, small, about thirty-five years old, quiet and polite, who listened very intently to everything the doctors and nurses told him, as if the key to this thing were to follow instructions as precisely as possible. Just now he snoozed, under the covers and partially elevated in his bed, clutching a copy of *National Geographic*, his balding head tilted back, his glasses slightly askew.

"I mean . . . first the chemo worked," Dale said. "Finally. And then . . . this, I thought . . ."

"You're doing really well. Everybody has said that. It's changing so much all the time. Research . . . I mean, there's just no way of knowing. All you can do is try to deal with what's at hand, I guess. You said your fever was down this morning."

"A bit, yeah."

"So . . ."

Dale took a breath and faced Eric.

"What did you want to know about Jay?" he asked.

"Where did you meet?"

Dale looked off again and then back. "We were judges the same year for the Miss America pageant."

"That's not true."

"Tell that to the winner."

"Did you live on your own after Mickey?"

"No," Dale said wearily. "I had roommates again. The curse of my young life. Three gadabouts in two rooms, that's what it amounted to. Lorne and Tad, where are they now?"

Dale looked toward the empty bed diagonally across the room, where the nameless, ageless man had finally died the day before.

"Three young men in search of closet space," he said. "The East Village seemed always to be full of irresistible clothing opportunities. Hours were spent in that apartment debating potential hairstyles. And then out, out for the night: dancing, drinking, usually ending up at the baths, separated at the doors to our rooms, if we were lucky enough to get them, reunited hours later, in the morning light, collapsed together across mattresses on the floor of the apartment, drunk and drugged and exhausted enough, I suppose, not to notice how we were living.

"I met Jay at the baths. Afterwards, he wanted to take my picture, so we went back to his place, uptown a little ways. But he never got around to it. We had sex again instead and slept, and when I woke up, I remember taking a stroll around that giant apartment and thinking that I wanted that again, to make a real home with someone.

"The sex was not as good as with Mickey, but the lifestyle with Jay was better, more what I'd always envisioned when I'd imagined myself in a relationship.

"It seemed that he loved me. He was certainly physically attracted to me. But I was aware very early on of not quite feeling these things in return, you know? He often wanted to have sex when I didn't. We locked horns over simple romantic gestures—a good-night kiss, a blow job in a parked car.

"But then of course Jay became quite successful. I even had my picture in a couple magazines as you recall, on his arm at this or that event. I mean it was very seductive, I suppose. And he wasn't bad looking."

"I always thought he looked like Isak Dinesen."

"Well, he did. But I thought I could learn to live with that."

"You weren't . . . monogamous with him, were you?"

"No-o-o-o-o.

"I don't remember exactly when I started that business. Again. We had been together at least a year, and once I'd cheated on him the first time, I know I did it several times in quick succession, as if I couldn't get enough. I remember being so relieved to have unencumbered sex again.

"I suppose I wanted to get caught. I mean I seem to have set it up that way, so the whole thing would blow up in my face and be over with. A friend of Jay's spotted me with someone; then another friend saw me at the baths. Jay himself came home early from an out-of-town shoot and found someone in the apartment." Dale laughed.

"I was in the kitchen making coffee, and, thinking quickly, before Jay had seen anything, I said a friend of mine had had too much to drink and slept over. Which was sort of inane because he more or less knew all my friends and, anyway," he began to giggle, "just then the guy came striding out of the bedroom buck naked with a hard-on and, apparently unaware of Jay's presence, grabbed his dick, shook it at me, and said, 'Hey, babe, you got any use for this?'"

Dale laughed until he coughed.

"He'd always been something of a bitch," he said when his breathing had quieted. "He'd get frustrated over something in connection with his work or money that was owed him, things that had piled up around the apartment, and the anger would momentarily consume him, black out every other emotion in his face. He'd throw things, sometimes breaking them. Once he pulled down a shower curtain, rod and all, along with a piece of the bathroom wall. He'd pound his fist against things, sometimes hard things, a desk or a table. He broke a small bone in his hand. And he'd chant something inane over and over, like 'bastards, bastards, bastards,' his whole body tense, his face red and twisted. And then he'd cry, he'd break down and cry, and inevitably close the experience by saying, 'I can't live this way. I can't go on living this way.'

"He always claimed that it wasn't specifically me he was referring to in this declaration, but it was hard not to take it personally. Especially with a split lip and a black eye."

"I remember."

"Once he threw me across the room so hard I had plaster in my hair.

"And then we'd make love. He would cry, and we'd make love, and that was the closest we'd come to having good sex."

Eric's mind tripped over the words "good sex." People often graded the quality of it this way, he knew, couldn't wait to find out "how" someone was in bed, as if it were a sport, or an art, instead of an awkward stringing together of bits of pleasure caught on the wing.

"Since this didn't seem particularly healthy," Dale continued, "I slowly began making plans to leave."

Actually, it hadn't been quite that civilized. Eric remembered. Jay, in fact, began giving Dale a taste of his own medicine by having an affair with one of his models, and Dale responded by ferreting out every photo and negative of the boy he could find, dumping them in the middle of Twenty-first Street, and setting them on fire.

"So I left him a long letter," Dale went on, "attempting to explain that I cared for him and basically wished him well and that I didn't think it was worth his ruining his life over this . . ."

But that was not at all what had happened. Jay had fallen madly in love with his new boyfriend, whom he had to spend a lot of time with now, reshooting pictures, and Dale had gone half-crazy with plots to get even. Why was he telling the story differently now? Didn't he realize Eric would remember? And what else of what he'd told him was untrue?

"Well, what can I say?" Dale said to wrap things up. "Another suitcase in another hall. Don't cry for me, Gramercy Park." And he lifted his arms like Evita, and bowed his head ever so slightly.

chapter fifteen

The women in Wardrobe at M-G-M used to circle Judy Garland and comment on how difficult her figure was to work with. She got her revenge by learning to ease one shoulder up as they measured her, so that she'd appear to be straight but when she put on the finished clothes they wouldn't hang right.

"How's my little hunchback this morning?" Louis B. Mayer would call in greeting.

Eric looked up from rereading his dogeared copy of *The Making of the Wizard of Oz* to see Grace standing in the doorway to his office behind the most beautiful young man Eric had ever seen. It struck him with just that kind of finality, a simplicity he hadn't felt in years.

"Eric," Grace said, "this is Glenn Merritt. He's starting upstairs."

The young man smiled and Grace's hand on the door squeaked it open a little farther.

"Eric?" she said.

"Oh . . . yes." He jumped up. "Sorry." He extended his hand. "I'm Eric."

Glenn Merritt had a very strong handshake. He was a little on the short side and extremely well built. When he shook Eric's hand, his biceps bulged alarmingly beneath the short sleeve of a dressy green shirt he was wearing buttoned all the way up in front.

"He knows about the tie," Grace said.

"What?" Eric asked.

"The tie," Grace said. "An article of clothing the company requires men to wear. You know, the one that hangs down in front."

"Oh . . . yes."

Glenn appeared to be in his early twenties. He wore his dark hair stylishly long on top and razored at the back. His lips were very pink and appeared to be wet; his eyes had more black in them than seemed usual.

"Well, welcome aboard," Eric said.

"Thanks," Glenn replied with enthusiasm. "I've been wanting to work in a bookstore for a while actually. I'm glad I finally applied."

"Good," Eric said. "I guess I'll see you around then."

He thought that Glenn stayed in his office and held eye contact with him just a little longer than was necessary, and though he suspected this was just his imagination, it had been so long since he'd cared about such things one way or the other that he pulled the excitement to himself and hugged it.

"We're all glad you applied," Grace said as she walked Glenn down the hall. "Aren't we, Eric?"

A second or two later she ducked back into his office to mouth silently, "Straight."

"What?" Eric said too loudly.

"He came in with a girlfriend," Grace whispered. "He's straight." She left the office again but then ducked back once more. "And I'm Mamie Eisenhower," she added.

At home that night Eric lay on his bed with a beer, Simone asleep on his chest, the TV flickering with the sound down on a recap of the day's Iran-Contra hearings.

What Grace hadn't said, of course, was that Glenn was replacing Dale, who had now officially lost his job. She and Eric had fudged time sheets for a while, trying to get other employees to pick up the slack and keep him on the payroll and thus covered by Blue Cross. But they could only reasonably do this for so long, and that time had just run out.

Even when Dale got home from the hospital, he wouldn't be in any shape to come back to work. Eric had warned him the week before that his time on the payroll would have to end soon, and that they should start the ball rolling on whatever other sources of support were available to him. But he wasn't sure Dale had really heard him, and now he had the disturbing feeling that Dale thought he would be coming back to the bookstore "as soon as I'm out of here," as he had taken to saying about a lot of things.

The immediate result of the change in the time sheets, however, was Glenn.

Eric downed the last of his beer and dropped the bottle with a clunk to the magazine- and newspaper-strewn floor. He scratched Simone on the top of her head and watched her scrunch up her eyes and purr in ecstasy. "You're so easily pleased," he said.

He reached behind him and turned off the bedside lamp, a black metal cylinder clipped to one of his bookshelves. In the light from the streetlamp behind his battered and streaked window shade, he stroked Simone and, as a warm evening breeze drifted through the slightly open window, thought that summer was definitely on the way. Dale dated everything from the Academy Awards, which he claimed always occurred on the first warm night of the year. This year he had hacked his way through the choice of *Platoon* as Best Picture in his apartment with Eric, who at that time was still struggling with Dale's reluctance to go to the doctor about his cough. Even post-stroke Bette Davis running amok at the end of the broadcast failed to elicit much response from Dale beyond an aggravated clearing of his throat. And he was sullen and uncommunicative for days afterward. Finally, in a quiet moment, almost wincing, hardly able to look at Eric, he said, "Ridiculous as it may seem, once upon a time, I believed I would win one of them."

For Eric everything just seemed to be going by very fast now. Twenty-eight, twenty-nine . . .

He stretched out his legs and ran his hand across the rumpled surface of his big, unmade, half-empty bed. He remembered buying his first double bed, in the spring of 1977, a week after his eighteenth birthday. The middle-aged woman who sold it to him, on the top floor of the Hudson's Bay department store, was very helpful but spoke with a slightly wry tone, raising an eyebrow as Eric looked for the firmest mattress for his back. He tried several beds, bouncing a bit and then reclining, imagining on each of them that he was sleeping with Thomas Stroud.

Presumably because of his age, the woman had initially said, in the friendliest tone she would use in the encounter, "You're looking for a single, are you?"

"No," Eric had replied, and then he could not quite suppress a smile as he added, "Queen size."

"I see."

She stood watching him test out the mattresses with a look on her face that many of her generation seemed to wear throughout the entire decade of the seventies, a kind of reluctantly tolerant, shell-shocked disgust.

"This is the one," Eric said, still bouncing a little on the third bed from the end.

"Oh really?"

He double-checked the price on the laminated tag and then said, "Yes. I'll take it."

He sat at the woman's little desk and arranged the details of payment and delivery. He paid her in cash, peeling off one at a time the hundred-dollar bills he had withdrawn that afternoon from his savings account at Toronto Dominion. At that point in his life he had never even applied for a credit card.

The bed was on a list of things that had stacked up in his mind behind the phrase "if only . . ." It seemed that the lack of these things was all that kept him from the adulthood he craved, the success, which now almost exclusively took the form of romance, success in love.

He took the escalator to the basement of the Bay and walked briskly out the exit to the mall and through the teeming underground to the bookstore, feeling lightheaded that another hurdle had been leapt. Particularly he felt, meeting male eyes in the sexy Friday night of the mall, that he was somehow better equipped to trick now, that he could cruise with less of a handicap.

Everything in the seventies seemed to be about sex—sex as the freeing, long-suppressed something that would change all for the better. And this attitude was epitomized by the world of the mall, where Eric first experienced the flush of independence, where he first made a living, and where he was first cruised.

The clothing stores, with names like Xanadu and Big Steel, a style of shop for young people that seemed virtually an invention of the decade, played the same music as the discos. The clerks, male and female, would stand in the doorway to their particular piece of the tunnel and bop to the ubiquitous beat as they made eyes at the passersby.

Eric's copy of the *Thank God It's Friday* soundtrack skipped when he got it home, so he took it back to Sam the Record Man in the corner of the upper level of the mall, where the woman behind the counter slapped it on their turntable to test it and ended up selling three more copies in five minutes, everyone in the store having been swept up immediately in the seductive inanity of the music.

Eric felt at that moment like an ambassador from this nightclub culture, gay culture in essence, that seemed to be everywhere then, that everyone wanted in on.

His parents drove over to pick up his old single bed. He helped his father carry it downstairs and strap it to the top of the car, to be hauled back to North Van for safekeeping. To his mother and father, he had stressed the space advantages of the larger bed, because of his height, but they obviously hadn't really bought it. And they weren't as jovial about this as they might have been under different circumstances—no nudging innuendo, no liberal acceptance of the swinging times. Homosexuality seemed to have come closer than anything to taxing their tolerance level, and this pleased Eric in a way that surprised him. He had always thought that his quest for worldly approval represented a rebellion against his parents' lax attitude, but now he wondered if what he really sought was just something, anything, that would make them pay attention.

No one answered the phone at all now at the end of the hall in Thomas's dormitory.

The campus had burst into a sweet spring, the tree-lined malls budding in the sun-warmed air, everything seeming to whisper of the life to come.

Eric tried to figure out who in the gay club had classes with Thomas, but apparently no one had seen him recently. Murray was particularly uninformative. "Sometimes," he said enigmatically as he scanned the bulletin board in the club office, looking for a summer rental, "it's best to leave well enough alone."

He hunched in the bushes at the side of the road leading to the swimming pool for three nights, but Thomas didn't show. By the third night Eric felt the pull of the glass himself, walked over to the building and stood as Thomas had, the rippling blue water hypnotic, like a view into a separate reality, of agile, exposed limbs, of athletic grace and effortless camaraderie, the night sky echoing with the boisterous hollering of young men on the inside.

At home in the West End, he switched from Craven A's to herbal cigarettes, and from Dan Hill to Rod Stewart. He leaned against the window late at night and gazed toward the campus in Point Grey, puffing on the sage that smelled like marijuana, and listening to

Atlantic Crossing: "I can tell by your eyes that you've probably been crying forever . . ."

He camped on the floor outside the door to Thomas's third-floor room, which he had never seen.

The hallway simmered with a tense collegiate sexiness, a feeling oddly like coming home and running away at the same time. There seemed to be young men everywhere in various states of undress or behind closed doors shouting in voices that somehow sounded naked. By the time Thomas wheeled around the corner from the staircase, Eric almost didn't care that he was angry.

But he pounded his fist against the door above Eric's head and said, "What makes you think you have the right to invade my privacy this way?"

"Uh . . . ," Eric said and got up off the floor. "I was worried?"

Thomas looked around uncomfortably. "I'd send you away," he whispered tightly, "but you'd only make a scene."

He opened the door to his tiny room and went inside, without holding the door for Eric, who followed.

Thomas stood in front of the window across the room, facing away, the sunlight fading on his thick black hair as he played with the yellowed pull cord of a blind. "What do you want?" he asked.

"To see you," Eric said.

"I have work to do," Thomas said and turned to his desk; he didn't seem to be in the middle of anything.

Two walls of the room were almost entirely covered by postcards and photographs taped or tacked up in giant collages. Eric stood, mesmerized, looking at the wall next to him. His gaze settled on a sexy black-and-white picture of Thomas with a beard. He moved toward it and reached out with a hand.

"My butch phase," Thomas said quietly, suddenly behind him.

In another picture, a skinnier, more effeminate boy, out of focus, held a cat to his chest in what looked like the backyard of his home.

"I was younger then," Thomas said.

There was a picture of him with his parents on the wall behind the bed, on a trip through Europe, as well as many postcards from that trip, mostly artwork from various museums. In the picture, the three of them stood before the drab facade of an official-looking building, wearing dressy vacation clothes. Thomas looked a lot younger than now, but sullen even then, less than fully present. His father, to one side of him, wore a like expression, and was built similarly, but stooped, heavier, his features having settled in on themselves. His mother, on the other side, appeared to have been pasted in from another photo, something more professional; though hardly glamorous, in a picture hat and a sundress, she stood like an actress from another era, proud to have hit her mark.

Thomas put a classical record on the turntable that took up part of the desktop in the corner by the window. He sat in the orange plastic bucket chair in front of the desk.

He took an actual orange from a drawer behind him and began to peel it with a penknife he'd slipped from his pocket.

"There's a correct way to do this," he said, starting a spiral of peel from the top, "so that the whole thing comes off without breaking."

"Do you want a piece?" he asked when he had successfully removed a complete coil of orange peel.

"No, thanks."

For a moment Thomas ate the orange in silence but for the slurping sounds of his lips and tongue.

Then he said, "So how do you like the show so far?'

"Hmn?"

It was dark in the room by then. The floodlight in the courtyard surrounded Thomas in an aura and left his features indistinct.

"Our . . . relationship. How do you like it?"

"I like you."

"Yes, but why do you like me?"

Eric couldn't answer that right away, and Thomas said, "I suppose that's unfair, because I never know why I like the men I like." He ate another section of orange. "Still, one wonders."

Eric didn't say anything. Thomas finished his orange, then looked about holding his hands like limp claws in the air. He tore a piece of lined paper from an exercise book and wiped them. Then he opened another drawer in the desk and took out what appeared to be a little black address book.

"You see this," he said and began to flip through the pages. "The first part is for friends. Name, address, phone number." He flipped to the back. "And the second part," he said, "is for sex. Name, if I get it, possibly phone number, seldom address, brief physical description." He closed the book and looked up. "I keep the two sections very separate," he said.

"I see."

"And I don't know where to put you."

Eric played for a moment with the spartan gray blanket that covered Thomas's narrow bed. "Will you lie down with me?" he asked.

"Hmn?"

"I want to hold you so bad I can't talk."

Thomas lay curled sideways in Eric's arms, with his head against his chest, and Eric let his face drift through his hair, inhaling his orangey scent.

"I was in love once," Thomas said.

"Hmn?"

"It was on that trip actually." He turned his head toward the wall next to them. "That trip I took with my parents."

He curled back against Eric. "I met him in Paris. My mother was having a time when she didn't want to be thought of as a mum, you know, didn't want to be seen all the time with the kids in tow. My sister had already left home, and my mother seemed impatient for me to do the same, although I was only sixteen years old. My father was a buyer for Marks and Spencer, and my mother was the wife of such a man, but oh how she craved culture! So while she dolled herself up and dragged my father to the theater without me, to the opera without me, to museums without me, and so on, I found out which parks the men went to.

"I spent several days with this one man, a native, much of the time having at it in his flat. Although that doesn't begin to describe what I was feeling. By that age I had had plenty of sex, with all sorts of men, but this was different—this man wanted to be with me even after the sex; just to hold his hand was close to overwhelming—I almost couldn't breathe.

"We wrote letters back and forth for months after I returned to England, and then at last I got away to Paris for spring break to be with him, and we were deliriously happy—or so I thought. One hears things differently when one is young."

"You're still only eighteen."

"Yes, but I am no longer young," Thomas said. "I mean, he said the most incredible things to me! How he'd found his soul mate, his lost younger self. He'd come home from work early because he said he couldn't bear to be away from me any longer. 'I'm so happy just to be here with you,' he'd say as we lay, just lay still, as we're doing now, for hours it seemed.

"But when I returned that time to London, I learned that my parents had found the letters of his I'd saved, and they threatened to take him to court, for corrupting a minor or some such nonsense.

"I felt I had to tell him what had happened. Although later I wondered why I hadn't just kept quiet about it and tried to appease my parents somehow. I didn't expect, you see, that he would be so . . . frightened.

"I'd acquired a secret postal box but suddenly my letters all came back marked 'undeliverable.' When I snuck away from the house to telephone him, he would say he couldn't speak to me and hang up.

He spoke as if there had never been anything between us, this sublime connection, as if I'd dreamt it. Finally, the phone just rang."

Thomas turned to face the ceiling. "He was a swimming instructor," he said. "He taught young children to swim. I suppose he was frightened for his job, which meant a great deal to him.

"I used to meet him at his work sometimes. I'd watch him with the children, in the water. They loved him. He was gentle but very firm. He taught well."

Thomas propped himself up on an elbow then and looked at Eric, ran a couple of fingers tenderly through Eric's hair and looked at him almost as if for the first time. And then kissed him, and the flavor of him was becoming familiar enough for Eric to take it in with delicious slowness. Thomas probed him as if in search of something. And Eric felt what seemed to be the beginning of an ability to open to this, this careful attention from another man.

But then Thomas stopped. He pulled back and smiled, but the old smile, the familiar smile that always bordered on contempt. "I'm tired," he said and flopped back on the bed. "I'm suddenly very tired."

Eric awoke to find his arms empty.

He got up and went to the window. He ducked his head beneath the blind and watched a stout figure scuffle determinedly through the eerie floodlight of the courtyard, on a mission of memory, it would seem, east through a portal to the mall, across the spring night to the swimming pool.

Later that week, in a flash of boldness or loneliness or just plain horniness, he decided to try his luck again at the Gandydancer, the bar he still had not succeeded in entering.

The Gandy was located on False Creek, at the corner of Hamilton and Davie Streets, in a warehouse district dark and echoing as you wandered through it during club hours, the pulse of disco music

faint in the distance and then louder and louder as you trotted down-
hill on Helmcken, past more and more parked cars, and round a
corner to the sizzling neon sign that bathed gay figures in blue light,
grouped about the thrumming enclave or bursting through its giant
slatted wooden doors to let a gasp escape into the night—of Donna
Summer, of ten thousand beer bottles, of a couple hundred gay men
trying to meet each other.

The Gandydancer was for men only, the hottest gay club in town.
Its name had once referred to itinerant railroad workers of the 1920s
who roamed from job to job slinging tools forged by the Gandy
Manufacturing Company of Chicago, but the name had come to
mean only one thing to Eric: sex—the free expression of adult love,
the thing all the songs and all the clothes, the movies, the ideas of the
time revolved around, the thing he craved instinctively, demanded,
even though he could never seem to do it right.

Ironically, despite the supposed heat of the place, more seasoned
veterans of the scene referred to the Gandydancer as an S&S bar:
stand and stare.

This mattered little to Eric, however, as he approached that
moonlit night. And discovered that the fates of admission were
finally with him. Despite his intense nervousness as he turned that
final corner onto Hamilton, he found himself throwing open one of
those tall wooden-handled doors, paying his cover, and checking his
coat with the casualness of a regular, no one but Eric batting an eye.
He held his fist out to the burly bouncer, and received the stamp of
approval that floated him to the bar, which was right before him, a
square in the center of everything. The tingle of the verboten colored
his every step, but also the thrill of acceptance, and the soon to be
forgotten pleasure of growing older.

Beer in hand, he located himself against a wall across from one
side of the bar, in shadow, not wanting to attract too much attention
just yet, and proceeded to stand and stare.

In front of him pulsed figures on the strobe-lit dance floor; around the corner was a quieter alcove with tables. It was a week-night and not too crowded, probably one of the reasons, he knew, that he had been let in, but it was still early. He had not yet mastered the art of arriving at the clubs fashionably late. By law the bars in Vancouver had to close at one, but the fashionable hour to arrive kept getting later and later anyway, so that a lot of men seemed to spend all evening getting dressed or dawdling over dinner or a movie, only to dash to a club shortly after midnight, down a couple of quick drinks before last call, and then frantically try to connect with someone.

As the Gandy began to fill that evening, Eric noticed some extremely handsome men there and that a couple of them were looking his way. But he felt glued to the wall where he stood. It still seemed as if he could be thrown out of the magic kingdom at any moment, and he was afraid to move.

And all this opportunity was dizzying. The sex act, as incomplete as it generally felt to him, remained tied in his mind to particular men, one at a time, and the secret of the Gandydancer seemed to be that this was not the way, that the world was in fact full of men and one was meant to unite with them all.

Before he had time for one gulp of his second Blue, he saw Murray coming in the front door.

It flashed through his mind in an odd mixture of panic and pleasure that Thomas might saunter in after him, but instead Roy followed, beaming artificially as usual.

As he walked toward Eric, Murray was passed by one of the handsome men, on his way out, and he indicated his opinion of the man by turning toward his back, opening his mouth wide, and pointing in with a finger, as to say, "This end up."

"Eric," he purred, "what a surprise," and headed for the bar.

"We were just talking about you," Roy said enigmatically, and Murray slapped him on the arm.

Some more guys from UBC showed up. Henry Wilson, the shaggy-haired botanist, began to talk to Eric about the giant flowers he was growing in a lab on campus.

The DJ played "San Francisco" by the Village People, the first time Eric heard it, the song that would become a kind of anthem that summer, performed by the prefab group that would forever be a symbol, however embarrassing, of the gay seventies.

Henry got Eric off his perch by asking him to dance. They set their beers down and moved toward the floor, Eric discovering along the way that navigating a room like this could be an art in itself.

He had spoken with Henry at several gay club meetings. He was skinny and cute and warm, likable and smart, and years later, when Henry had found a lover and Eric visited Vancouver one summer when the boyfriend was out of town, Eric pushed his way into Henry's bed with the weight of a sadness that sex failed utterly to articulate. You were there, the sadness said. You were there and I chose him.

Henry went back to his friends from the club, who were around the corner from the dance floor, in the nook where there were tables and tall, dark wood shelves filled with books no one read.

Eric, drunk at the bar, saw Murray's face multiply three times in front of him.

"You know him," he heard himself say. "You've known him for some time. He's close to you."

"Come on, honey," he seemed to hear Murray say, "it's time to put you in a cab."

"Don't you love him?" Eric said. "Don't you want him? How can you be that near him, how can you be that lucky, and not know it?"

"Oh, Mary," someone said.

"Yes?" Murray replied. Then to Eric: "Look, honey, you just picked the wrong guy, OK? It happens to the best of us. He's not available—to anybody—right now."

"But he was . . . once."

"*Le professeur?*"

"You know?"

"If I hadn't, I could have guessed. One day you'll realize that everybody has a story, Eric. The trick is to find the one you're in."

He ordered Eric a coffee from the bar, and as he drank it, his mind began to clear a bit.

"Best go home and sleep it off," Murray said.

And soon Eric headed out to do just that, weaving a little on his way to the exit through which he had so amazingly entered just a couple hours earlier, grabbing for his coat and trying to look non-chalant as he fell through the wooden doors into the darkness, leaving behind the handsome men, Murray, Roy. And Henry Wilson, who may have wondered at Eric's mood swings, aloof earlier, then so drunk and emotional with Murray. Or perhaps Henry hadn't seen him later, reeling into the night; perhaps he only wondered at his odd coolness on the dance floor, his seeming self-sufficiency.

Then again, perhaps, as Eric headed tiltingly uphill back to the West End, Henry had hardly given him a thought, had only taken another sip of his first and last beer and continued to search calmly for his future boyfriend, whom he would live with eventually, and whom he would meet one openhearted night, in an undiscovered corner of the Gandydancer.

———

Eric discovered gay porn that summer. He had known about it before, but he had never actually bought any of the slick magazines that danced out at him from all the newsstands in the West End. He'd confined his jerking off fantasies to the pink pages of the *Advocate*, the occasional *After Dark*, and his own imagination. He'd been preoccupied with the pursuit of romance with a live person, and as well had lacked the nerve to admit tacitly to some news vendor, and anyone else who happened to be present, that he was on his way home to whack off looking at pictures of naked men.

But as Thomas Stroud receded and no one rose to take his place, that long, hot summer of 1977, ticked off on his Donna Summer *Four Seasons of Love* calendar, belonged increasingly to the men of *Blueboy*, *Mandate*, and *In Touch*. Eric remembered details of their faces and bodies as if they had been lovers.

The bars were more corporeal, if nothing else, although the experience was not unlike a more time-consuming issue of *Blueboy*.

Eric began to go to the clubs more and more as that year progressed, and for the first time to go home with men he met there. His nineteenth birthday, when he would finally be legal drinking age, was now within reach, but he was rarely asked for ID anymore.

He began his second year of university lackadaisically. It was depressing for him to see Thomas Stroud as a casual friend, to revisit the haunts of their brief romance, if it could even be called that, mostly to grieve for what he had hoped would be.

And toward the end of the year, near Christmas, he began to see Thomas in the bars, and to see him go home with other men. Which always took Eric straight to another Blue, or two or three, and hopefully the arms of someone, anyone, someone else's home, someone else's life for a while.

The burly horse breeder who drove him what seemed miles and miles outside the city, to Richmond, and sucked his cock in front of a table full of trophies.

The black man who took him to breakfast at McDonald's and bitched about his wife the whole time, and who the night before had complained that "All you young boys ever want to do is snuggle. What is this snuggle shit?"

The hippy who'd just gotten out of jail for a drug conviction and talked about death after Eric fucked him one torrid July midnight. "It's just another trip," he said, lacing up his boots on the other side of Eric's apartment, "that's the way I see it. Death is just another trip."

He began to keep a list of his tricks, like notches in a belt, and to worry if too much time went by without adding a new one. The Luv-a-Fair had opened on Seymour Street, and Eric might go there to dance, but eventually, in the same evening, he'd end up alone over on Hamilton, striding drunkenly toward the traffic along False Creek, throwing back his head and all but baying at the moon over the Gandydancer.

He began to watch intently the men he saw Thomas Stroud leave with. They were all older, at least a few years past student age. They all had mustaches and were well built, certainly bigger than Eric.

He would strip before the mirror in his mildewy bathroom at the Garth and with the aid of a hand mirror study cruelly, minutely, his thin, scarred young body.

He joined the YMCA just a block away from his apartment and started to work out, to swim, to jog. And miraculous changes occurred. He gained five pounds of muscle in six months. He fussed and bothered over the sparse beginnings of a mustache, but in the darkness of a disco it looked fuller and aged him, the thing he wanted most of all.

He dressed now to accentuate his body—small-size T-shirts that fit more tightly than medium on his arms and chest, blue jeans that threatened to cut off circulation—and he raided the Army and Navy for a supply of plaid shirts and work boots.

The change in his reception at the bars was almost unbelievable. Seemingly overnight he went from being a potentially exploitable sweet young thing to being something more threatening, eliciting overtures from a whole different class of men. And more of them. If he'd just pumped up at the gym, sometimes the number seemed to double.

He was no more sexually adept than he'd ever been, but as man after man after man crossed his path, this seemed to matter less and less. The perception now was that he was "sexy," and appearances were everything.

He dropped out of school. He had never really understood the purpose of his studies anyway, but he dropped out to escape—from memory, from hope—and to seek a degree, cum laude, from the Gandydancer.

And then even that wasn't enough. He needed to move on. He had to get out of Vancouver; he had to get out of Canada. Like someone plotting a cockeyed career, an insane résumé, he thought, If I'm this successful night after night at the Gandy, I should move up— San Francisco, maybe. L.A. New York!

The sky was the limit.

chapter sixteen

Dale took all the mirrors down from the walls of his apartment.

The shelves of the medicine cabinet stood exposed now. ("It's easier this way," Dale said.) In the bedroom he must have struggled privately to unbolt the heavy wooden frame on the back of his dresser and stash it behind the clothes in his closet.

The bathroom scale disappeared.

He and Eric seemed suddenly to be living in two different realities, and guilt hounded Eric in his. Here he is trying to get back in the swing of things, the voice of guilt said, and all you can think about is death.

It was hard for Eric to decide which was worse: the physical state Dale was in or the fact that Dale acted as if nothing were wrong.

He began to circle auditions in *Backstage*.

When he would force himself to sit up on the couch and talk to Eric, his bony knees all but stuck through the legs of his pants, his feet barely seemed to exist in his shoes, Kaposi's spots were visible on his upper arm and face, and he'd perspire profusely, whether the air conditioner was off or on, his temperature fluctuating widely but seeming to have no bearing on this constant purging of his body. He'd form the words of normal conversation, but the bones in his sunken face made the speech look painful.

"Do you think Grace will rehire me when I'm better?" he'd say. "I think I'll take a trip. Maybe I'll go to California, visit Mickey." Or "That boy on the second floor wants me. I think I'm gonna run out of sugar."

And if Eric didn't play along, didn't chime right in with something equally enthusiastic, an anger would spark in Dale's eyes and he'd start hinting that Eric should leave.

"You fired me," Dale said.

"We didn't fire you. We kept you employed there longer than we really were supposed to."

"I can't believe this. All this time I've been working my way back to health with the idea that at least I had a job, at least I had that."

"We did everything we could."

"Well, it wasn't enough."

Dale's voice seemed sometimes disembodied now, it was so much the liveliest part of him, his voice and his eyes. He continued to sleep a lot, and not necessarily from the pentamidine he was still taking, but from a general exhaustion that had overcome him. Eric had had to dress him when they left the hospital, pulling on socks and underwear and tying each shoe.

In addition to the pentamidine injections, he was now taking AZT—every four hours, with a wristwatch alarm set to remind him—and experiencing side effects from it—nausea, chills, and headaches—that required drugs of their own. When he wasn't asleep, he was in pain, sick to his stomach, or being injected with a drug that would *put* him to sleep.

He spent an amazing amount of time alone in this diminished state. Eric had never realized how sick you could get and still be left so alone. He had naïvely assumed that there would be someone to look after a person this sick, but no—bedridden, nauseated, wracked with pain, Dale fended for himself much of the time. And despite the fact that a visit to the bathroom often seemed a major physical challenge, he would sometimes tell Eric about trips he'd taken, to the laundry room in the basement or the corner grocery.

Eric wondered if Dale knew how sick he now looked. The slightest physical exertion seemed to drain him completely, so that wherever he went, however he got there, if he was upright, he would be looking for something to lean on. Eric wondered if people encountering him on these trips recognized Dale's problem, or if they said or did anything to give it away if they did.

But if anyone asked him about his health, Eric knew that Dale didn't tell them the truth. He had been with him one day when he explained to a neighbor that he was suffering from a reaction to a flu shot.

Glenn was built like a small refrigerator, but he could move sometimes with an odd diffidence, a shyness as Eric watched him every opportunity he got.

"You seem to be doing an awful lot of store reports these days," Grace observed as she watched him roam the floor with a clipboard.

Glenn was from Levittown, which seemed somehow perfect to Eric. "You make it sound like Paris, France," Glenn told him when Eric kept repeating the name.

Eric found him asleep one day on one of the benches in the lounge, and he sat on the other bench and pretended to read his newspaper so he could watch him.

It was like a meditation, watching this young man's powerful chest rise and fall in a crisp white shirt splashed by a colorful tie. Eric wanted to hover over this warm body and breathe the exhaled breath.

It was a contemplation of beauty but also something more, a long-lost feeling, a tightening in the stomach, as if muscles were coming into play that hadn't been used in years.

If you exist, the feeling seemed to say, then I'll take the world as is. Because whatever else God may have done, he, she, or it created you.

———

"Shi-i-i-i-i-t," Dale would moan when Eric gave him his shot, and then he'd hide his face in the pillow.

"Not much more," Eric would say and his gloved hand would shake as it injected the syringe into the back of Dale's scrawny thigh.

The pentamidine apparently didn't mix well with the blood-stream: It burned into the muscle and spread out in stinging waves; the shots were leaving a map of welts across Dale's shrinking skin.

He was in a lot of pain now just because of the sores and muscle stiffness from being in bed so long, and he had developed a herpes rash across the backs of his legs and on one arm, which made him gasp or cry out whenever it was touched.

Eric had never given anyone a shot of any kind before; he'd always been a little bit squeamish about getting them himself. In his suit and tie each June morning, gulping a third cup of coffee through a ragged hole in its plastic lid, as he cabbed it to the Village, he could have passed for a doctor, but he didn't feel like one.

"OK," he'd say and press an alcohol-soaked swab of cotton against the needle and extract it. He'd hold the swab against Dale's leg while he carefully dropped the syringe into a plastic bucket next to the bed. He'd wipe a little back and forth, lift the cotton away for a moment, and then drop it in the pail, too.

Usually Dale would lie still while the pain ebbed. Eric wished there were some way to make it cooler in the room. Air-conditioning was not agreeing with Dale these days, and in mid-June it was really too early for it anyway. But even with the windows open, there was a closeness, a sick smell, in the bedroom that Eric felt sure was seeping into the walls, to stay for years.

Cruising back uptown, he seemed to pull farther and farther away from that stale air in Dale's bedroom, so that by the time he left the cab, strode into the bookstore, and spotted Glenn, it was as if he'd taken a hit of pure oxygen.

Glenn's legs were thick and stocky; his bottom curved voluptuously in a pair of company-approved dress pants.

Eric wished to kiss and rekiss the downy dark hair he'd glimpsed one day beneath Glenn's creeping shirt, fanning out at the base of his spine.

He'd be walking along the street and suddenly the thought of Glenn would fill him with the most goodwill he'd felt in years. Just the thought of Dale now, at almost any given moment, would fill him with the greatest sorrow and fear.

"I dropped out of premed a little over a year ago," Glenn said when Eric hesitantly struck up a conversation with him in the staff lounge. "My girlfriend is still going," he added, one of many, many times he mentioned his girlfriend to Eric, a woman his age he'd met at Cornell. "But I just didn't have her . . . discipline, you know."

He frowned then and wrinkled his forehead. He seemed to take his life very seriously, reminding Eric that at Glenn's age he had also.

Glenn had the most beautiful voice, something in the lips and tongue that created the most sensual, crippling sound, but Eric was still too shy to talk to him much.

He'd watched him meet Theresa, his girlfriend, at the front of the store a couple of times after work. He accepted Glenn's heterosexuality; he had no genuine hope of anything romantic happening between them. In fact, running through the intensity of his feelings in the solitude of his apartment or walking back and forth in the warm wind along the East River late at night, Eric recognized that part of what produced the rush around Glenn was his normalcy, the protection locked inside his dazzling form, the cleanliness, the upstandingness—lust with a strange permission and safety Eric hadn't realized he was missing until he experienced it again.

———

Dale's friend Paul came by the apartment one heavy late-June evening when everyone staggered indoors with that pallid, damp limpness Manhattan produced such an awful version of, quickly emptying sad stores and restaurants where the AC was on the fritz.

Dale's apartment sometimes felt like one of those places, when his own personal temperature swings made him turn off the window units in both rooms on hot days. Then sometimes he would insist the AC be left running during a milder spell, when only the lowest setting even got the cooling to kick in.

On this night, however, Dale's body temperature was apparently in synch; the apartment was comfortable and he was wearing shorts and a baggy T-shirt with a picture of Tammy Faye Bakker on it, her tearful mascara spilling down the front.

Paul had once, years ago, been Dale's strictly platonic roommate, and up until the time of Dale's diagnosis had still been one of his best friends. What Eric most remembered from Dale's stories of living with Paul was that he would spend several hours each morning in the bathroom primping, adjusting his hairstylist's latest variation on the Jheri curl, before heading to his favorite subway men's room to give and, primarily, receive blowjobs. He'd visit another rest room on his lunch break from work as a tour guide at Rockefeller Center, another on the way home, and then retire once again to his and Dale's bathroom, to get ready to go out dancing. Eric wondered if Paul still did anything like this, wherever he was living now. According to Dale, Paul had always insisted—even though the evidence was far from unequivocal—that at least his lifestyle was safe.

Paul had not been around much at all since Dale's diagnosis. Partly this was because Dale kept all his friends except Eric in the dark about what was happening to him, and partly it was because Paul seemed peculiarly sensitive on the subject.

Dale insisted that Paul had fainted when he finally told him about his diagnosis, although the story kept changing. When last heard, it had expanded to include the Riviera Cafe. "There we were," Dale said, "about to have coffee, and the woman just keeled over."

Apparently he was coming around, because he sat there this evening and asked Dale all sorts of questions about the various treatments he had undergone. Paul had always had this brisk efficiency about him, this near-mania for the giving and receiving of information. Whether it was a recipe you needed, or how to get a spot out of your necktie, or send a package UPS, Paul was a walking catalogue of dos and don'ts.

He also asked a lot of questions about how Dale was paying for his treatment. Dale's welfare payments had not begun yet, but supposedly they were on the way. Eric had gotten the forms from Ed, the GMHC buddy he had finally convinced Dale to accept, carefully filled them out with Dale, and taken them downtown to the welfare office.

Paul got funny toward the end of his visit. Apparently he'd come straight from his job, and he sat there on the sofa in his powder-blue button-down shirt, his second-skin black jeans, and his shiny dress shoes, with something more than the hot weather in his eyes, a quivering in his fingers like a volcano.

"I'm sorry," he said suddenly and all but leapt off the sofa.

He did an odd pacing bit of a dance then, almost as if Eric and Dale were no longer present and he was warming up before delivering a speech to an anonymous audience.

"You see this is all very new to me," he said in a rush, "and I'm not quite sure how one goes about bringing it up. I'm not quite sure what the procedure is."

"Well, Harriet," Dale croaked, "I wouldn't put yourself—"

"I was afraid, you see," Paul said. "I didn't want to be around you because you would only remind me. But no-o-o-ow," he almost sang, his voice rising in pitch, "it seems I had reason to be afraid."

He sat on the couch and with furious fingers unbuttoned his shirtsleeve and shot it up his arm.

On his black skin, the spot was dark, though not exactly purple.

When Eric looked up he saw that Dale and Paul were staring into each other's eyes, as if he no longer existed.

"I want Mickey," Dale said, sitting forlornly in the corner of the sofa late one weekday afternoon as the light outside turned to evening.

"Hmn?" Eric asked, drinking a bottled beer on the other side of the room, his tie across his knee.

"I want to see Mickey. I want you to call Mickey and ask him to come out here."

"Shouldn't you call him?"

"I'm too tired, and besides it will be more convincing if someone else does it."

"Convincing?"

"I don't want to beg."

"He doesn't even know you're sick, does he?"

"No. And I think it's time someone told him. The number's in my book."

Mickey turned out to be older than Eric had expected. He'd imagined the Mickey Dale described from long ago. He was still handsome, and still an ex-hippy, but with a neatly trimmed salt-and-pepper beard and a ponytail.

Dale was asleep when he got there.

He stood shyly at the door of the bedroom. "Hey, snuggy," he said.

And when Dale opened his eyes and turned, years seemed to fall from his face.

Later, Mickey came quietly out of the bedroom and shut the door behind him. "He's asleep," he whispered.

"Are you staying in town long?" Eric asked.

"I don't know if I can get the time off work."

"Oh . . . I thought you painted. Aren't you an artist?"

"Huh? Oh, no, not really. I haven't really done that in years."

"Oh."

"I work for a software manufacturer. I do design work for a software manufacturer, and I don't get—" He stopped suddenly and looked embarrassed. "Uh," he said and put a hand to his eyes. "Is there a Kleenex?"

Eric scrambled around for a box and handed it to him.

"I don't want him to hear me," Mickey said in a voice like a hushed wail. He blew his nose a couple of times and sat rocking on the couch. "I just can't believe," he said, "what's happened to our lives."

Homosexuality must be all right if it means loving you.

Eric remembered this feeling so vividly now, from when he first came out of the closet, this feeling of redemption in the eyes of a young man.

And the delight that coursed through him at the thought of Glenn was a kind of contagious lifting, a brightness he seemed to communicate to others, so that they smiled at him more, clerks in stores and strangers on the street. He seemed to know the right thing to say to people without even saying it; his presence construed some kind of radiance. He saw the world, and particularly he saw Glenn Merritt, as God must.

———

He arrived one evening to find Reg, Dale's friend from ACT-UP, trying to convince Dale to go off AZT.

The pentamidine injections had been discontinued a while back, and Dale was now inhaling that drug in a new aerosol form, so that AZT was currently his biggest medical expense. And it produced so many side effects that Dale ended up taking several pills just to counteract it.

The apartment was stuffy that night, though not unbearable. Dale had shut off the air conditioners and closed all the windows, but it was only about seventy outside.

Dale sat on the sofa, wrapped in an afghan, his donut-shaped cushion, which he now had to put under himself when he sat on any hard surface, flung nonchalantly at his feet. Reg sat cross-legged in khaki shorts on the floor across from him, spouting statistics in a firebrand style.

Eric couldn't keep up with everything Reg was saying, but a nostalgia snuck up on him as he listened. He'd felt it earlier, too, at work that day, while he tailed Glenn with an empty pad of yellow paper on a clipboard. I am following my heart's desire, he had thought as he glanced at the back of Glenn's dark brown head, his muscular body somehow caged in a shirt and tie, as though the material were about to catch fire. I have not followed my heart's desire in years.

And now, in Dale's apartment, he found himself listening to the kind of speech he had not heard since his university days.

"You should come," Reg was saying, to both of them it seemed. "At least come to a meeting. It helps a lot to deal with the frustration if you get out and do something. And once you start figuring out how much of this we didn't *have* to go through, if the government had just gotten off its ass a little earlier, if they were just more willing to so something now, if the perception wasn't that it's just a bunch of fags and druggies getting this disease, you get *so* angry you just have to go somewhere with it, take it to the street. It's like when you first realized it was OK to be gay, you know, that you had just been lied to your whole life. It's that kind of clarity. Did you see us on the news yesterday?" he asked. "We stropped traffic in front of the Stock Exchange."

Eric raised his eyebrows and smiled.

Dale sighed deeply. "The only time I ever stopped traffic," he said, "was in my Maidenform bra."

And then he gestured in an odd way he'd begun to use with Eric recently, a haughty flick of the wrist.

"I must leave you now," he said to Reg. "Eric will show you out."

chapter seventeen

One day Dale seemed to be morbidly accepting the finality of his illness, the next he seemed to be wildly optimistic.

"I think that's it," he said as Eric walked with him along West Street next to the Hudson on a Saturday afternoon in early July. He had refused to get a cane to help him move about, so he leaned against Eric and seemed sometimes about to cut off the circulation in his arm. With his free hand, he made a sweeping gesture through the air. "I think it's over."

"You think what's over?" Eric asked without thinking. He squinted in the bright sunlight and thought for the thousandth time that he should buy a pair of sunglasses. As with any potential fashion statement, however, the thought of purchasing a pair, making sure he got the "right" kind, the kind everyone else was wearing, filled him with terror. So instead he squinted.

"My illness," Dale said. "I feel this wave of health coming on. Just the way I felt right before the chemotherapy finally worked. Just the way I felt last month before that clean X-ray. I beat the two biggies. Surely I can handle this odd collection of pesky diseases no one's ever heard of."

Eric tried to agree with him, to say something appropriately upbeat, even though he could feel the bone in Dale's arm next to his own. Apparently he wasn't very good at hiding his true feelings, because Dale got pissy.

"Why do you have to look at me like that?" he demanded.

"Like what?" Eric asked. He hadn't looked at Dale at all. If anything, that was the giveaway lately.

"You don't think I can do it, do you?" Dale said, bringing them to a standstill and letting go of Eric's arm. Eric turned to face him and couldn't help noticing that even in illness, Dale had managed to get ahold of a pair of bright green retro sunglasses with round frames, the kind, Eric suddenly realized, that everyone was wearing.

"You think I'm kidding myself," he went on. "Why don't you just say it?"

Dale had taken off the jacket Eric had made him put on back at the apartment and tied it around his waist. The breeze billowed his white T-shirt, this one with Joan Crawford on the front saying, "I never touched those damn kids!"

"How am I supposed to get well," Dale continued, "with you around? You're so totally wrapped up in the disease that you can't see the forest for the trees."

"I'm sorry. I didn't mean to give that impression. I think it's wonderful that you feel this health . . . wave thing or whatever . . ."

And then Dale launched into another one of those speeches he'd been making a lot recently, like the dying matriarch in a TV movie. "Oh, I see," he said in a tone worthy of Joan herself. "I'm not making sense. I suppose that's the first sign of senility setting in. I can see your brain clicking away now. Lock him up. Put him away. It's obvious the disease has begun to affect," he paused dramatically, "his mind!" His eyes bulged and his head swung up at an angle that made him look remarkably like Gloria Swanson at the end of *Sunset Boulevard*.

They walked back to the apartment in silence, and when they got inside, Dale announced that he was going to "fire" Ed, his GMHC buddy.

"You can't 'fire' Ed," Eric said, "he's a volunteer."

"Well, whatever, I'm letting him go," Dale said.

It had been hard enough to get him to agree to have Ed come in the first place. At first Eric hadn't known what to make of Dale's buddy. With his two-tone hair and black clothes, he seemed a little too young and East Village for the job. But he came over or called every day, and tried to do things for Dale, who resisted his help.

"What's the sense in having some street kid skulking about the place when I'm perfectly capable of doing everything myself?"

"He isn't a street kid."

Dale sat on the sofa. For a moment he didn't say anything.

Then he picked a magazine up off the coffee table and flipped through it. Eric stood on the other side of the room in silence. Dale looked up at him once and then down again. He continued to page slowly through the magazine.

"You know," he said finally, "I don't quite know how to say this, but *you* don't have to come here every day anymore either."

"Oh," Eric said and flushed.

Dale continued to flip through the magazine.

"Well," Eric said and thought for one hysterical instant that he was going to cry. Then the feeling jelled as anger. "Very good then," he said tightly. "You let me know if you need anything."

With his hand on the doorknob, he added, even though he knew it sounded farfetched, "It'll be nice to have my evenings free again."

He tried to slam the door on the way out and ended up hitting himself in the back of the leg instead. He limped down the stairs, and in the vestibule at the front of Dale's building, he beat his fist, just once, against Dale's mailbox.

He called Paul. He called Reg. He called GMHC, and through them he contacted Ed. He made sure that someone would be looking in on Dale on a regular basis.

His agitation momentarily diffused the sadness and fear that had been surrounding Dale in his mind, but a different sadness took its place. He felt more alone than he had in years.

Feelings from childhood seemed to resurface, especially at night, in the darkness, the realization at too early an age that the world would forever be a place he visited, his finest, sharpest emotions misunderstood.

He almost hated Glenn Merritt some days now, for his easy perfection, his magnetic eyes, his tanned biceps curling beneath the short sleeve of a dress shirt as he toted his gym bag out the door night after night after night.

Above the line of his sleeve his skin was oddly the color of alabaster. "I would have thought you'd be at the beach every weekend," Eric commented somewhat snidely.

"I hate the beach," Glenn said.

Paul called Friday night about a week after Eric's banishment, when Eric was home alone, slightly drunk, and unreasonably angry that the *Full House* that night was one he'd seen.

"He now believes," Paul said, "that AIDS is happening to gay men because of the way we've . . . expressed our sexuality or something. He's been reading all that Louise Hay and Bernie Siegel jazz, which is fine, I mean I'm reading it, too—who isn't?—but Dale seems to have boiled it all down to guilt. As if the disease were somehow our fault. He says we're obsessed with image. He says we learn at an early age to lie, and by the time we're adults we can't tell the difference between truth and illusion. Our sexuality is based entirely on image, never on intimacy, really getting to know the other person. He says that's why KS is particularly common among gay PWAs; it's an image disease, and really the whole syndrome is—it destroys the way we look. If I sound like I'm delivering a lecture, it's because it was delivered to me several times while I was there."

Eric's mind whirled. He was so thankful to be getting a phone call from anyone, he just wanted to keep Paul talking. "So what does all this mean," he said finally, "I mean, in a practical sense? What good is all this theorizing now?"

"Well," Paul said, "call me Elisabeth Kübler-Ross, but I think this is 'Bargaining.' It's part of this whole purification thing he's going through. He's begun to make a list of all the carcinogens to avoid in food and so on. He's thrown out bags of stuff; he's eating seaweed— I don't know what to tell you. He says he's swearing off sex. Well, honey, to the best of my knowledge no one's breakin' down the door, if you know what I mean."

Eric leaned back on his bed. His air conditioner hummed under the window beside him; Simone sprawled in the middle of the floor, legs in the air. "So . . . ," he said, "does he ever mention me?"

For a long moment Paul didn't say anything. Then finally he said, "He resents you."

"Well, you know, all I did—"

"No, he always has."

"Huh?"

"Haven't you ever noticed the way he treats you? He thinks of you as this good-looking guy who fits into the straight world and is never going to get sick."

"What?!" Eric giggled nervously.

"I'm serious," Paul said. "Why do you think he singled you out for the honor of being at his beck and call?"

"Well . . . I don't know. I always figured he thought I was pretty inept to tell you the truth."

"No— He hates you. It's different."

Eric lived in such a cloud as to other people's feelings about him that whenever anyone expressed such a strong one it fascinated him, as if he'd finally discovered someone who spoke the native tongue.

"Don't get me wrong," Paul said. "He also loves you. But I don't think he can tolerate much of that."

Dale's theory of AIDS trailed Eric about in the following days. It whispered hotly that it was no big surprise all these gay men were getting sick, that he had never really experienced it as such, that something in him had always said, "Of course. I *knew* this would happen."

Watching Glenn Merritt with his girlfriend, he couldn't help thinking that this was a *real* relationship, this was human feeling of some value, whereas his own feelings for Glenn were merely surface infatuation; he barely knew the man, and he had made no real effort to get to know him.

"So . . . your girlfriend is still in school?" he asked, looking up from his unread newspaper in the staff lounge.

Glenn was leaning forward on the table, his head resting on his strong, folded arms, his retro-nuevo pompadour slightly mussed. "Yes," he mumbled against the fine dark hair on his broad forearm. He sat up and ran one of his peculiarly small hands through the dark mop, brushing it back from his forehead. "Which makes me feel just great, let me tell you."

"You're kidding, you mean?"

"I'm kidding," Glenn said and leaned back against the park bench.

"What branch of medicine were you planning to go into?"

Glenn clasped his hands in front of him on the fake woodgrain table. "I was still trying to decide," he said, "when I quit. I was thinking about either obstetrics," he said, pronouncing the word as if it were foreign, "or plastic surgery."

"Plastic surgery. That's a laugh."

"It is?"

"No, I just mean— So now what are you thinking of doing?"

"I wish I knew. The trouble is that none of the things that interest me will pay the rent, you know. I should have done what my brother did—set myself up with a little business, get married . . ."

"You don't plan to get married?"

"Hmn? No, no. Not in the immediate future anyway." He took a breath. "Maybe after Theresa wins her first Nobel," he added and smirked.

"So," Eric said and tried to look relaxed against the hard back of the other bench, at a right angle to Glenn's, "what is it that does interest you?"

"You mean instead of marriage?"

"No, I meant in terms of career."

"Oh . . . well . . . who knows? I . . . sculpt," he said and held his tiny hands cupped in the air before him. "Sometimes," he added and dropped them. "Expensive though, and unprofitable." He pronounced this last word the same way he'd said "obstetrics," as if enunciating something strange, and then he licked his lips.

Eric loved the sound of Glenn's voice. He could listen to him talk for hours about where he'd left his name badge or what books he was planning to reorder for the Coin Collecting section; having a legitimately interesting conversation with him was almost more than he could bear. "That's great," he said.

"How's your friend?" Glenn asked.

Eric had forgotten that he had even told Glenn about Dale. "He's . . . OK," he replied cautiously.

"A friend of mine used to volunteer at that hospital. Maybe he even saw your friend. He used to read to people, which I thought was sort of a neat idea."

"Dale's not quite that far gone. Yet."

"Oh. Sorry."

"No— I didn't—"

Glenn put his head down again.

"Tired?" Eric asked.

"M-m-m," he murmured. "I'd like to go home and sleep after work, but they're showing *Indiscretion of an American Wife* at the Cinema Village."

"You're kidding."

"On a double bill," Glenn said and looked at Eric over the crook of his elbow, "with *I Confess*."

Glenn was a big Montgomery Clift fan. It was one of many things about him that didn't quite add up. He had even used the word "infatuated" once. He had said, "I'm infatuated with Monty," and then, as Eric recalled, he'd joined Theresa at the front of the store.

She was pretty enough, Theresa, but not as pretty as Eric had expected. In fact, he found that his affection for Glenn only deepened when he met her, that there was something touching about this walking perfection, this dazzling specimen, picking out a girl this side of plain, and an egghead to boot. He almost wished Theresa had been some sort of plastic moron—then they both would have been more dismissible.

"He's obviously a closet case," Dale had said the one and only time Eric tried to talk to him about his replacement at the store.

"Why do you say that? Why are you so sure?"

"Oh, you can always tell," Dale replied enigmatically.

"But you haven't even met him."

"Just from the things you've told me."

It wasn't as if the possibility hadn't crossed Eric's mind, and pleasurably, but he still thought Dale was jumping to conclusions.

"Look on the bright side," Dale said finally, to end the discussion, "it's inevitable you'll meet up one day at a revival of *Judgment at Nuremberg*."

Now Eric wondered if he even wished for Glenn to be a closet case. In the funk he'd been moving through recently, he couldn't fathom why anyone with half a choice would want to be a homosexual of any kind in this day and age.

"Well," Glenn said, and stretched his exquisite arms, "back to *verk*." He stood and ambled out of the lounge.

Impulsively, Eric moved over to Glenn's bench, lay back, and stretched his legs. Glenn didn't use aftershave; he left behind a warm, sweat-stained aroma, tinged with the more medicinal perfume of deodorant.

Eric's eyes rolled toward the floor, where Glenn's backpack rested, partly open, against the opposite wall. He could see a library book inside, the title of which he couldn't read, a half-filled bottle of what looked like apple juice, a Bic pen, and a collection of pamphlets of some kind, on one of which he could make out the words "Image Changing Consultant."

He played with these words in his mind a bit, drifting dreamily on the hard bench. Image Changing Consultant. What could that mean? And then he remembered Glenn's medical career goals. Obstetrics and plastic surgery, he'd said.

Dreams die hard, Eric thought.

chapter eighteen

August 12 was Dale's thirty-second birthday. And he decided to throw a party for himself. He had often done this in the past; in fact, it seemed that most of the parties Eric had attended at his place had been birthday parties.

Eric barely remembered the date of his own birthday; Dale generally began mentioning his about six months ahead of time, and seemed to put everyone on trial based on his or her response, as if assessing whether or not to renew the friendship for another year. If no one else seemed about to throw a party, he was sure to do it himself. Amid the tumult of his illness, he had managed to drop many of the usual hints over the previous weeks, sometimes with virtually no sense of fun, just a painful earnestness, almost a fear. But Eric, as usual, had failed the test and forgotten about it.

He heard about the party from Paul, over the phone at work. "He's *what?*" Eric said.

"Yeah, I know," Paul said. "But I'm going to help him with it. Now, he's invited a lot of people—"

"He hasn't invited me," Eric said and sank back in his chair.

"Well . . . he's gonna get around to it. I think. Anyway, the deal is that everybody is getting a little speech that there's to be no death and disease talk at this party, nothing but upbeat encouragement and support. If people feel they can't be enthusiastic, he's telling them not to come. He's serving nothing but health food, or what he's calling health food, which is mostly stuff I simply don't recognize, and I'm an educated person. Who the hell knows, he may get us all to sit in a circle and chant or some damn thing."

Eric tilted back in his chair. In a weird way the sense of absurdity he was feeling was a relief, because for a while he seemed to have become unable to feel anything at all about Dale. "So . . . how is he? I mean, physically, how is he doing?"

Paul thought for a moment and then said, "No better really. I mean he's going to need a lot of help, and I'm almost hoping a number of these people don't show."

Finally Eric found a brief, straightforward invitation on his machine when he got home from work one evening. Dale delivered the message with aplomb; it sounded for all the world as if he were inviting an old friend he hadn't seen in ages, someone he only half-expected to show and wasn't intimately concerned with one way or the other.

At least for once Eric didn't experience a surge of dread at the thought of attending one of Dale's parties. Was this because something had changed within him? Or was their fight just obscuring his other feelings? Or, even worse, was it maybe true that the only way Eric could feel relaxed at a party was if the host had a terminal illness?

On the train downtown, he had a fantasy of showing up with Glenn on his arm, and in the fantasy they were oddly attired in tuxedos, with bright red bow ties. "He loves me," Eric told Dale, "and all we do is have sex."

Paul got his wish: Not that many people showed up, about fifteen maybe, drifting in and out during the evening, and it was a different crowd from the one at previous parties.

Reg was there, and was pleased to learn that Dale had followed his advice and gone off AZT. In fact, according to Paul, Dale was going off quite a few of the drugs he'd been taking.

"Apparently," Paul said dryly, "it's all available in bean curd."

Eric wasn't exactly sure why more people from Dale's old group hadn't shown. Partly he knew it was because Dale had cut himself off from these people following his diagnosis, but maybe it was even worse. He had no idea how rudely this disassociation had been accomplished, or if these friends of Dale's were even still around.

Alcohol was one of the few exceptions in tone at the party; Paul had all but begged Dale to let people drink. The food, as Paul had reported, was pretty much unrecognizable, but Eric never ate at these things anyway. There was no loud music, which was a relief, but in the background some sort of prolonged bass note kept welling up, almost a whine at times, and Paul later informed Eric that they were listening to whale sounds.

The apartment was more familiar to Eric than it had ever been at Dale's parties before. He seemed to realize all at once what an enormous amount of time he had spent there over the past year, but the rooms also held the sadness of a familiar place revisited after a separation, when one has become a stranger to it.

Dale looked brighter, anyway, sitting on the couch in black jeans and a pretty white shirt with a string tie, all new, surrounded by gift-wrapped presents. But he still didn't look well, and he seemed more than a little frustrated by the turnout and by the fact that he couldn't be up and flitting about as usual from guest to guest.

Everyone seemed to be abiding by his dictum about optimism, but it was possible that those who wouldn't have had simply stayed home or not been invited. Eric was still not entirely sure how he had sneaked through.

Grace was there, which at least provided Eric with someone to talk to. She seemed shocked by Dale's appearance. She didn't say anything; her eyes just fastened on Eric with an unsteady intensity he'd never seen there before.

Paul began to shoo people out by about eight-thirty, and Eric noticed that Dale's eyes were fluttering. He had said he would save his presents for later.

All he had said to Eric the entire evening was a generic "Glad you could come" as Eric handed him his gift. Eric had debated for a long time what to bring, longer than he had wanted to, longer than he'd tried to tell himself Dale deserved, and finally he'd surprised himself by buying something he thought was a fairly naked attempt to win back friendship: a Louise Hay tape and a crystal pendant.

As usual, he was one of the last to leave. Grace said good-bye to Dale and told Eric she'd wait for him downstairs and they could share a cab uptown. When Eric turned from speaking to her at the door, Dale, along with everyone else, was gone. Eric looked in the kitchen, but there was no one there. He dropped his plastic glass in the pail under the sink, then headed down the hall to the bedroom. He froze near the open doorway when he heard a sound, something so raw it stopped him in his tracks. Then he looked up and saw Paul standing in the bedroom and Dale sitting on the bed, his head cradled against Paul's stomach as he sobbed and sobbed.

When Dale saw Eric, he turned his face away and wiped his eyes as if he'd been caught by a parent—no, worse than that, a friend, an *acquaintance*, with whom he just wasn't intimate enough to share this kind of emotion. And then Paul came toward Eric, took his arm, and walked him out of the room before he had a chance even to say anything.

"Sorry," Paul said at the front door, but Eric barely heard him.

The old isolation had closed in, and Paul was on the other side now, mysteriously included, in the know, the place where Eric could never be.

Then, without any fanfare, or explanation, he was admitted back into the fold. On Dale's behalf, Paul invited Eric to the apartment for one of Dale's macrobiotic dinners, and during the evening, Dale behaved pretty much as if there had never been any trouble between him and

Eric. As Eric was leaving, Dale suggested he drop by after work someday that week.

It seemed that Dale was being friendly at least in part because
Eric had volunteered to accompany him to the Harmonic Convergence in Central Park, which apparently no one else had been available or willing to do.

That weekend Dale had bouts of terrible nausea and diarrhea,
and leaving the apartment wasn't possible. But Eric was sure he'd
read that the Convergence would be going on for a few days.

However, when they arrived Monday afternoon at the clearing
near West Seventy-ninth Street, the place had a distinct look of
abandonment about it. A ragtag group of maybe ten people hovered
over a sand pit, where a bunch of burned-out candles and some crys-
tals lay scattered about. Incense wafted from the pit, and there were
matches, as well as butts of various kinds, scattered about the sand
and beyond.

A couple of people sat cross-legged with open palms extended,
lost in some kind of trance state; one extremely well-built young man
wore next to nothing as he struck yoga-like postures and glanced
at Eric and Dale as if they didn't exist; a middle-aged woman in a
mu-mu was saying that she didn't like the attitude of the thin,
younger man sitting next to her, who had a long, scraggly beard. "It's
not about judgment, Dino," she kept saying.

"This is pathetic," Dale said as he and Eric stood near the
entrance to the clearing. "Are you sure they said it was going on for
three days?"

"Yeah," Eric said a little doubtfully. "That's what the *Times* said."

"These people look like rejects from a bus and truck tour of
Godspell."

"Maybe we should go back to the apartment," Eric suggested. "I
heard that you could meditate in the privacy of your own home and
still have some effect."

At the apartment, Dale did just that, in the bedroom, sitting cross-legged on the bed, his new crystal pendant around his neck.

As cytomegalovirus ate away at his optic nerves, Dale went blind from a distance, like a camera pulling out of a zoom. First the horizon disappeared, then the long shots. The doctors were also concerned that the virus would begin to affect his brain.

In some sort of mad dash to escape the loss of vision, he started to cover one wall of his bedroom with pictures and objets d'art, clipped from magazines and elsewhere, the gaudiest, most colorful things he could find—classic works of art alongside body builders and soft drink advertisements and an actual McDonald's french fry carton. It reminded Eric of the collage of photos and postcards in Thomas Stroud's dorm room, an eclectic time capsule, a daily reminder of identity that all but jumped off the wall. Dominating the whole thing, off to the right-hand side, was a real traffic sign Dale had found somewhere that read, like a terse summation of his future, "Photo Opportunity Ahead."

"I always had good eyes," he said to Eric with a chill in his voice. "I always prided myself on that. Twenty-twenty."

Eric began to visit him after work a couple of times each week and on weekends, always calling first, trying to behave as if they would be getting together as friends rather than PWA and helpmate. Dale often seemed to be in despair during these visits, which usually entailed nothing more than sitting around the apartment with a drink of some kind for about an hour, maybe watching a video, about all Dale was physically capable of.

But he wasn't articulating his despair, if that's what it was. He'd grown quiet, which was extremely unusual for him. He sat on the floor a lot now, sometimes on a cushion, sometimes not, even though he hadn't gained any weight. He locked his arms around his knees and rocked; he stared dully into space with something too relaxed in his face.

And then he'd lash out suddenly over some little thing. His GMHC buddy, Ed, had returned, been "rehired," and none of the food he bought or prepared for Dale seemed to satisfy him. He was moving off the strictness of the macrobiotic regimen, but the disease and the medication had so affected his appetite that it sometimes seemed there was nothing left he could enjoy eating. He yelled at Ed if he didn't like the food he was brought. He yelled at Eric for not reminding him it was time for *The Facts of Life*.

Paul tried giving him pep talks, emphasizing that though it was good for Dale to be getting in touch with all this anger, it was not so good to be making a habit of hostility.

Whenever he watched Paul with Dale now, Eric was struck by the resourcefulness of this energetic man who had gone seemingly overnight from being a person so preoccupied with appearance that no one else could get into the bathroom when he lived with Dale, to being someone disfigured (he now had Kaposi's spots on his face, neck, and arms), possibly dying, certainly out of work, and volunteering hours of his time not only to Dale but to others through GMHC.

We are on a journey here, Eric thought. We are being shown something.

Ed got Dale a wheelchair, but as with the cane, he refused to use it. He left it sitting in the corner of the living room, though, which was almost disappointing. Eric expected him to demand its removal from the premises.

"Why do you do this anyway?" he snapped at Eric one day. He had complained that he wanted the air-conditioning on in the bedroom and then seemed to change his mind. Eric was fiddling with the controls. "Why are you always hanging around here? Haven't you got anything better to do? You're like an ambulance chaser."

"I should probably just ignore this," Eric said.

"Oh, Miss Priss. Can't you get a date, for Christ's sake? Can't you do something normal for a change?"

Eric got very rigid and sighy about the face then and stalked out of the room. He finished up a few things in the kitchen and left the apartment with a curt good-bye called from the front door.

But the moment he had closed the door, he knew that the question would stay with him, as it had, he supposed, for the last ten months. Why *was* he doing this?

"I don't know," Glenn said, "I've always... I have a lot of gay friends— Well, not really a lot, but I have ... I've always had gay men friends, so ..."

Eric couldn't even remember how they'd gotten onto this. "That's great," he said.

"Yeah. I guess," Glenn said. And then suddenly, like a bullet: "I'm straight, OK?"

Eric took a moment to catch his breath and then said, "OK," with what he thought was beautiful calm. In the back of his mind, though, was something about the lady doth protest too much, which was Dale and Paul's influence, he knew.

They were both convinced that Glenn was gay. Dale had never even laid eyes on him. Paul had, one day when he dropped by the store while running errands in midtown. "So where's the Adonis?" he'd asked through clenched teeth, with the wry look of someone expecting another person's enthusiasm to turn out to be hyperbole. However, when Glenn was pointed out to him, as subtly as Eric could manage, Paul fell against Eric, his mouth literally hanging open for several long seconds.

What exactly it was that so convinced Dale and Paul that Glenn was gay Eric couldn't quite figure out. He was an extraordinary-looking young man, someone who by doing what most people did every morning gave the impression of having fussed over his appearance for hours. And he did talk a lot about gay people and gay issues, but then, Eric reasoned, maybe twenty-one-year-old straight men in New York were doing that now. There was the Montgomery Clift thing, of course, but then Eric had a Judy Garland thing and that didn't make him straight. ("That," Dale said when Eric offered it up, "is easily the silliest thing I've ever heard.")

Was it just wishful thinking? Jealousy? Thomas Stroud had once told Eric that gay men in England referred to a certain class of straight men as CBHs—Could Be Had. Eric's whole romantic history seemed to have been built around such men—"could be had," not "*want* to be had."

"But I've never had any problem with the gay thing," Glenn was saying. "I mean I'm not . . . prejudiced about it or anything."

"I'm glad," Eric said.

"And neither is my girlfriend," Glenn added.

Dale began to forget what he was saying sometimes, halfway through a sentence. Sometimes this surprised him. "Ha! I can't remember what I was going to say," he'd comment with a puzzled tilt and then shake of his head, as if he had no clue what might be causing this. Sometimes it embarrassed him, and he'd try to cover it by saying something like "Oh, whatever—it's not important" or "You know what I mean." Sometimes it infuriated him, and he'd spit something like "Oh, who cares anyway?" or "I can tell you're not really interested, so why bother?"

He'd forget individual words and substitute something similar, something that rhymed, or sometimes a word that wasn't related at all.

"What am I going to do with this damn . . . spare renditioning?" he yelled. "Get me a . . . spankit."

"Where's the clover? Where's the clover?" he called, looking for the topical acyclovir Dale's new doctor, Dr. Edelman, had prescribed for the Herpes rash that had broken out again across the backs of his legs.

He'd use some even less specific term and get very angry if someone couldn't figure out what he meant. "Bring me the ... thing," he'd say. "Where's the ... you know, where is it?"

And Eric noticed that he had also begun to ask questions and make statements three or four times in a single visit. "Where's Ed?" he'd ask Eric suddenly.

"He's not coming today. What do you need him for?"

"Nothing. I just wondered why he wasn't here."

And Eric would continue cleaning the bedroom or applying Dale's salve or whatever might be going on, and a few moments later, with a fresh surge of intensity, Dale would look around and ask, "Is Ed coming today?"

One day he asked Eric, "How long have we known each other?"

"It must be ... six years now," Eric said. He was sitting at the foot of Dale's bed, in a dining room chair someone had brought in and placed against the wall, almost like the hospital now, Eric thought, only with Dale lying dressed on top of the bed.

Then Dale asked, "Do we work together?"

And Eric turned then, ever so slowly, to look into the eyes of someone who didn't recognize him, who was trying to puzzle out who he was.

Eric couldn't speak. And Dale apparently sensed he'd said something wrong, because he broke eye contact and looked out the bedroom window, an expression on his face of cool, almost casual confusion.

chapter nineteen

Eric called Dr. Edelman, who told him that to pinpoint the precise cause of Dale's mental symptoms, he would have to undergo a series of tests. And this would mean broaching the subject with him, which Eric didn't relish the thought of.

"What do you mean 'forgetful'?" Dale demanded. "What are you trying to say?"

"Look, it's no big deal," Eric said. "The tests are pretty routine under the circumstances, and if there's nothing wrong, then no harm done, right?"

"And how did Dr. . . . Edelman come up with this idea? I suppose you called him, did you?"

"I was worried, that's all. You seemed to be having difficulty articulating your thoughts sometimes . . ."

"Oh, well, thank you very much, Funk and Wagnall's. The next time I want a critique of my language . . . thrills, I'll know where . . . to go." His face fell. "It's the damndest thing, isn't it?" he said in a smaller voice and chuckled awkwardly. "The tests won't damage my eyes any more, will they?"

"No. In fact, as I understand it, they might help them learn more about what's causing the loss of sight."

But Dale still resisted. Until one night in the second week of September he had a seizure of some kind, in the middle of the night, when he was alone in the apartment, and woke up on the floor of the bedroom, his body sore all over as if he'd been knocking against things. His muscles hurt for days, and he remembered a dream in which the room wouldn't stop spinning.

The tests turned out to be fairly elaborate. They did a spinal tap and an electroencephalogram and a CT scan to photograph Dale's brain. He was also interviewed by a psychiatrist, who asked him questions like "Who's the President of the United States?" To which Dale replied, with mock earnestness, "Uh ... that would be ... Barbra Streisand."

There turned out to be nothing structurally or psychologically wrong with him, but blood tests showed a high level of CMV, and the spinal tap indicated that the HIV virus had entered his nervous system. The symptoms, Dr. Kroll, the brain man, said, were bound to get worse.

"So ... ," Eric said and looked up at Glenn, in the chair across from his desk, where Eric had invited him to sit for his break, "who are these gay friends you mentioned?"

"Well, there's really only two of them," Glenn said. He was eating a yogurt, which reminded Eric of Dale sitting there what just then seemed to have been years ago. Glenn didn't linger over the snack the way Dale did; his movements came closer to gobbling. "There's my friend Grant, who's my age, from the restaurant I used to work at." He took in another couple spoonfuls and swallowed. "And then there's Theo, who was a teacher of mine, an older man."

"I see."

"Theo believes," Glenn said, "that we're all basically bisexual anyway. And ... I guess I pretty much agree with him."

"Really?" Eric watched Glenn's arm flex when he lifted the white plastic spoon. "Really," Eric repeated thoughtfully. "I guess I've always figured that was true."

"What?" Glenn said suddenly. "About *me*?"

"About *you*?" Eric asked with equal intensity. "No ... no, I mean, the idea, in general. I mean I know I've been attracted to women at different times, so I've always assumed it more or less worked the other way."

Glenn nodded slowly, a serious expression on his face. "Well anyway," he said abruptly and stood. He held out the spoon and the empty yogurt container.

"Where's the garbage?" he asked.

Theresa showed up at the store that afternoon. On his way out at five o'clock, Eric passed her waiting for Glenn at the front door, a bright yellow video bag clutched to her flat chest.

"What are you renting?" he asked.

"Oh," she said, as if it had never occurred to her to check. She opened the bag and looked in. *"From Here to Eternity,"* she said and looked up. "Is it any good?"

Eric arrived at Dale's apartment one night to find Paul there, obviously upset. Dale was on the floor in the corner of the bedroom, wearing only a T-shirt and a pair of jockey shorts, his arms wrapped around his knees, sobbing.

"He's been like that for almost an hour," Paul said. "We took a walk. We went to the grocery store, and when we got back he said he wanted me to put some of the acyclovir on. As I was doing that, he just started to sob uncontrollably. I keep asking him what's wrong, but all I can get out of him is something somebody did, something mean; somebody did something mean."

"What's the matter, Dale?" Eric asked.

"Mean," Dale said immediately.

"Who was mean?"

"The man."

Eric sat cross-legged on the floor. "What man?"

"In the . . . in the . . . you know."

"The store?" Paul asked and sat on the bed.

Dale looked up at him. "You didn't do anything to him," he said sharply, almost a whine.

"No, I didn't," Paul said and then looked at Eric.

Dale continued to sob.

"Look, Dale," Paul said and leaned forward, his hands clasped between his knees, "the thing is we're having trouble figuring out why you're sitting here on the floor crying like this, OK? So can you try to explain a little more clearly?"

"I'm sorry," Dale said.

"What are you sorry about?" Eric asked.

"I'm sorry I'm like this."

"We know it's hard," Paul said.

"Not fair to you."

"Don't worry about us," Eric said. "What happened?"

Then Dale started pointing to his face with a finger, touching his skin in different places.

"What's that?" Eric asked.

"Oh," Paul said. "He's talking about my KS, I think."

Dale nodded and continued to sob. "So . . . ," Eric started, "what? Somebody said something, OK. Somebody said something in the store . . ."

"About me?" Paul asked, and Dale nodded.

For a moment no one spoke.

"Well, that sucks, Dale," Paul said finally, "but you don't have to get this upset about it. People have said mean things about me all my life. As a black gay person with AIDS I don't exactly expect to be showered with roses." He took a breath and closed his eyes for a moment, with one hand raised in front of him, as if to say, "Enough of that." When he opened his eyes again, his face had relaxed into its more familiar shape, and he said to Dale, in a calmer voice, "I mean I think you're overreacting here, OK?"

Dale looked up and sniffed. "OK." His brow furrowed in concentration, and he stopped crying. "I'd like a Kleenex," he said dramatically.

He began to stay in this highly emotional frame of mind for long periods of time. Despite his obvious exhaustion, despite the fact that he wasn't eating enough and now weighed under a hundred and ten pounds, he wandered, he shuffled, about the apartment, talking to himself, stopping to look at simple objects for several minutes, an hour at a time, occasionally letting out a cry or a moan as he circled the furniture, and falling to the floor to keen, his arms wrapped around his stomach.

If you held him when he cried, he'd fold up in your embrace like a child. "I love you," he'd say. And he'd keep repeating it, fixing you with an unsparing gaze, until you replied, "I love you, too."

There were nights when Eric sat late into the darkness of his apartment, unable to sleep, and thinking of nothing but this naked emotion of Dale's.

No one outside of his family had said "I love you" to Eric in years.

During his increasingly rare periods of lucidity, Dale seemed to have only a vague memory of his more extreme behavior. And he felt guilty about it. "I'm sorry," he'd say over and over and over again. "I'm sorry I'm this way."

This apologizing took on a craziness all its own. "I'm sorry," Dale would say for the fifteenth time, with a fervor that suggested he'd never said it before. "I'm sorry, I'm sorry, I'm sorry," he'd repeat, almost muttering, a litany. "I'm so-o-o-o-ry," he'd wail, tears in his eyes.

It got so that Ed and Paul and Eric barely heard the words anymore. "Yeah, we know," they'd say. "But what the hell good does it do?" or "The only thing you have to be sorry about is that you won't stop saying 'I'm sorry.'" Dale would turn his head and look at them a certain way, and before he could speak, one or all of them would say, "Yeah, we know. You're sorry."

No one could apologize for anything without getting a laugh. "Where's the *TV Guide*?" Eric asked. "Oh, shit," Paul said, "I think I threw it out." And they looked at each other for a beat before chorusing, "I'm sorry!"

Paul got so sick of it, he combed the city until he found a 45 of Brenda Lee singing "I'm Sorry," which, when he couldn't stand it anymore, he'd slap on the turntable and play at full volume. Even Dale would smile at the music and sway a little in time to it. Everyone present would end up grabbing something to use as a mike and lip-synching a few bars.

At any time, with no warning, Dale would come up to each of them, put his arms around him, and say, "I love you."

He was taking a drug called Dilantin to control the seizures he'd been having, but apparently it wasn't working or the dose wasn't strong enough, because he started to have them again. The trick was to keep him from hurting himself. You had to hold him as still as possible on the ground or the bed or wherever, while his limbs jerked and flailed every which way. You had to get something into his mouth—a towel, a napkin, whatever you could find—so he wouldn't swallow his tongue.

The seizures generally lasted a minute or two, and when they were over, Dale was always exhausted and would sleep for hours.

His behavior was becoming more and more stereotypically crazy. He picked a fight with the people in a neighboring apartment because he was convinced they were leaving garbage outside their door and that he could smell it in his place. As Eric arrived one evening, this argument was reaching a high pitch. "You're nuts!" the man down the hall said. And Dale pulled down his sweatpants, exposed himself, and appeared about to start peeing in the hall.

"Uh . . . ," Eric said abruptly, "you don't have to do that, Dale."

He pulled Dale's pants up and turned to face the man down the hall. He appeared frozen in place, his eyes alive with the uniquely New York realization that if something has actually managed to penetrate and shock you, your life may well be in danger.

"Uh . . . good night," Eric said and hustled Dale back into his apartment.

One night Dale stood suddenly at the table and began to remove his clothes.

"Well, isn't this special," Paul said.

Dale was talking about his family, which he seldom did. Eric couldn't remember what had gotten him onto the subject. Recently he had asked Dale again, more than once, in the sanest moments available, if he wanted someone to contact them. And Dale had said, as he always had before, that he didn't want them to know anything about "it." "I don't want to give them the satisfaction," he said.

"What's that supposed to mean?" Eric asked.

"It's like they've won," he replied.

Now, naked at the end of the table, he kept repeating, "My own family. My own family, and they don't even know I exist. My own family."

Paul and Eric proceeded as best they could with their meal. Unfortunately, this approach sometimes just led to Dale's turning up the volume.

He lifted a water glass and held it in his hand for a brief moment before hurling it through the passageway and onto the kitchen floor, where it shattered spectacularly. Then he stared into the kitchen for a moment as if somewhat in awe of his own theatricality.

And as Eric watched him stare at the broken glass, he suddenly knew with a horrible certainty what was coming next. "No!" he shouted and jumped up to grab Dale, just as he began to move toward the kitchen in his bare feet.

He struggled against Eric's arms. "Get a broom or something," Eric yelled, and Paul dashed to a closet. Eric was a lot stronger than Dale, but that didn't stop Dale from wrestling to the best of his ability, his naked body so thin Eric feared he would break something as Dale squirmed against him and they swayed in a strange dance at the end of the table.

Paul swept diligently, collecting wet glass in a dustpan, emptying it under the sink, and going back to check for more. He kept making busy little remarks as he worked, like a mantra: "All in a night's work." "Just another day at Petticoat Junction."

Gradually, Dale calmed, and the rhythm of his body against Eric changed, became more sensual, almost lascivious. He turned toward Eric, rubbed against him and moaned softly, pressed his face to Eric's neck. Then he shifted gears and got angry again; he struggled momentarily and then stopped, locked in Eric's arms but digging his heel into the top of his foot, just enough to really hurt after a while. He got a hand free and tweaked the biceps of Eric's right arm with two of his fingers until the stinging drove him crazy. "That's hurting, Dale," Eric said, and he stopped immediately. He caressed the muscle then, in an almost fraudulent way, like a child who wanted to make it all better.

When Paul had swept the floor a half dozen times and was on his knees still searching for glass, and Dale had calmed into repeating "I'm sorry" over and over again, Eric let him go. He sat in one of the dining table chairs and said, "Do you want to put your clothes on now?"

"Want" did not seem to be the operative word, but Dale was *willing* to put his clothes on. Eric helped him, but Dale had gone all sloppy, so they ended up collapsed in the chair, Dale only half-dressed, asleep in Eric's lap.

When Paul left the kitchen and came back with a flashlight, Eric yelled at him, smiling, "Paul!"

"What?" He looked up innocently.

"I think you got it all, OK?"

Without quite realizing it he had begun to rock Dale back and forth in the chair.

Paul extinguished the flashlight and sat down across from them. "One of us is going to have to move in here," he said.

chapter twenty

"How's your friend?" Glenn asked every day, once Eric had moved in.

"Oh ... about the same," Eric would usually reply. And it was true, which seemed neither good nor bad, since with AIDS it often felt as if stasis was the best you could hope for.

Sitting across from Glenn in his office, where Glenn now habitually took his break, a part of Eric was overwhelmed by pleasure. But just as the joy of Glenn's presence, and particularly of his taking an interest in Eric's life, seeming actually to *like* him, had reached the pitch of near delirium, it would crash-land in a feeling like heartbreak, as if Eric could not possible survive it.

He could handle Glenn as a fantasy, at night especially, sometimes sexual, oftentimes not. He spent many idle moments on the couch in Dale's living room imagining simply lying, fully clothed, in Glenn's strong arms, his head resting against Glenn's perfect chest, as they engaged in hours of casual, comfortable conversation, about everything—even Glenn's relationship with Theresa; in Eric's fantasies there was nothing they didn't share.

But up close he found himself more and more tongue-tied. And more than that, he felt as if this ongoing, day-to-day relationship with an actual physical person was threatening his relationship with the fantasy person he'd become so emotionally dependent on. And if he could have only one or the other, he feared there was no question which he would choose.

Late one afternoon he headed into the men's room and encountered a sight oddly reminiscent of something he'd seen Dale do almost a year ago, when his lesions had first begun to appear.

Only this time it was Glenn who turned suddenly away from the mirror, as if caught.

As Dale, Paul, and Eric lounged on the bed one night watching *Lethal Weapon* on cable, during a scene near the beginning of the movie where Mel Gibson wandered nude through his trailer home, Dale suddenly got up and started to undress again.

"What are you doing?" Eric asked, and Dale just moaned a little and did a bit of a dance step.

Then he continued to strip. Paul finally looked away from the screen. "Oh, Jesus," he said. "Hide the stemware."

Dale's eyes had never left the TV. When he got down to his jockey shorts, he began to masturbate. He lowered his underpants to his knees and grabbed hold of his erect cock.

By now Paul had buried his face in a pillow on the bed, giggling uncontrollably.

"Isn't he cute?" Dale asked, his eyes on the screen, as if his response were the most normal thing in the world and the odd thing was that Eric and Paul hadn't joined him. "Don't you think he's cute?"

He began to have long conversations with people who weren't there, intimate exchanges that didn't make a lot of sense, partly because Dale jumbled the language and partly because in perfect English they wouldn't have quite added up.

"I realize you don't have a farkson of what the methodology calls for," he muttered, his eyes lifting to meet those of someone apparently sitting opposite him in the living room. "Kennebunkport, Kennebunkport, Kennebunkport. How could I have foreseen the farksickle of the final pissbowl?"

In the night, he'd wake up screaming.

"They're there," he yelled very early one morning, running into the hallway. "They're in the bedroom again."

"Who?" Eric asked, roused from sleep on the couch.

"The people," Dale almost whined. "The people with the heads."

There was no point in arguing with him. "Well . . . How about a hot drink or something?" Eric suggested.

"Let me sleep with you," Dale almost demanded.

"Huh? There isn't room . . . on the couch."

"That room isn't safe," Dale said and thrust an arm out to point down the hall.

"All right," Eric said, "I'll sleep in there."

"No," Dale said, his voice becoming more childlike. "I want to sleep with you."

"Well . . ."

"You don't want to sleep with me."

"Oh, for Christ's sake—"

Dale got under the covers on the couch and patted the small space beside him.

Eric was tired. And he felt a little silly standing there in his T-shirt and underpants, so he got onto the couch next to Dale. They struggled for a minute or two in the narrow space—Eric almost falling on the floor twice, Dale giggling—and finally found a way in which the two of them could fit—Dale turned away from Eric and facing the back of the couch and Eric curled behind him facing Dale's back. But then Eric didn't know where to put his hands.

Finally Dale took hold of one of them and brought it around his frail body to the front.

"There," he said.

Eric arrived after work one afternoon to find the apartment empty. He went from room to room calling Dale's name, even checked the closets, but he wasn't there and there was no note from him or Ed or Paul or anybody explaining where he had gone.

Recently they had all been strongly discouraging Dale from going out by himself. Even in the apartment, they tried not to leave him unattended, but sometimes it just wasn't possible.

Eric phoned Ed but couldn't reach him. He called Paul, who had no idea where Dale was. He said he would come over right away and wait in the apartment while Eric went out and looked in the neighborhood.

The Village had never appeared so foreign, as Eric moved from store to store, bar to bar, searching for Dale, finally beginning to ask people if they'd seen him. He visited bars he hadn't been inside in eight years; he went to the porno bookstore at the corner of Christopher and Hudson, which he'd never been inside. In his suit and trench coat, he felt like a messenger from some sort of clean-cut alternative, the middle-aged parent in one of those movies from the sixties, searching for his offspring among the flower children.

"Excuse me," he shouted at bartender after bartender over the sound of music that was current but also somehow old, mostly echoing off the walls of near-empty places. "I'm wondering if you've seen a friend of mine in here. I was supposed to meet him and he hasn't shown up."

No one had seen Dale. Not in Boots & Saddle, not in Ty's, not in Badlands, not in the new porno shop on Hudson, where Eric felt bathed in sex, glowing off the shelves and in the eyes of the men who turned to watch him enter and approach the heavyset guy behind the counter.

Outside again, he pushed on through the growing dark, trying not to think of all the possible things that could have happened to Dale. As he ducked into one sparsely populated place after another, he wondered if AIDS had really cleared the bars, or if it was just too early in the day for a crowd.

When he walked through the door of one anonymous place on West Street, the four or five aged, mustachioed denizens looked up as if from a time warp. A ceiling fan spun distorting shadows through the bar murk, and for a moment Eric couldn't figure out what the sense of concentration in the room was, the sense that he had interrupted something. But then he saw a thin, dark-haired man in the corner sitting behind a glass tumbler full of bits of cardboard, one of which he held in his hand. "Under the B, nine," he called hoarsely and took a drag on his cigarette.

On the street again, Eric stopped at a pay phone and called Paul to see if Dale had come back to the apartment, but there'd been no sign of him.

He hung up and stood looking about helplessly. The week before, holding Dale in his arms on the couch, he had felt the strangest combination of feelings—something almost sexual, his body suddenly feeling so incredibly vital and strong pressing to him the skinny frame of his friend. But that was just it, it was his friend, his friend he was having these feelings for, and that seemed about to break open something inside him so well protected he must have been born with it.

He finally found Dale down by the river farther along West, just as the light was about to fade completely. He knelt in the grass by some benches and threw a Frisbee to a little boy and girl who ran to retrieve it and then seemed to try to keep the game between themselves for as long as possible, despite Dale's obvious desire to play.

"Hi," he said when he saw Eric. He had a big smile on his face.

"Hi," Eric said. He took a breath. "We were worried about you."

"Silly," Dale said and picked at something with a stick in the dirt.

"Do you want to come home now?"

Dale looked slightly petulant for a moment, but then, elongating the sound with a mock tolerance, he said, "Ohhhhh-kaaay."

He got up, and Eric saw that he had wet his pants.

"Oh," he said. "Look what you've done."

"I'm sorry."

"That's all right," Eric said.

He put an arm around his shoulder and walked him home.

At home, he began to "forget" to use the bathroom. This became more and more of a problem, until finally they were left with no choice but to start diapering him. Around the same time he developed a lung infection, not PCP apparently, but enough to force him into bed again and bring on chronic diarrhea with it.

The diapering itself, like so much associated with the disease, could be gotten used to after a while, more than Eric ever would have thought, more than he ever would have wanted to believe, as if all people lived much closer to this kind of destruction and finality than they realized. "Just think of yourself as June Allyson," Paul would say as they rolled Dale in and out of his new undergear.

The smell began to permeate the apartment. Dale was sweating and losing weight again, and they had almost to force him to drink liquids so he wouldn't dehydrate. They were all afraid that Dr. Edelman was wrong, that the coughing really did mean PCP, but so far the doctor had not seen fit to hospitalize Dale. It was hard to tell what that meant.

They decided to rent a hospital bed, since it didn't look like Dale was going to be getting up much for a while and it would be easier to look after him in a bed they could raise and lower and put sides up on.

Eric went shopping for this at a medical supply company, and standing there, looking about at the various orthopedic devices that filled the room, listening to a balding, middle-aged man in short sleeves and a nondescript tie describe the different beds, he felt a stab of pain near his left shoulder blade.

He thought suddenly of Glenn Merritt, and when he did, he felt so old and decrepit he all but collapsed onto one of the stretchers against the wall behind him. What would it be like, he thought with the weariness of a question he'd wanted answered all his life, what would it be like to be perfect?

"What do you think?" the man asked, and Eric realized that he had been putting on quite a show raising and lowering one of the beds.

"I think we'll just take this one," Eric said and pointed to the least expensive model. The man's face fell, and Eric tried to cheer him up by telling him they would also be needing a bedpan and a urinal.

Dale was as sick as he had ever been. He sweated profusely, he coughed off and on all day and night, he barely ate a thing. His eyesight was continuing to fail, but it hardly seemed to matter, since he often lay in his own excrement without saying anything, talked very little in general, and made virtually no sense when he did.

When he started coughing up blood, Dr. Edelman finally hospitalized him again, which meant that they ended up canceling the entire order from the medical supply place.

"Have to keep your deposit, you know," the man told Eric in a chipper voice over the phone. "Can't do anything about that. You always lose your deposit."

chapter twenty-one

In the wide open spaces of the intensive care unit, Dale seemed to be shrinking. Would I have even recognized him if I hadn't seen him in two months? Eric wondered. How would I have found him?

Tubes ran from his nostrils, carrying dark liquids from somewhere inside him, and his mouth was plugged in the choke hold of a respirator, which hissed familiarly beside him, the background score from countless TV shows.

Three bottles were slung up on the intravenous stand next to his bed, in what the nurses called a piggyback system: One held pentamidine, another a sucrose mixture because Dale wasn't eating, and the third a saline solution to prevent dehydration, from perspiration and from the diarrhea that still plagued him.

Dale had been diapered and catheterized, and now he was attached to this dreaded, hissing machine, expanding and retracting his lungs like clockwork. Even when his eyes were open, he had a slack, vacant look about him.

"He's gone blind," Paul said when Eric approached him in the corridor of the ICU.

"What?"

"Edelman says he's developed retinitis from the CMV. He's gone totally blind."

"Christ."

"We have to call someone," Paul said. "We can't—"

"I know. I know. I think I'll try the sister."

Paul started toward the main room, then turned. "Did he ever make out a will?"

"No," Eric said sadly. "Not that I know of. I kept meaning to mention it, but I just couldn't."

Paul nodded, and the two of them slipped into the room, where the rhythmic hiss of the machines engulfed everything.

Eric couldn't reach Dale's sister, Valerie, in Wichita. He called first every half hour and then every fifteen minutes until about ten-thirty, when he began to despair of reaching anyone while he was still sober.

He was trying to imagine as positive an outcome to his efforts as possible. They'd always known Dale was gay, for example. They'd just been waiting for an excuse to have a giant family reconciliation. All past misunderstanding would fly out the window in a concerted effort to rally round Dale and make his last days as comfortable as possible.

Since the older brothers seemed as frightening and less useful than the mother and father, at ten-thirty Eric switched numbers and called the farm in Russell.

A man answered on the first try.

"Hello," Eric said. "Is Mrs. Corcoran in, please?" She seemed to be the one to speak to first.

A long pause followed. "You selling something?" the man finally asked.

"Excuse me? No. No. I'm not."

"Who is it?" a woman in the background asked in a high-pitched whisper.

"I don't know," the man answered.

"Well, did you ask?"

"No."

"Well, give me that thing then."

Some fumbling and then: "Hello?"

"Hello, Mrs. Corcoran?"

"Yes?"

"My name is Eric Summerfield. I'm a friend of your son Dale's."

"Oh," she said and nothing more.

"I'm afraid he's very sick."

"Who is it?" Eric heard Dale's father ask.

"It's just some salesman," Mrs. Corcoran said. "Go back to your paper."

"You don't know how to get rid of them, Marie. That's your problem."

"Hello?" Eric said.

"Yes, I'm here." Then in a whisper she asked, "What's wrong?"

"It might be better if we talked about the specifics when you got here."

"Got there?"

"Mrs. Corcoran, I don't want to mislead you. Your son is *very* sick. He's been sick for a long time now. He's in the hospital. And the doctors seem to feel that he won't live much longer. And I think that someone from his family ought to be here."

"I'll come out there," she said, still talking quietly. "Give me your name and telephone number."

Eric gave her the information and asked that she call him when she got into town. Then she hung up in an odd, fragmented way, without saying good-bye, as though she'd just suddenly dropped the receiver.

In the middle of the next afternoon, Eric got a call at the bookstore from Mrs. Corcoran, who had arrived, with Valerie, and checked into the Milford Plaza a few blocks away. He left work early and went to meet them in the hotel bar.

Marie Corcoran looked younger than her age, late sixties, but was a little heavy and on the short side, Dale's height, with dyed blond hair. In the bar lighting, Eric couldn't tell if it was a good dye job, but even in the darkness she appeared to be dressed stylishly, although in a way that somehow suggested she was used to being a big fish in a small pond.

Valerie was taller and thinner, with shoulder-length, overtreated dark blond hair and an angular face a bit too heavily made up. She wore large glasses and was much more casually dressed, in a loose cotton blouse and blue jeans. She was nine years older than Dale.

They glanced up at Eric when he entered the bar, and since they were the only two people in the place who remotely resembled a mother and daughter, he made his way toward them, which caused both women to fidget and look away as if they were about to be attacked or at least solicited in an unpleasant fashion. A part of Eric couldn't believe he was doing this, approaching two complete strangers with this kind of news, he who sometimes had trouble talking to his deli man.

"Mrs. Corcoran?" Eric said as he approached, and held out his hand. "I'm Eric Summerfield."

"Yes," she said, and took his hand noncommittally. "Marie Corcoran, and this is my daughter, Valerie Fortunelli. Valerie raised her eyes once and then brought them down again, her hands encircling a water glass.

"I'm sorry to have brought you here under such mysterious circumstances," Eric said when he had sat, slipping without thinking into a habitual politeness that he did not at all trust to encompass the situation at hand. A waiter came by and he ordered a beer.

"What's the story?" Marie asked.

"Dale is very sick. He's in an intensive care unit."

"What happened? What's wrong with him?"

Eric had tried to rehearse an easy way to say what he had to say, but he couldn't find one. He glanced up now to see how the waiter was progressing with his beer. "AIDS," he said, and realized how seldom the word was used. "Dale has AIDS."

"Shit," Valerie said immediately.

"I don't know how much you know about the disease," Eric continued, trying to find his way back to politeness as the waiter set an Amstel Light in front of him and poured, "but I'm sure you know that it's particularly common among gay men, and that's how Dale got it."

The two women were drinking iced tea, but Valerie now eyed Eric's beer hungrily. She looked at her mother. "Oh, Mama," she said. "I knew this was going to happen."

This struck Eric as a good sign. Maybe they had known more than they let on . . .

"Dale has AIDS?" Marie asked. "Why weren't we notified?"

Eric took a sip of beer. "Well, it's not automatic that you get notified," he said and then thought that sounded stupid. "I mean Dale was the one who had to notify you, and . . . I mean, we tried to convince him to get in touch with you," he continued, recognizing a familiar desire to boost his standing with the older woman, "but there was only so much that any of us, his friends, could do. I'm sorry."

"I figured he was gay," Valerie said, in a tone Eric thought suggested she expected the Nobel Prize for the deduction.

"Yes," he said and found himself gulping his beer, "I think he said he thought you knew."

"Well . . . ," Mrs. Corcoran said a little frantically, looking around, irritated all of a sudden, "where is he? I want to see Dale. This is ridiculous."

"We can go over there now," Eric said, "but I have to warn you." He took a deep breath. "He's unconscious much of the time. All the time, really. He's on a respirator. That breathes for him. He's lost an extraordinary amount of weight and he has Kaposi's sarcoma lesions on his skin. The AIDS virus has infected his brain, and even when he was last conscious, he often didn't recognize people or make much sense. His brain has also been infected with a virus called CMV, which has caused blindness."

The two women remained motionless, staring at him.

"I don't understand," Mrs. Corcoran finally said. "I don't understand how all this could have happened without us being notified." She turned to Valerie when it seemed that Eric wasn't going to give her an answer.

"Blindness?" Valerie asked, as if she could only digest this one piece at a time. "You say he's blind?"

At the hospital, Mrs. Corcoran still didn't seem to believe Eric. He caught her checking Dale's ID bracelet and chart to be sure that the curled, cow-eyed, spotted body afloat in the giant bed was in fact her son.

chapter twenty-two

Eric began to look at Glenn with an odd, exhausted spite, born of sadness and frustration and the lust and love he feared would remain forever confused in his mind.

He discouraged Glenn from sitting in his office on his breaks. He claimed he had work to do, an assertion that was, as ever, silly.

Some days he believed that Glenn was one hundred percent heterosexual, and on those days he hated him for the luckiness of it, the freedom that the girlfriend and the perfect body and all those white teeth gave him. He hated him for being young, for being so unconscious of his luck, for taking it so for granted that he would always be wanted.

"I have this problem with gay men sometimes," Glenn had said, "in that they tend to be attracted to me, I guess, it seems, *a lot*."

Don't worry about it, Eric now found himself wanting to say. Time will take care of that problem very nicely for you. I give you another three, maybe four, years, five tops, before it all starts to fall apart.

And then other days, he was convinced that Glenn was what Dale and Paul had said he was all along: a closet case, and maybe a closet case waiting for Eric to make a move. And on those days he hated him for that, for this dance of the seven veils he kept doing, this taunting, cowardly sashay around the subject, talking near-obsessively about it and then complaining because the gay men just wouldn't leave him alone.

But he saw something like genuine hurt in Glenn's eyes the day he sauntered into Eric's office with his yogurt and newspaper and was greeted by Eric saying icily, "Would you mind eating that in the lounge? Thanks."

Eric couldn't seem to stop himself. It was as if, one way or another, Glenn was a constant reminder of what could have been.

On nights in the ICU there was a tall, thin, dark-haired nurse in her late twenties, named Sandy, who had a religious bent. She claimed to have watched hundreds of patients die, and each time, she said, she'd seen a kind of light, a spark, flash out of the person's head at the moment of death. She had thought she was crazy for a long time, until she read about a survey conducted among medical personnel that revealed most of them had had this experience, but that, to a person, they had never told anyone about it.

Sandy seemed to have taken it on as her private crusade to see that people knew. "It's information," she told Eric sotto voce. "I mean frankly I think it's a hell of a lot more helpful than most of the medical theories they dispense around here. But," she added with a sigh, "you can't make much money in a place like this if you prove people survive death, now can you? Beating death is the name of the game around here; everything else is failure."

When Eric got to the hospital with Dale's mother and sister on the night after they arrived, Sandy was pacing the ward in a distracted manner, and he wondered if she were hunting for sparks.

Marie and Valerie seemed to have had time to think things over and were no longer quite so stunned by everything that was going on. They had questions now. "Who is his doctor?" "What treatments has he been given?" "How did he get to be so deteriorated?" And other, more personal, somewhat inane, questions. "How can you be so sure Dale is gay?" "Aren't other people getting this disease?" Marie was certain she'd heard that was true.

She sat and Valerie stood near Dale's bed for almost half an hour, speaking only occasionally, and then only to each other. When they were ready to leave, Eric suggested that the three of them get a drink back at the hotel.

"I realize," he said, when the waiter had brought his beer and their gin and tonics, "that this is a lot for you to take in all at once. But the condition that you see Dale in now, he's been in for several days, and for several weeks he hasn't been much better. Even on the respirator, the doctors are certain he won't live long. Either the cancer or the pneumonia or something else will kill him. And during that time he will be either unconscious or out of his mind. If you give them permission to disconnect the machine, he stands a much better chance of dying relatively peacefully, probably within a few days."

For a moment no one spoke, and then Valerie seemed suddenly to snap to. "I'd need to know just a whole hell of a lot more about this situation before I'd be willing to make a decision like that," she said, her face flushing, her eyes not meeting Eric's.

"Well, Dr. Edelman wants to talk to you," he said. "They won't do it unless they're positive you understand exactly what's involved. I just wanted to prepare you." He took a hefty gulp of beer. "What is it you feel you don't know?" he asked.

"Well . . . ," she said, still very tightly, "for example, I don't know who you are. I don't know what your relationship to my brother is. I don't know what sort of life he's been living out here, how he came to be in this condition."

"I thought we'd been over all that. I'm not Dale's lover, I'm just a friend. He had two relation—"

"Oh, I don't want to hear about that," Marie said wearily, flicking her hand up in a dismissive gesture and turning away.

"Why couldn't he have told us?" Valerie asked.

"Told you what?"

"That he was . . . you know," she said angrily, as if it were Eric's fault she couldn't say the word.

"I think he was afraid that you wouldn't take it very well."

"We may not be as unsophisticated as you think," Valerie said haughtily and threw her drink back so quickly she almost tossed ice cubes in her lap. "I realize that we don't live in New York . . ."

"I'm just guessing at what Dale thought."

"Well, I know what Dale thought," she said. "The few times he even came out there he looked down his nose at everybody. I haven't seen my brother in three years, because Wichita was just too far away for him to take an extra trip when he was visiting Mom and Dad. His nieces and nephews barely know who he is."

A long silence followed. The muzak in the bar played "Moon River."

"If all this . . . gay business is true," Marie said finally, "I think he would have told me. I just can't accept that. I think I would have known."

Something was beginning to ignite in Eric. This was definitely not moving toward the bedside reconciliation he had envisioned, which would have allowed them fairly effortlessly to fade to black and go to commercial.

"What?" he asked. "You think I'm making it up?"

"I don't know what I think. I want to talk to my son."

"Well, you just may not be able to do that."

"Don't you raise your voice with me, young man."

"Mrs. Corcoran," Eric said, trying not to spit the words, "when I called you the other night, you lied to your husband, you didn't tell him who was calling, you said it was a salesman. Why did you do that?"

Valerie searched the bottom of her glass for something, anything, to imbibe.

"Dale and his father have never seen eye to eye," Marie said and sipped her drink with an aloof air. "I . . . Whenever Dale was in trouble, I always tried to keep Ty out of it. It never did any good for him to get involved."

"Well maybe," Eric said and took a jagged breath, "it was that kind of environment that made Dale think he couldn't tell you about his life. Maybe he wasn't being condescending. Maybe he was just being realistic."

"What do you know about it?" Valerie mumbled.

"Nothing," Eric said. He sat back in his chair. "I know nothing. Talk to Dr. Edelman."

The next night, Eric stood at the foot of Dale's bed and spoke to him.

"I'm just going to say this," he started awkwardly, "in case there's some chance that you can hear me and understand me, OK?" The respirator hissed. He sensed Sandy hovering about in the background. "First of all, I know you didn't want your family involved in this, but what happened is that the only way we could arrange to have this machine turned off was to have a relative of some kind give permission. So I called your mother. I tried your sister first actually, although now that I've met them I'm not sure why. In any case, I couldn't reach her, and then they both ended up coming out here anyway.

"If that was wrong . . . for us to do that, to contact your family, I'm sorry." He glanced toward the reflection in the dark window next to Dale's bed. He felt as if he had to shout to be heard over the respirator, and then it seemed that his words were bouncing off the walls of the cavernous room, lit like daytime twenty-four hours a day.

"But what I most want to talk to you about," Eric continued, "is this machine, this tube that's down your throat. It's more or less keeping you alive at this point and will go on doing that for quite a while apparently. In the meantime, you have a number of serious infections that are threatening your life and will continue to do so. In other words, one way or another the doctors are certain that your body is not going to hold out much longer. With the respirator, this process will be drawn out, that's all. You won't get better. That's not what the machine does. And since what you're living right now doesn't seem like much of a life, to me or Paul or the doctors, we thought you might be better off without the respirator, in which case you might only live another few days, if that."

He took a breath, which just then seemed the most luxurious thing in the world. He felt as if he had talked more in the past week than in the whole year previous.

He moved around to the side of the bed and took hold of Dale's free hand, the one without the tubes. "If you can hear me," he said, "and if what I've described to you, about turning off the machine, is . . . If you want us to turn off the respirator, squeeze my hand once, OK? If you don't want us to turn it off, squeeze twice. OK? Once for yes, turn it off. Twice for no, leave it on."

Eric waited, watching Dale's tiny, bony hand resting, still, in his own for what seemed like several minutes. Then he chuckled. "I could have sworn this worked in the movies," he said.

He let go of Dale's hand and started to turn away. Then he turned back suddenly and knelt on the floor beside the bed.

"This has changed me," he said. "In ways it will take me a long time to understand." He took a breath. "You were a good friend to me. I want . . ." His voice trailed off strangely, as if the giant hissing room could only tolerate the truth. "No," he said and sat back, "you weren't. What a funny thing to say. That's not at all what I meant to say. But I'm just suddenly remembering that I've *never* been comfortable around you. I don't think I've ever been comfortable around anyone, but couldn't a good friend at least have been compassionate about that, instead of picking at me all the time, getting such a charge out of hurting my feelings? You could never wait to give me bad news. You fought for the opportunity to do it . . . a kind of sick gleam in your eyes—especially news you knew I'd be sensitive about. I guess you thought I could take it—the logic of much of your behavior suddenly escapes me. Hurting me, I know, was part of your 'fun,' and you were good at 'fun,' weren't you? It charmed the hell out of people who didn't know you well enough to see how cruel you were being. I've never been 'fun,' I've never been able to play the game, I've always bored and alienated people, but at least I've tried to be a good person, and right now I can't remember a single truly honest conversation we had with each other. I can't remember ever being listened to. I suddenly can only remember you talking incessantly about yourself, always swinging things back to you, you, you. And what a chump I was!" He stood. "To just take it! I always felt *bad* when I came away from being with you. I always felt put down. Isn't *that* a coincidence? Why did you hate me so fucking much?" he shouted, and then felt Sandy move in to stand in the background. He was filled with a rage so pure it seemed to redefine the world in its own terms.

"He talks to me sometimes," Sandy said.

"What?"

"In my dreams."

"Oh."

"You can take it seriously or not, but I have dreams about a number of the terminal patients that are quite vivid and not really like dreams at all, they're so precise."

Eric looked hesitantly down at Dale. Somehow Sandy's voice was pulling him back to the former world, and he didn't want to come.

"You can take it seriously or not," she continued. "But I'd say you don't have to bother turning off that machine."

The most remarkable thing about death, Eric would think later, was how nonchalantly it entered your life, as if totally oblivious to the fact that you'd spent years denying its existence.

The hospital didn't even call him. They called Dale's mother at her hotel, and she called him, around seven-thirty in the morning, to say, "He's died," in a slightly disgusted tone, as if it were Eric's fault.

He kept waiting for the swell of music on the soundtrack, the camera pulling back to frame him in beautiful mourning clothes, his brow attractively furrowed beneath windswept hair, his handsome lawyer lover at his side. Instead he was standing in his underwear in his messy apartment, he had a morning hard-on, and he had to pee real bad. And Dale was dead.

Mrs. Corcoran wanted to take the body back to Kansas. Paul was planning a service among Dale's friends in New York, but since Dale hadn't made out a will, it was unclear who had a right to the body, and anyway, after a while, when it became apparent they'd have to fight Marie for it, the whole thing began to seem slightly inane. "Let her have it," Paul said finally. "His body was all she ever had to begin with."

Eric was inclined to agree. But he wasn't in a mood for driving wedges between people. He'd been thinking about his own family a lot. It suddenly seemed that so many things in life were so incredibly fickle that no matter what the problems, in the end you'd value most what had been consistent. And even that was gone too soon.

Marie wanted to see the body. Something about helping her accept the death. Valerie refused to accompany her downstairs to the hospital morgue, so Eric did it.

He felt the strongest sense of Dale's presence he'd experienced in a while as he and Marie walked along a basement corridor toward the morgue and he was suddenly positive the doors would be thrust open

by Dale in nurse drag, fixing Eric and his mother with a bizarre stare
and announcing that there was "Room for one more, honey."

But watching Mrs. Corcoran, he knew that she was not experiencing this relief, of Dale's humor, a side of himself that hadn't flour-
ished in her presence. She sat quietly next to the gurney and brushed
Dale's hair gently, repeatedly, back from his forehead, something Eric
had never seen her do upstairs.

Then she stopped and sat back with her hands in her lap. She
looked up at Eric with an expression that was almost awestruck.

"He was my baby," she said.

Days later, in the apartment, Eric and Paul found a stash of the letters Marie had sent Dale, and which he had saved but never opened.
Eric couldn't bring himself to return them to her, so he took them
home with him, and one night he sat cross-legged in the center of his
unmade bed, with a knife and a third beer, and opened them. There
were about twelve letters in all, dated a few months apart, sent over
the past three years.

Dear Dale,
Had a moment free from my canning enterprise, so thought I'd
drop you a line. The garden was particularly lush this year . . .

Dear Dale,
The shop is slow this time of year, so thought I'd write you a
few words . . .

Dear Dale,
Weather has been plain lousy here. Seems spring doesn't want
to start. Saw on TV that you've had pretty balmy weather there
for this time of year . . .

What most struck Eric as he read the letters, as he opened one
after another after another there on his rumpled bed in New York
City, was how steadfastly Marie had reported the mundane news
from Russell. There was hardly an original thought in the batch, and
there was never a mention of the fact that Dale didn't respond. Just
this faithful reportage:

> *Still can't get over what a difference it's made having Walt*
> *back on the farm. He and Dad have made real headway this*
> *year. Not quite the same as when we owned the place but Dad*
> *was getting so he couldn't handle it alone. Walt says we did*
> *better this year than last. He thinks we should buy more hogs.*
> *Jenny and kids are settling in, too. Sarah and Ben now go to*
> *the same school you kids all went to. It's changed some of course.*
> *The three of them are in town for the day.*
>
> *Had a visit from Valerie, Ron and Vanessa last weekend.*
> *Vanessa is now 4, and she couldn't get enough sledding on the*
> *back hill. They still like it in Wichita.*
>
> *Gene is not too happy at the plant just now but I don't think he*
> *and Louise will move with the boys almost through high school.*
> *Can you believe it? Tim graduates in a month!*

Pictures of the children spilled out of some of the letters: high
school photos of Gene's boys, looking more radiant than Eric could
remember high school ever being; Sarah and Ben in snow suits on
the back hill and Vanessa looking up from a sea of wrapping paper,
their enthusiasm, and the diligence with which they had been photographed suggesting—miraculously, Eric suddenly thought—that
they were the first children ever to do these things.

The seasons came and went, the notepaper turned from pale blue to pink, different flowers sprayed the corners of its pages, and over and over and over again, Marie used phrases like "Nothing much new here," or "Things are pretty much as usual at this end," or "Not much to report," and yet she had.

There were occasional glimpses into what Dale and his life may have meant to her:

> We see so much on TV about that incident in your subway, and I just cannot believe you live there. Are you taking good care of yourself? Mothers worry, you know.

> Do you remember Mrs. Cudmore? You kids used to make fun of her. Well, she drops by the shop quite often when I'm there and is always interested to hear about my son in New York!

And Dale was right, she spoke with the most pride and interest when talking about her job in the beauty salon. And she seemed to reach out to Dale most here, too, as if she wanted his praise, or maybe just his articulate friendship. There were detailed descriptions of several processes she had learned to put the town's ladies' hair through, and the results—sometimes successful, sometimes not so, and these were related with humor. She loved the fact that she got a discount on the merchandise they sold and used at the shop, and that she could get her own hair and nails done anytime she liked. The job had made her a local beauty expert, but one who was still insecure enough to yearn for big city approval.

"Hope you can drop us a line," she said often, with no hint that he never did. "Call collect," she suggested. And each letter closed with "Dad sends his love," and then "Mom" signed beneath the words "Mine too."

The traffic noise from First Avenue had died down. A bus huffed its way to the stop at Eighty-third Street. Through his slightly opened window Eric heard the jingling of someone walking a dog past, then the faster pace of a more animated group on the other side of the street.

He looked around his apartment, at the weird shadows his bedside lamp cast across the books and papers on the floor, the clumps of dirty clothes, and Simone, sipping prissily at her water dish, next to a stack of empty pizza boxes waiting to be dumped.

A year ago he might have found Mrs. Corcoran's letters ridiculous, filled with denial and absurdity. But he had begun to see life as a more fragile thing, and her attempt to communicate, against all odds, suddenly struck him as noble, and terribly sad.

He carefully returned the letters to their envelopes, and noticed that a number of the stamps had been canceled—six months ago, three years ago—with the Kansas state motto: *Ad Astra Per Aspera* (To the Stars Through Difficulties).

The service Paul planned was very nice, held in St. Luke's Church at Christopher and Hudson. Grace was there. Mickey had flown out with his new lover, Gene. Jake and Tony showed up, and Ted Myer, and others Eric recognized from parties over the years.

Paul spoke eloquently about Dale's courage. Reg started out somber and then segued into something more volatile, as if they should all tear off their funeral clothes, grab placards, and hit the streets. Ed related some of the funnier moments from his time as Dale's buddy. Someone from the Gay Men's Chorus sang "Fire and Rain." It was all pleasant enough, but Eric drifted through it.

Paul had asked him to say something, but he didn't trust himself to make a speech like that. He couldn't wait to get outside, where fall was coming on strong in the form of a rainstorm.

As he stood on the sidewalk in front of the church, under an umbrella, he cursed himself for thinking of Glenn, for wishing Glenn was there. He saw himself crying against Glenn's strong shoulder, saying, oddly, "I'm sorry. I'm sorry. I'm sorry."

Just then Sandy, the nurse from the ICU, came up behind him.

"How nice of you to come," he said flatly.

"I wanted to talk to you," she said, and Eric felt an urge to pull away.

"The morning your friend died," Sandy went on, "I dreamt about him."

"Oh?" Eric didn't meet her gaze. A taxi was barreling up the street, and he ducked back to avoid being splashed. Sandy followed him.

"Yes," she said, from under her own, tiny blue umbrella, "I often do that. I'd gone home earlier, when my shift ended, and fallen asleep right away. I saw him as a healthy man, so I knew that he had left his body. I asked him, in the dream, if he had died, and he said yes, he had."

Eric looked around for someone, anyone, he recognized leaving the church, but they had all congregated inside the front door.

"Anyway," Sandy went on, "I think he must have had some sort of . . . religious experience . . . awakening, conversion. Whatever."

"What?" Eric turned.

"They'll do that in the end sometimes, you know."

"What the hell are you talking about?" Eric almost shouted.

"I asked him if he was in heaven," Sandy said, totally unfazed by his anger, apparently still perplexed by what she was describing, "and he said yes. And then I asked him what heaven was like." She looked into Eric's eyes, as if maybe he could puzzle it out. "And all he said was . . . St. Mark."

chapter twenty-three

Eric, Paul, and Ed were left to clean out Dale's apartment. Paul contacted the guy Dale had been illegally subletting from, who now lived in Maine, and he decided to let the apartment go. The landlord wanted to rent the place again by November 1.

It was amazing, Eric thought, what got left in an apartment when someone died. Marie and Valerie hadn't shown any interest in any of it, but Eric and Paul still planned to mail them a box of the more G-rated stuff. Paul was a godsend, in his element, organizing the whole project, seeing to it that everything none of them wanted got assigned to someone else or donated to charity.

There was a lot of food left in the kitchen: canned goods and spices and things stuck way in the back of cupboards, much of it useful but bulky; Eric took a couple of boxes home. He was also given some of Dale's dishes and pots and pans, and his track lighting, which Paul promised to help him install, and offered his sofa, which was too big for his place. He could have used the dresser from the bedroom, he supposed, but Ed expressed interest in it, and really Eric felt emotionally encumbered by everything he was taking from there; he said yes just to keep things moving.

During lulls in the work, he found his mind worrying over the previous year. "I wonder sometimes," he said as he and Paul sipped mugs of coffee and lackadaisically emptied one of the hall closets into cardboard Random House boxes, "if it wasn't all that chemotherapy at the beginning that really did him in ultimately. I don't think it was really necessary, do you?"

"Different people have different opinions," Paul said and dropped a stack of towels into one of the boxes. "And it keeps changing. It seemed to help at the time, didn't it?"

"I guess."

"It still hasn't shown up inside me," Paul said, and Eric felt again the shockwave that had been visiting him more and more recently. He kept forgetting who had this disease and who didn't; it had once been such an unforgettable thing. "That's why my doctor hasn't wanted to get into any of that, the cancer treatments. If it's primarily cosmetic, they don't bother now."

From the top shelf, Paul took down the blue blanket Eric had spread over Dale so many times. Then he stopped as if caught unawares by something. "I keep thinking I should have helped out sooner," he said.

"You didn't even know he was sick. He didn't tell anybody," Eric said. "Except me."

"But even after that, I mean after I knew, I think maybe, you know, maybe he wouldn't have had such a hard time of it . . ."

"It all went by so quickly," Eric said. "It's like we just didn't have time to get it right."

Within a week the apartment was completely empty. Eric stood watching Paul do a final sweep of the floors Dale had had refinished just a little over a year ago. He realized that Dale's death had left more than the gap of a missing person. A project, a battle, he had been engaged in for months, which had consumed his life, was over, with no clear victor. He had no idea when, if ever, he would see Paul again. Suddenly, he couldn't imagine what he was going to do with all that time.

He retreated. He slept more, and began to watch television again for hours at a time. He went through the motions at the bookstore, barely speaking to anyone there.

And then one night Paul called to say he was making a patch for Dale to be included in the Names Project quilt, which was to be unfurled for the first time at the national march on Washington for gay rights in October.

"I can't go," Paul said. "I really don't feel up to it, and besides the guy I'm a buddy to right now is real sick and I don't want to be away. But I want someone to go and check it out, so why don't you?"

Eric caught himself mentally coming up with the old excuses, the resistance he used to put up almost automatically with Dale.

"Sure," he said. "I'll go."

He didn't see the patch before Paul sent it off, but he promised to look for it in Washington. By the time he left, he was cranky again. He avoided the special "gay" trains and buses chartered for the march and bought his own separate train ticket. On board, he wondered why he was bothering to go at all. The quilt didn't seem like such a big deal and the thought of the march frightened him.

But once there, in Washington, and checked into his hotel near the Capitol, he began to feel a little more excited. He had never been to Washington before, and he hadn't traveled to a new city in years.

He took a bus tour of the monuments and wandered around past the government buildings, all ancient in architecture, lending a bogus sense of history to the place. The White House was amazing—like every good Canadian, Eric had imagined it sequestered on some enormous estate, but there it was smack-dab in the middle of the big, bad city, a matter of feet from a Burger King and an all-night liquor store.

He noticed a lot of gay people walking about, couples hand-in-hand, individuals wearing pink triangles or otherwise making their orientation pretty clear. At the Lincoln Memorial he stood with a lesbian couple and another gay man, their necks arched back to read the words of the Gettysburg Address.

He was going to take a tour of the White House, but he ran out of time, and the next day was the unveiling of the quilt, which he'd promised Paul he would attend. He figured he'd go early, near sunrise, when they said they were going to begin, so that he could get it over with before the crowds arrived.

As Eric approached the Capitol Mall the next morning, with light just beginning to crack the darkness, he heard footsteps slowly collecting about him. More and more, as he got closer to the mall and could see a small group of figures up ahead, where the ceremony had apparently begun, he sensed a forward momentum all around him. It took him a while to figure out what it was that felt so strange. It was the silence. No one was saying anything.

Across the damp grass of the mall they made their way toward the group ahead. What drew people most seemed to be the sound, somewhere beyond those immediately in front, of voices amplified, one at a time, echoing in the still distance. Eric couldn't hear what was being said until he drew up next to the loose gathering of people along the perimeter of the quilt. The voices were reading names. A fair number of people had already shown up, and more and more were arriving by the minute to form a ring around the site, where Names Project volunteers were unfolding the quilt one section at a time. And as each section was spread on the ground, someone at a microphone near the other end of the field would read the names of the individuals memorialized in it.

The silence surrounding the names was unimaginable. Eric had never been present in anything like it before. Soon there were a couple hundred people there, and still such silence. "David Arcone. Kyle Johnson. Ron Carey." Only this sound in the coolness of the morning air, as the light continued to break across a cloudy sky. "Roger Ellis. Charles Skipper. Charles Thompson."

Eric could hear people breathing next to him. The movement of news reporters to take photographs some distance away traveled

across the ground with nothing to stop it. A middle-aged man in a
suit stood next to a well-dressed woman at the microphone and read,
"John D. Smith. Louie Galacia. And . . . our son . . . Tim Harris."

Eric was astonished to find tears rolling down his face, but the
astonishment was not so much that the event had turned out to
be so powerful so immediately, but that the tears were like air that
morning, like breathing. The man to Eric's right was crying and the
woman to Eric's left was crying, and the most extraordinary feeling
grew up inside him, from the earth through his feet, that nothing,
nothing he would ever experience in however long his life turned out
to be could ever, ever, ever feel like this.

"Fernando Delgado. Bob C. Mike Melig." The sound of hundreds of people crying, of their tears christening a silence all their
own, filled the dawn as more and more joined, people from all over
the nation, the world, gay people but also their family and friends,
drawn together by what suddenly seemed to Eric, for the first time, a
tragedy of almost unbearable dimension. "Jay Rindal. Rueben Dana
Holland. And my lover, Larry Nelson."

The quilt was being laid out in a grid with pathways of fabric
crisscrossing it. Each section, containing thirty-two patches, first
rested in the middle of its square of ground, and when its time came,
a team of volunteers unfolded it and turned it in a kind of dance
around the twenty-four-foot square before letting the cloth drop
carefully to the ground.

"Paul Neesom. Herman McNeill. Don Beavers." There were some
celebrities reading at the podium. Joseph Papp was there, and Harvey
Fierstein; Whoopi Goldberg was supposed to show up later. There
were people from the gay community, from the gay presses, from parents' groups, who were there in greater numbers than Eric had ever
seen at any other gay event. "Jim Schroeder. Debra Lenard. Brian
Tadesco."

The sun began to warm his face. He wiped it with his hands and held one above his eyes to shade them from the light, reflecting now on the Capitol dome in the background. "Andrew Finochio. Richard Bledsoe. A. Sydney Gadd III."

A giant fruit picker stood at the side, ready to lift news photographers high above the finished quilt. "Mel Wald. John Patrick Quinn. Gary Christopher." The readers often teared up themselves, were unable to go on for a moment, the sound of crying in their voices as natural as the wind. "Bob Sullivan. Joe Frattini. Eric Walker." My own name, Eric thought, my own life; it could be my life laid out here.

"Chris Page. Rock Hudson. Sergei Shuiiski." It was bright now, despite the overcast of clouds, and there were hundreds of people gathered. Eric backed off from the crowd at his end of the quilt and began, as others were doing, to circle the growing creation, to look from a different angle and just to walk free, to break away from the sadness. But it followed. "Richard Garcia. Charlie Braun. David Reed."

And then Eric heard something that for some reason surprised him, hadn't occurred to him. There was such care and dignity in it, there alongside the rest, as if all the last year had been watched over somehow, protected and preserved. A man's voice Dale didn't recognize read, "Wayne McGee. Dale Corcoran. Bill Colby."

Eric broke into a sob so loud it frightened him. He had never made a sound like that in his life, and he buckled to his knees on the grass. Ahead of him in his blurred vision he saw a bearded young man with red hair tied back in a ponytail, who moved immediately to his side on the ground. He put his arms around Eric and rocked him gently, sobbing himself as well. "That was my friend," Eric managed to say, as if an explanation were required. "They just read my friend's name."

———

The beginning of day, advancing toward noontime, brought more people and a greater freedom to move, to begin perhaps to try to speak, as the sound of the names became more and more familiar, filling in the background.

When the readers were finally done and the entire quilt had been laid, it formed a stunning panorama that filled an area the size of two football fields and at that represented only a handful of the total number of people who had died of AIDS. Whoopi Goldberg led off, pushing a friend of hers in a wheelchair, and the crowd followed in an orderly fashion down the pathways for a closer look.

The mood shifted slightly then, became a little looser, but still quiet, respectful. They were handing out a guide to the quilt, with a list of the names of everyone on it and a map keyed to show where each person's patch was located. And for the first time in weeks, Eric suddenly heard Dale's voice in his ear. "I finally made it," he said, "into Grauman's Chinese."

People were now locating the patches of their own friends and relatives, and the sound of grief, which had been collective earlier, began to cut the air with specificity. The sorrow of parents and friends and sisters and brothers, the sight of so many people falling to their knees, keening, reaching out to smooth protectively the patch that commemorated a brother, a child, a best friend, embracing those they knew as well as strangers, burned its way into Eric's brain.

And the patches themselves—each in its individuality so obviously represented a life, an entire life, a unique life. And so many of them were gay lives. Wandering the maze of the quilt, Eric was stricken by the familiarity of so much of what he saw. I know these people, he kept thinking. I know who these people are.

The dates impacted him more than anything. So many of them began with his own year of birth, or later. He was just beginning to accept that people had actually been born in years like 1965 or 1968 and now they were dying.

Paul had found, in Dale's closet, the hamburger costume he'd made for last year's Halloween parade, and he'd used as background for the patch a big swipe of the cardboard bun that had circled Dale's middle. Beneath two photographs he'd spelled out "Dale Corcoran, 1955–1987."

One was of Dale in costume that Halloween night, balancing rings of all-cardboard patties, lumpy pillowcases passing as special sauce, and bright green rags torn like lettuce. His "hat" was the top of a smaller sesame seed bun set at a jaunty angle and tied under his chin with a big bow, brown like his turtleneck, his stockings, and his big leather shoes. He had asked Eric to be his partner in another costume he'd invented, a walking 7-Up bottle, but Eric had declined. He couldn't remember what he'd spent that night doing.

The other photograph was of the "real" Dale, taken by whom Eric couldn't remember, but catching Dale with a gentler expression on his face, turning against the sunlight in a window he was working on at the bookstore.

Eric arrived for the march the next day feeling shy and awkward, his old habits hovering about. They were giving away free leftover march T-shirts, and he took one, but then he didn't want to put it on in front of everyone, so he ended up having to carry it all day.

He watched for a long time as several groups with banners paraded by the starting point of the route, which would take them past the back of the White House and on down Pennsylvania Avenue to the mall, for a rally before the Capitol. The ACT-UP contingent moved by, and Eric saw Reg, who waved him over and gave him a big hug. Eric's face reddened, but he was glad to have been recognized by someone.

"Act up! Fight back! Fight AIDS!" Reg and everyone else in the group chanted. At first Eric remained silent, as he did when stage performers tried to get the audience to sing along, too shy to speak and yet self-conscious to be the only one not doing so. Finally, though, almost of its own accord, the voice rose within him, and never had he felt more entitled to shout.

At the rally, Reg drifted off and Eric once again felt the isolation he seemed so peculiarly prone to. He sat by himself on the lawn and listened to the various speakers and performers, including Jesse Jackson, who was running for president, and began ever so gingerly to look around at the amazing crowd. He thought suddenly that he was looking for the red-haired man who'd held him the day before, but then it seemed maybe he was just looking for that quality in everyone and anyone, a way to express that quality more in himself.

At dusk, with the speeches and songs and cheers dying down, and many people heading back home, Eric still sat alone. He stood, brushed the grass off the seat of his blue jeans, and started back to his hotel with his new shirt.

But on the way there, strolling along Pennsylvania Avenue, flanked by the massive Greco-Roman buildings, he saw the red-haired man walking alone ahead of him.

He was younger than Eric, a little shorter and thinner, more delicate, although not effeminate per se, in fact kind of tough-looking with his beard and his torn, faded blue jeans and sleeveless white T-shirt. The setting sunlight glistened on an earring, a gold hoop as Eric recalled, in one ear, and the man's ponytail was tied back with a pretty pink ribbon. He was about a block in front of Eric.

At first only the old reflexes were there: Who knew what sort of person this guy would turn out to be; what were the chances of the two of them really hitting it off in the long run; it would probably at best be a one-night-stand sort of thing and Eric just wasn't really interested in that anymore—a thousand and one excuses not to make a move.

But then it was as if someone, someone familiar, put a hand on his shoulder and nudged him, whispered in his ear, "There isn't time for this." And he found himself walking, and then almost running, forward until the red-haired man turned to see who was coming behind.

"Hello," they both said at the same time. The man smiled a little, although underneath he still seemed sad. They walked side by side.

"This was better, huh?" the man said. "Today?"

"Yes," Eric said and felt his face flushing. "It was . . . exhilarating. As if we could channel some of the . . . grief from yesterday into the anger today."

"Are you a reporter or something?"

"Huh?"

"You sounded a little like you were writing an article about it."

"Oh . . . sorry."

"Don't apologize. I wish I knew more . . . thoughtful people."

"Oh . . . well . . ." Eric had never heard the description "thoughtful" as a compliment before. "So . . . ," he went on, "uh . . . where are you from?"

"New York."

"Me, too! Did you know someone who . . . was in the quilt?"

"Several people. Unfortunately."

They walked a little farther in silence.

"It was something, wasn't it?" Eric said.

At the corner of Seventh Street, the red-haired man stopped and turned. "Listen," he said, "I'm about to meet some friends and we're going to drive back to the city in about a half hour. I'd offer you a ride, but we've already turned down a couple people so I know there's no room. But if we can find a pen or something, I'll give you my phone number in the city and maybe we can get together. OK?"

"Sure," Eric said and began, he hoped not too frantically, to search for some sort of writing utensil. The red-haired man found the stub of a pencil in the pocket of his jeans. "Do you have something to write on?" he asked, and then they both searched again, the man finally coming up with a crumpled matchbook from Tracks, a local bar, which he tore carefully in two.

"I'm Brian," he said and handed half of the matchbook to Eric. "Turn around."

"What?" Eric asked and then followed Brian's hand motions and found himself facing away. Brian put his half of the matchbook against Eric's back and wrote.

When he was through, he turned Eric back around, said "Your turn," and faced the other way.

"I'm Eric," Eric said and wrote out his name and telephone number on the crumpled bit of cardboard. He could smell the sweetest odor emanating from the red-haired man named Brian, not really a cologne, more human than that, and when he was through writing out his name and number, he shoved the pencil and matchbook into the back pocket of Brian's jeans, and before he could turn, caught him with both arms, pulled Brian toward him with his hands cupped against his firm chest, and kissed him very gently just under one ear. Brian snuggled against him for a moment, and when he turned, he had a big smile on his face.

"I've . . . ," Eric said. "I've never done anything like that in my life."

As he walked away, Brian said, "Let's hope it's a new beginning."

chapter twenty-four

His first day back in the city, Eric asked Glenn to join him for dinner after work. Grace had told him Glenn was taking some vacation time the following week, and Eric wanted to talk to him soon.

He seemed surprised but then maybe sort of pleased by Eric's invitation, and the two of them left the store together and went across the street to the Beanstalk in the McGraw Hill building.

It took Eric the longest time to figure out exactly what was so different, but then it hit him with the most amazing clarity: He was less afraid.

He watched Glenn maneuver his mouth beneath the hamburger he was eating, to catch a string of onion. "I just have to tell you," Eric found himself saying, "that you are easily one of the most interesting, nicest, handsomest men I've ever known."

Glenn stopped in mid-bite. "Oh," he said when he had swallowed a chunk of burger. "Well . . . Gee."

"I'm sorry if that embarrasses you, but recently I find I'm of a mind to say these things. Sometimes when you stand near me I shake inside I want so bad to hold you."

Again Glenn stopped with his mouth full, and then after a moment swallowed with a gulp. "Oh," he said. "Gee . . . I'm sorry."

"I like feeling this way."

"Yeah, but . . . I mean, I appreciate, you know, you being honest with me and that, but, I mean, I'm straight."

"That's OK. I forgive you."

They ate a moment in silence.

"So are you and Theresa going away somewhere next week?"

"Hmn?"

"Grace said you were taking some vacation time."

"Oh. No. I'm not going away anywhere. Really." Glenn frowned and continued to eat. He stopped and seemed to weigh something. He looked up at Eric again.

"Actually," he said, "I'm going into the hospital."

"The hospital?" Eric stopped eating.

"Yes."

"What's wrong?"

Glenn chuckled embarrassedly. "I'm getting...I'm getting a breast implant," he said quietly, and looked from side to side.

"Huh?"

"You'll probably think it's stupid."

"Stupid?"

"I was born with this thing," Glenn said, "where some of the muscle on one half of my chest was missing." He gestured vaguely toward his torso.

"What?"

"The major pectoral muscle on my right side never grew. It's called a Poland Anomaly. Because it was first discovered in Poland."

Eric felt as if he needed a translator, so completely was the underpinning of the conversation shifting. Had the lights dimmed? He realized that he was staring at Glenn's chest.

"Most people don't even notice it," Glenn said, "but it's always bothered me. I mean, like, I *never* take my shirt off in public, for example. I'm just too self-conscious. And guys in gym class were fond of pointing it out." He took a sip from his water glass. "Theresa thinks I'm crazy to be doing it," he said. "My friend Theo says he thinks a slight... imperfection like that just makes someone more... attractive, whatever."

"I don't understand," Eric said. He was still not absorbing this properly.

"You never noticed, I suppose."

"No. Not at all."

"Well," Glenn said with an air of finality. "Now it's all you'll see."

Eric left the next morning on a trip to Head Office in Toronto, following which he had decided to take some time off and fly out to Vancouver for a few days. He hadn't been back in almost two years.

His stay in Toronto was typically uneventful. He tried to stay alert through Jane Frost's excited talk of the coming Christmas ("Ta da!" she said and brought out the elves she reconceived every year), but he was reminded more than ever of the passage of time, and he began to wonder how long he would keep this job. Paul had mentioned something about a friend of his opening his own bookstore upstate, and Eric made a mental note to call him about it when he returned to the city.

On the plane to Vancouver, he began to daydream about moving back there, leaving New York behind him for good, returning to the simpler life he had so impetuously abandoned as a youth.

But he hadn't seen Vancouver in a while. Even when he'd been out for Christmas in 1985, he'd spent all his time in North Van with his family, hiding out it now seemed.

He stayed with his parents again this trip, but he found himself softening toward them.

For a long time, his mother had attempted frequently to bring up the subject of Eric's back operation, with a strange nostalgia in her voice, as if she were remembering a family camping trip. A younger Eric had thought that she got some charge out of remembering him in such a diminished, infantalized state, and it would enrage him the way she'd keep trying to sneak the subject into conversation, particularly if she was getting sloppy late in the evening.

His father had always approached the memory as he approached everything: with a storyteller's instinct for theme, for tying up loose ends; they had all grown from the experience, it had brought them together as a family. Eric had always felt diminished by this sweeping, happy generalization of an experience that had traumatized him with such specificity.

But suddenly, one night this trip, without his even remembering how they got there, he found himself listening to his parents tell the story of what they'd done the night of his operation.

"Dr. Hodges had told us he would call when they were through," Eric's mother said. "He'd also said the operation would take five hours. God, that was a wait! And then he didn't call. I think we started hoping to get the call about a half hour before he'd said they'd be done. But he didn't call. He didn't call and he didn't call and he didn't call. And then you went to Mac's, remember, Jack?"

"Yeah, because we thought for sure he'd call then."

"Your dad went out to buy some milk and things we needed, and sure enough, he wasn't out the door more than two minutes and the phone rang. And I'll never forget that voice, I'll never forget that voice telling me that you were all right, that you had come through it fine.

"You were in the recovery room when we got there. On that terrible Foster Frame. Oh, Eric, to see you in that giant room, tied to that bloody thing, all the way at the other end of the room! You weren't allowed to eat or drink anything, but you could suck on ice cubes, they let me feed you ice. Do you remember?"

No, he didn't. And he'd never heard her describe it so vividly before. He'd never let her.

That night, drifting to sleep in the bedroom of his youth, he thought suddenly of what his mother had feared that night so many years ago: that something would go wrong, that the doctor would call and say that Eric had died. And he was plunged suddenly into the horror of it, how the whole family would have been shaped from then on by the disaster of his death, instead of having been to some degree shaped as they had, by his recovery, his growth to adulthood.

Closer to sleep he found himself standing in the doorway of the room and looking at a hospital bed in the middle of it, where a teenage boy slept, his long blond hair splayed out on the pillow beneath him, his one arm thrown to the side, the other resting across his pajama top, which covered a plaster cast.

Eric entered the room and knelt quietly by the side of the bed. The boy's breathing hesitated a moment and his forehead creased, but then a steadier rhythm returned. And Eric reached a hand out and touched his brow.

This is me, he thought, for the first time. I was, I am, this boy.

He climbed into the bed beside the boy, who stirred only slightly. He curled his knees up and turned his face to the boy's soft hair and smooth face. He rested his head against one arm and with the other he circled the hard plaster atop the boy's chest.

He closed his eyes and slept.

He went into the city more often this trip, and discovered that it had changed dramatically. Expo '86 had given Vancouver international publicity the previous year, and an influx of people it had never known before. The population had been growing steadily for years anyway.

A rapid transit system had been built in time for the exhibition, a much cleaner system than New York's, computer-operated, most of it elevated (the "SkyTrain") and filling the air with an odd whine, which seemed to follow Eric about, and to symbolize the strangeness the city now exuded for him.

There were many new buildings in the downtown skyline; a giant stadium had been built on False Creek. His old neighborhood, the

West End, was virtually unrecognizable. He counted two business establishments on Robson Street that had been there when he lived in the area; the rest were all new and very flashy. "It's the Upper West Side of Vancouver," he overheard someone say.

When Eric was a kid, if he wanted to see a copy of the *New York Times*, he had to make a special trip overtown to the international newsstand in the Hotel Vancouver, where you could get the Sunday edition several days late for about five times the local price. Now the daily edition was sold routinely throughout the city. On Robson a bookstore was called the Manhattan Book Co.; the theme of the windows at the Bay was "On Broadway"; and from a bus, Eric glimpsed the hoarding around a half-built condominium complex and saw repeated all along it the image of a giant Statue of Liberty. It was as if the whole city had caught the disease of discontent he had thought was only his own youthful folly.

The Garth was still standing, and Eric wandered down the alley behind the building to have a look up at the window of his old apartment. Someone had hung a birdcage there.

He was filled with a stunning nostalgia. When he was younger, he had found it strange that people approaching thirty became so moody and unpredictable.

He wandered down to English Bay. He had lost touch with everyone he'd known in the city and would have been a little frightened just then to run into any of them. But still he wished perversely to see Thomas Stroud.

Maybe not really, not now, not at age twenty-eight. He wanted to see eighteen-year-old Thomas again. He wanted to breathe the air of first love that had blown off the bay in 1977, to have hope in this city again instead of feeling like a tourist, whose whole life seemed to have boarded a jet plane, when once it had appeared to stand still.

On the last evening of his stay he dropped by for a drink at the Gandydancer. Walking toward False Creek, past the silent, night-enshrouded warehouses, hearing the familiar beat grow louder as he neared the club, he thought at least some things don't change. But immediately upon entering the place, he was all but thrust onto a dance floor—crowded with men and women.

After a moment's apprehension he figured out that the place was still gay, but now women were admitted, which Eric could agree with politically but which still disappointed him somehow.

The bar had been moved to the back; the bookshelves were long gone. But what most amazed Eric as he looked around the Gandy-dancer was how young the men were.

He hadn't been inside a gay bar of any kind, to stay, for a long time. In his own days of Gandy glory, he had rejected many young admirers in pursuit of the older, mustachioed men he held out for then; around thirty-five he used to think was just about right. Now, standing there at twenty-eight, working on his second beer, and noticing that a few of the young men were flirting with him, he finally understood the fear he used to see flickering in the older men's eyes when he'd approach them, the insecurity, the look that, whatever the outward appearance, at some level seemed to say, "*You* want to go to bed with *me?*"

He finished a second beer and then staggered out, as he had many nights years before, through the tall double doors onto Hamilton Street, where he weaved a path uphill, away from the water and toward some sort of bright light ahead.

As he neared the light, he saw that an intersection had been cordoned off and that a number of people were standing around near a couple of truckloads of what appeared to be television equipment. As Eric drew closer he saw that a man in the group was wearing a baseball jacket across the back of which was bannered "21 Jump Street."

"Bloody hell," Eric muttered drunkenly when he tripped over a sound cable and all but fell against one of the technicians. "Thomas Wolfe was right."

On the plane east he felt freed of something, a sense of home being someplace off there in the distance to be reclaimed. All you ever had were your memories and they were portable—you could carry home around with you wherever you happened to be, even New York City.

He ordered a vodka tonic on the plane from Toronto and leaned his chair back to look at the black night.

When Eric had next seen Glenn, in the bookstore, in his white shirt and snazzy tie, he had been dumbfounded to see how his eyes had deceived him, how far from reality it was actually possible to live without knowing it.

The physical abnormality that seemed to preoccupy Glenn was of no ultimate consequence in the sense that he was still an incredibly handsome young man, but what amazed Eric was that when you looked, it was certainly there to be seen, especially when he turned profile or a deep breath filled out his work shirt—as if the bottom half of the left side of his chest were missing—and yet Eric had absolutely not seen it. He had looked at Glenn and seen a perfect body, and he had put himself at great distance from this perfection, even though in actual fact, it wasn't even there. Far from being distanced from this body, Eric was almost organically related to it. His back was imbalanced on the opposite side to Glenn's front; only if you put the two of them together could you get anything approaching perfection.

And Eric realized that he had done this thing, this distancing from other people, his whole life. He had blamed it on many things—his parents, his gayness, his scoliosis, the men he fell in love with, other people's neuroses—but suddenly he began to wonder if he didn't have more choice in the matter.

There was virtually nothing Eric could do in public without concern over what other people would think. Checking for oncoming traffic when crossing a street, ordering a sandwich in a deli, taking a walk in the park, removing his jacket in a restaurant—*everything* was self-conscious. And he suddenly saw to the heart of this shyness and realized it rested on the fundamental assumption that he was different from other people, and that he had fed this sense of difference over the years, with his intelligence and sensitivity, instead of using those same qualities to try to transcend it.

Looking about the airplane, he saw people in a strikingly new light. Rather than noticing how different from them he was, he grasped for the first time their common humanity—and the comfort of it, the joy.

At LaGuardia, waiting for his bag to appear on the carousel, he remembered his dinner conversation with Glenn, and the immediacy of what Glenn had said hit him with a kind of aftershock: He was planning to have surgery, surgery Eric hadn't even known existed for men, to make himself... what? More perfect, more like everybody else. And this operation struck Eric suddenly as a kind of terrible sacrilege, which he absolutely had to stop Glenn from committing.

How could he have not said anything? he thought frantically as the taxi sped along the empty late-night streets. How could he have let this happen?

He didn't even know Glenn's phone number, and it wasn't listed, so he had to toss and turn till morning, and then at the bookstore he was greeted with something that still seemed to be sleep-induced, a nightmare. Grace said, "He's gone to the hospital."

"What?" Eric yelled.

"Yeah, he went last week, too. The same one Dale was in."

"This is horrible!"

In Admitting, they didn't have any information on Glenn in their computer, but behind the woman Eric was speaking to a younger woman turned, and with a slightly goo-goo-eyed expression, said, "He's that guy who asked you for the sixth floor about an hour ago, remember?"

The older woman at the counter didn't seem to know what the younger woman was talking about, but Eric had heard all he needed to know. An hour, he thought. There may still be time!

On the sixth floor, when he asked about Glenn, the woman at the reception desk thought a moment and then said, "Oh yeah. He's in six-twelve. Are you with him?"

"With him?" Eric asked and then remembered how Byzantine visiting regulations could be. "Of course. Yes. I'm with him." And he raced to room 612, feeling more and more trancelike in his motions, as if the weight of the night, the year, maybe his whole life, were in his every step, however swift.

He threw open the door to the room and was greeted by startled expressions on two faces: the man in the bed by the door, who was probably about thirty-five but whose face had been ravaged by AIDS, and the young man who sat beside the bed reading to him.

"Hi, Eric," Glenn said.

Eric stood frozen in the doorway, trying to get his bearings. "I thought . . . ," he finally muttered. "I thought you were the patient."

"Oh," Glenn said, looking puzzled for a moment. "Oh," he repeated as he seemed to figure out Eric's mistake. "Theresa talked me out of it."

"Oh," Eric said. "Good. Good for Theresa."

"Why don't you hang around," Glenn suggested, "and when I'm done here we'll get a cup of coffee?"

"Great. Fine. Yes. All right. I'll meet you out front." Eric nodded to Glenn, and then to the man in the bed, who still looked a little stunned, and then he left the room.

Outside, still feeling a bit dizzy, he sat on a stoop around the corner, from where he could watch the entrance to the hospital. It was chilly in the shade of the cross street, so he sat with his hands in the pockets of his raincoat, watching the door as well as the traffic and the crowds of people moving by in the bright morning sunshine on the avenue.

When he saw Glenn emerge from the hospital, Eric started toward him, and as he walked into the light, he pulled his hands from his pockets, and with them the ragtag collection of objects he'd stuffed there. He looked down momentarily from the richness of Glenn's breeze-blown figure, more handsome than ever he thought, and examined the contents of his hands.

There was a pill in his left hand, a white banded-blue AZT capsule, and a receipt from Frank's deli, for two coffees. And in his right hand there was the back half of a matchbook, from a gay bar, emblazoned with a lightning bolt, and the telephone number of a man with red hair.

chapter twenty-five

"I'm sorry," Eric said.

He turned away, to face the unfamiliar ceiling of Brian's apartment.

"What's wrong?" Brian asked.

"I don't know. I guess it's been longer than I thought."

"No— I mean, why are you apologizing?" Brian rested his curly red head against Eric's shoulder. He ran his hand along Eric's chest and rolled a nipple gently between two fingers.

"I thought you were getting impatient," Eric said.

"Not particularly."

"Sometimes it's hard for me to come the first time I'm with someone. But it's OK. I mean, I have a good time anyway."

Brian propped himself up on an elbow and looked at Eric.

"What?" Eric asked.

Brian pushed the hair back slightly from Eric's forehead and bent to kiss him on the lips. With his other hand, he reached for Eric's cock. Any pleasure Eric felt in the touch was eclipsed by his concern that the effort was now beginning again: to get him to come. A cold rigidity entered his body, from the head down.

Brian stopped and scrunched down in the bed to place his mouth on Eric's cock. The warmth and wetness and the affection of the motion only filled Eric with a sense of guilt and inadequacy. Brian had eased Eric down to his own cock earlier and Eric had blown him, he didn't think very well, and certainly without much enthusiasm, since this was an act he'd always felt a certain repugnance to.

The farther away from the person he could get, the more he enjoyed sex.

Brian was working hard. Finally, Eric reached down and pulled his head back. Eric's cock was beginning to feel slightly raw.

Brian looked up with a contented grin on his face.

He's faking that, Eric thought. He's impatient. He had come himself earlier, with Eric giving him what he thought was a misguided handjob. Brian had moved into it pleasurably, though, undulating his hard, skinny body and pulling Eric's mouth down to kiss him. Eric was sure all Brian wanted to do now was go to sleep.

"It's OK," Eric repeated. "I don't need to come."

"I don't think this is going to work," Eric said, and a familiar fatigue and disgust filled him.

With a lubricated finger, Brian massaged Eric's asshole. The sharp tenderness of the physical sensation made Eric want to run. He broke out in a sweat waiting for Brian to give up.

Brian popped his finger inside Eric.

"No— Please don't," Eric said, and hated the pissy tone in his voice.

He had been very surprised when Brian called and asked for a second date. After the movie, Brian suggested they go to Eric's place, that maybe Eric would be more comfortable there, and Eric had agreed with some degree of hope, but also a feeling of shame and rage that he had to be taken care of in this way.

Watching Brian earlier in the restaurant, particularly when he talked about his life—his job in a framing shop, the classes he was taking toward becoming a graphic artist, his family in Delaware— Eric had certainly wanted him, had wanted to pull Brian's white T-shirt over his head and yank down his pale blue jeans then and there, loose his curly red hair from its pink ribbon, and swing his freckled nude body onto Eric's lap, redheaded cock slapping friendly and happy as they eased into a kiss.

But now, back at Eric's apartment, in bed, it was the same old same old. And if anything, being in his own place made it worse. He kept thinking he heard neighbors in the hallway, and Simone eyed him suspiciously from her cushions on the floor.

"You do me, then," Brian said. He caressed Eric's balls and slipped his tongue between Eric's teeth.

It had been so long since Eric had been with anybody that the mechanics of safe sex were still foreign to him. In preparation for his initial date with Brian, he had bought his first ever box of condoms, and practiced to be able to put one on and take it off with the ease of a pro. Now the mask of experience had been so completely shattered it hardly seemed to matter how skillfully he did it.

He entered Brian like slipping into warm butter and again marveled at the easy availability of this man, the relish with which he gave himself physically. Eric could have wept with envy.

In the night Brian snored. And seemed to take up too much space in the bed. Eric sat up tired and annoyed and yanked the blankets his way. The smell of Brian's breath irritated him as well, and the rhythm of it threw off his own. It lacked the Downy pillowcase scent and soft deadness of the fantasy lover he'd curled against for years.

"Let's just start slow," Brian said.

"But you've come already," Eric said. "You don't want to do this. It's OK. Really. I had a good time anyway."

Brian held Eric's balls and stretched out beside him. He was considerably shorter than Eric, and Eric thought his legs looked cute turned against him, as Brian scooted up to give Eric a kiss. With his free hand he stroked the hair back from Eric's forehead.

"I think," Brian said, "that you need to explore your definition of 'good time.'"

"Huh?"

"Now, just don't get caught up in the idea that this is work, OK? I *enjoy* this. I *enjoy* being with you." He looked at Eric with a funny intense gleam in his wide eyes. "Even though I've already come," he added, mimicking Eric. "I know it seems radical to you, but it is possible to come more than once in a night. It is not absolutely necessary to roll over and go to sleep the moment you're done."

Eric smiled half-heartedly.

Brian reached for the tube of KY at the side of the bed and lubricated his finger.

"Here," Brian said and placed Eric's hand over his own cock. "Do the thing you most enjoy."

"It's boring. I'm boring."

"I like to watch you."

Eric turned to him.

"I do. I like to watch you enjoy yourself." He brought his hand down between Eric's legs. "You do the thing that's totally familiar to you, and just do it for as long as you like, and then, while you're doing it, we'll introduce a new element," he held up his lubricated finger, "and maybe," he said and kissed Eric on the lips, "just maybe you'll find you sort of like it, too."

He pulled back, but Eric had already begun to work his cock, and freed to do that, and with less guilt than he'd felt doing it in years, he looked up into Brian's eyes and a surge of gratitude welled within him, so that he grabbed Brian around the neck and forced his mouth back onto his own.

But he still didn't want Brian's finger down there. The moment Brian entered him he became distracted and self-conscious. He remembered that when he'd withdrawn from Brian the last time there'd been shit on the end of the condom. It's not natural to mix these two elements, he thought. I can't be alone in finding this whole thing somewhat off-putting. Why is it necessary? I'm perfectly happy just jerking off.

"What's wrong?" Brian asked.

He pulled Eric's flaccid cock from his hand. He took his finger out of Eric's asshole. Eric immediately grabbed two tissues from the Kleenex box by his bed and handed them to Brian.

"Oh, thanks," Brian said casually. He wiped his fingers perfunctorily and dropped the tissues on the floor.

He scrunched down in the bed and put his head between Eric's legs. Here we go, Eric thought, and Brian began to lick his balls, and then to move up to his cock, which was still limp.

The engulfing sensation only made Eric wonder at the logic of this action others seemed to find so irresistible. Again, he thought, Why would you expect the mouth to serve this function? Kissing was one thing, but this was substituting the mouth for . . . what? It occurred to him suddenly that no aspect of gay sex had ever seemed quite natural to him. When he asked the question where a cock should be put, the only answer that sat absolutely right with him was: a vagina.

Brian pulled up and shook Eric's limp cock again. "What are you stewing about up there?"

"I'm sleepy," Eric said.

As Brian slid to rest turned sideways toward him, Eric recognized a certain smugness in his attitude with Brian. To lie there so unresponsive as this man worked so hard to bring him pleasure had a strange feeling of command about it, because even though Eric had brought Brian to orgasm earlier, as he had every time they'd been together, this that he was withholding now, his own pleasure, seemed more highly prized.

Brian rolled to his back and sighed.

"But it isn't my birthday," Eric said and took the gift-wrapped package from Brian.

"I know. But I bought you a little present anyway. Open it."

They were back at Brian's place, a dark railroad apartment in the theater district.

Eric slid a long box from the wrapping paper.

"I found the box myself," Brian said. "I bought a rolling pin in it."

Eric lifted the lid from the box and saw resting inside a long, flesh-colored and extremely realistic replica of a penis.

"It's so you can practice," Brian said. "When you're by yourself."

Eric's heart sank. He wished, as he always had, that he could get into this sense of sexual play that all gay men seemed so preoccupied by, to find things like this hot and fun and all that other wonderful stuff, but he didn't. He found it all too overt and tacky and laughable. He was sure that all of this was written on his face.

But then he really heard what Brian had said.

"Practice?" he asked.

This Eric hadn't thought of. He had assumed it was Brian's intention to add this toy to their shared sex life, yet another gimmick, another effort, another step removed from what came natural to him.

Brian sat next to Eric on his musty couch. "Your anus," he said, "is an extremely erogenous zone." Eric looked at him. "Why do you think I like it so much when you fuck me? But when you're not used to it, having something up there just feels real uncomfortable and strange. So what you do is, when you're jacking off, you use this," he took the dildo out of the box, "and play with it back there."

"But it's huge."

"It's medium-size." He leaned forward and nibbled on Eric's ear. "Start with your finger," he whispered. "Then try two, and three. Work your way up."

It was all chop suey to Eric, but he smiled and thanked Brian for his gift.

Alone in his apartment a few days later, Eric was jerking off before bed, his mind, as it so often was during this act, on a fairly abstract fantasy: one of his tormentors from high school, naked after P.E. class, trying desperately to cover himself while Eric ushered in every attractive girl in the school.

Just before he came, however, Eric sensed another presence in the locker room, pulling him away to a sweeter place in the mind: Brian, who said sex could make you laugh. And with this new presence in his thoughts, without quite realizing what he was doing, Eric found himself reaching back and touching his asshole with a finger.

"You're getting downright sloppy back here, you slut," Brian said, as he eased the dildo a little farther into Eric, who worked his cock with his own hand.

It felt different when Brian did it. The first time Eric jerked off alone with the dildo, he had panicked afterward when he saw that he had bled all over the towel he'd laid neatly on his bed. He'd thought of infection and death, mess and failure; he couldn't imagine ever trying again. But he had, and discovered to his surprise that he soon stopped bleeding. The past few times, in fact, had been wonderful. But now, with the dildo under the control of someone else, he had the old feeling of impossibility again; the pleasure/discomfort ratio was out of balance and he was worried about the specter of blood, and certain he wasn't going to come.

After a while he stopped. And then he immediately wanted the dildo out of him.

Instead of removing it, Brian reached forward and took Eric's cock in his own hand.

"No," Eric said. "Please don't. Nothing's going to happen. I promise you. Take it out of me, OK?"

Brian carefully removed the dildo, with a slight sucking sound. He took it to the bathroom to rinse it, then padded back to the bed. Eric turned slightly away from him, a familiar agitation simmering inside him.

Brian set the dildo on the floor and lay down on the bed behind Eric. He put one arm up over the top of Eric's head and curled the other around his chest.

He reached down and took hold of Eric's cock.

"Why are you doing this anyway?" Eric asked.

"You fascinate me," Brian said.

"What? Am I some kind of experiment?"

"No. You know it's more than that. Haven't you been having a good time? I have such a good time with you."

"You're almost seven years younger than me."

"So?"

Eric sighed. "I should be the teacher."

"Life is full of surprises."

He ran his hand up and down Eric's nude body. He nibbled on an ear. Eric was hard again and Brian took hold of his cock around the shaft and moved it with a tight fist.

"Tell me what you want," he said. "Tell me if it's too fast, or too slow, or too tight or whatever. Or am I even holding it right?"

"It's hopeless," Eric said.

"Which is more sensitive? The shaft or the head?"

Eric took a breath. "That feels good," he said. "What you're doing now."

"OK, then—"

"Only a little slower," Eric interrupted, and Brian slowed down. "And . . . say things in my ear."

"Like this?" Brian whispered, and for a second Eric felt something, something he hadn't felt with anyone before, begin to break down there.

"Maybe . . . move your hand, like turn it a little this way." Eric gestured with his hand.

"Show me," Brian said. "Remind me of how you do it."

Eric took hold of his cock and pumped, while Brian played with a nipple and snuck his tongue ever so precisely inside Eric's ear.

"I see," Brian said. "OK. Let me." And he took hold of Eric's cock again, but this time with his hand rotated at a slightly different angle.

"Yes," Eric said with intensity, and again this something shifted down there, this cracking, this willingness. What are you afraid of? it seemed to ask.

"It feels like it's getting pretty close," Eric said.

"How's the speed?" Brian asked.

"Maybe just a little slower, and . . . keep on with my tit there, and don't stop . . . whispering to me."

Brian slowed his hand ever so slightly and slipped in closer to Eric. "You're beautiful," he said in his ear. And the feeling continued to hover, the feeling that this could almost finally happen.

But it didn't. Up, up, up Eric's breathing would go, only to plateau just short of release. And having seemed to get so close only made the sense of failure more intense.

Finally he reached down and touched Brian's hand. He had to almost grab it to make him stop.

"I'm sorry," Eric said.

"Don't give up," Brian said with intensity. "Don't give up this time. Just rest a bit."

Eric lay there, without closing his eyes. Brian flexed his fingers. The sheets had fallen to the floor. The radiator hissed.

Brian took hold of Eric's cock again.

At first Eric sighed and wished for Brian to stop, but as his cock grew hard again, and Brian once again played with his nipple and whispered, "I love doing this," Eric was surprised to find that the feeling returned, the feeling of possibility, even stronger.

Up, up, up he went and then hovered there, at the crest of this unfolding, almost as if his breath would be cut off if he didn't release it, but he couldn't, and then the frustration would pull in in a wave, but Brian wouldn't stop, and up, up, up Eric would go again, to hover there, while his mind jumped in with thoughts like *Even if you finally come, it's taken too long*—and down he'd plunge.

It was the most amazing thing to have these feelings controlled to some extent by another person. Beyond the frustration and failure beat the wings of a blissful freedom, and a binding to this diligent man.

He heard Brian reach for something with his free hand, but he was on his way up to the peak just then, lost in the hope. Both their bodies slipped and smelled now with sweat. Eric could feel his hair plastered to his forehead, and his eyes were rolling back in his head.

Brian held his free hand in the air to bring the lubricant to room temperature, then scrunched down more comfortably and continued to work Eric's cock, to drive him up the crest again, the road map the music of Eric's rising breath.

And when he sensed Eric teetering on that brink again, he eased his finger into his asshole, and Eric cried "Yes!" in a voice neither of them had heard before.

He began to play with his own nipple now and to writhe back on the bed, thrusting his buttocks toward Brian's finger and stretching out his arm to hover near Brian's shoulder and head, unable to quite reach him. "Oh, yes, yes, yes."

But still he got to the edge and began to think those destructive thoughts: *It won't happen. It's never going to happen.* And instead of going through the wall, he just pounded and pounded on it, so that the acute pleasure, strung out like that instead of moving forward, became almost like pain, and he sank down again. He pulled his hand away from his nipple; his other arm fell to the bed; he turned his head away.

Brian leaned in closer and whispered, "We have all the time in the world, my sweet beautiful man."

And up again Eric began to go, moved by the physical sensations but also by something that seemed both more exotic and so familiar he wanted to laugh: affection, genuine regard.

Again Brian slowed a little and reached behind him for something. Working his own nipple with one free hand and reaching forward again with the other, Eric whispered, "Don't stop, don't stop."

Brian ripped open the condom package with his teeth and slapped the lubricated sheath over his own erect cock. Eric was barely aware of what was happening.

Brian's finger was in him again, moving this time, and the loss of control had begun to seem the most delicious thing.

And then the finger was out and Brian was pressing against Eric with his cock, a move which in the past had always shut Eric down completely. Now, however, without thinking about it, he thrust back hungrily; for the first time in his life he realized that something down there wanted a cock, had hungered for it for years.

And his mouth, too. His fret for years about blowjob mechanics dissolved in the discovery of this desire to be filled. It came to him in a flash: You don't suck a man's cock just to please *him*; you do it because your lips and your tongue and the back of your throat crave it.

Brian continued to pump Eric's cock at what seemed almost the perfect speed and pressure, but it was really more that these things no longer mattered—in fact, the pleasure now was in not knowing the rhythm, being taken somewhere new.

He kissed Eric's ear; he licked him there and whispered, "You're fantastic," until finally the head of his cock popped in and Eric winced, and then gasped as the shaft slipped partway up.

Brian kept up the rhythm in front, and began ever so slowly to move in Eric, and then to slow the movement on Eric's cock, so that the two rhythms became one, and as he did so Eric was filled with a rapid progression from pain and tight fear to something else, an exquisiteness he'd never known. He began to cry.

The ripples traveling through his body, the closeness of this man, and his acceptance of Eric, of his problematic self, seemed to bind them in something so sublime Eric did not know how anyone could survive it.

And the trip up, up, up was lighter this time, filled with a kind of laughter. And the arrival, when it finally came, had the solidity of real achievement about it; nothing hesitant, no need for it—just this quintessential human experience, this piece of God.

"Oh . . . my . . . god!" he cried. "Oh my god! Oh my god!"

His body arced back powerfully and his butt muscles pulsed around Brian's cock. And he screamed: "Aaaaaaaaaaaahhhhhhhh! Aaaaaaaaaaaahhhhhhhh!" And then spun down into tears and laughter, which Brian joined, licking his ear and sweeping his cum-covered hand up Eric's body.

He moved the hand past a nipple to his mouth and licked his fingers, as his eyes eased shut on a deep breath. And Eric, turning in the bed and opening one eye, watched Brian do this, feed himself this piece of Eric, and for the first time in his life, he did not have to ask why.

It amazed Eric how much it relaxed him to realize that other people were not that different from him. He had lived for so long with a crippling anxiety that he had only been able to put his

energy into managing it; it had never occurred to him that it could
be lifted.

It surprised him how soothing this was, to see himself as part of
a larger human picture, to recognize a kinship. It allowed him to say
hello to neighbors in the hall without even thinking about it, to talk
spontaneously to strangers, to hold doors for them, and to relax into
an energy he had been holding back for almost thirty years.

And as he made his way through these new days he thought often
of Brian, but also of what had led to him, the year with Dale, and he
knew that it was in part this death and dying that had allowed him
finally to live.

Eric realized that, in a strange way, even before he became so
sick, Dale had taught him. His methods may have been barbed and
mostly unconscious, but he had picked and prodded at Eric's veneer,
and he had steered him toward love.

Eric believed that he must now be going through something of
the rebirth his mother had experienced, first when she met his father,
and then later with the death of her own mother. Despite the best
liberal intentions, his parents seemed in the end to have passed on
only their own scenario, to be replayed, rewritten, relearned.

In Brian's arms Eric felt a new wisdom in his body, its ability to
connect with another inviolable, sacrosanct. It was as if he had never
understood before what people were talking about when they talked
about sex.

And he cried sometimes from the wonder, from the sheer release
of it, and he smiled and laughed to breathe free, to rest in the aware-
ness that body, mind, and soul had, finally, begun to move as one.

afterword

I was twenty-six years old when I saw Larry Kramer's *The Normal Heart* shortly after it opened at the Public Theater in 1985. I was stunned by the play: first of all, by its artistry, the dazzling way Kramer wove his AIDS polemic into a riveting dramatic story, and a story of men I felt I knew. I'd been in activist gay groups when I was younger, back in Vancouver, Canada, where I grew up, and all the infighting and passionate, if often ego-driven, arguing and rupturing of friendship in the play rang so true to me. But, of course, in Kramer's world, gay men were dying. And what most stunned me watching the play was the first solid, undeniable, horrible realization landing in my lap that they were dying in my world, too, that he and I lived in the same world, New York City in the 1980s, and AIDS had somehow snuck up and engulfed everything when I was barely looking.

I also thought: If you have any legitimate claim to the label of "writer," you have to try to write about this. It's happening in your own backyard. And so I began work on this novel, which was called *A Friend of Dorothy's* from the beginning, based on an old-time euphemism for being gay. I knew people who were sick, people who had died, but I had been spared the loss of a close friend. That was partly because I didn't have that many friends at the time. My earlier youth had been spent trying to become a happy, healthy, promiscuous homosexual, even though my sudden, what seemed intense popularity, following a high school career of being bullied and ostracized (until my last year, when my "blossoming" started), left me feeling overwhelmed and quite confused by all the attention. And my romantic bent never quite fit with the sex-centric gay male world bursting at the seams around me in the late seventies and early eighties. So I had retreated from all of it, and left quite a bit of the rest of the world behind in the process. Which may have saved my life, but also left me wondering what I could possibly have to say about AIDS, a phenomenon I felt completely impacted by, but, as with so much else in my life then, had observed from a distance.

My main character, Eric, was born when I got the idea to take a character like myself, isolated and handicapped by inhibition, turn up the volume even further on his almost unhealthy desire to fit in, and fear that he never would, and then launch him into the middle of the unfolding disease nightmare. What would he make of it? And what would it make of him?

Reading the novel now, at the age of sixty-five, I'm struck, as I often am by my early work, at the sheer audacity and ambition of it. Who wrote this thing? I want to ask. What was he thinking? But I also see themes and literary derring-do that would be echoed and refined in my later work. And I remember how diligently I toiled over the book, for years, honing and honing and honing. This draft, which would be the final one, was completed in the early nineties, when I was in my early thirties.

And I did that toiling with the help of many others, too many to fully acknowledge here. But I wish to give special mention to a couple. Edward Albee awarded me a fellowship from his foundation based on a short story of mine, and I spent a month working on the book at the Barn in Montauk, where I was lucky enough to get to know Edward. I'm told he liked me because I was always writing. "We wake up in the middle of the night," the German sculptors who were with me at the Barn told him, "and we smell coffee. Richard is working!" The writers had Edward over to hear us read from our work. When I'd finished reading from *Dorothy*, I vividly remember he said, "You do some very interesting things with language in there, are you aware of that?" "Um ... yes," I replied. "And it's also very funny, are you aware of that?" "Yes," I answered more definitively. He then expressed disbelief that I'd never been published and we moved on. And thus began what I like to call a friendship, carried on, mostly in correspondence, until his death.

Another writer I must acknowledge is James Wilcox, whose class I took at the West Side Y in the early nineties, and whom I credit with inspiring this final draft of the book. His class was called something like Details in Fiction, and he gently coaxed us over and over again to stay focused on the throughline of the book, for character and theme, and to pull out the details of that story we might have glossed over. He's the one who made me realize there was a scene missing from the end of the book, and it became the scene people most often talk about.

In 1993 I won a Tennessee Williams Scholarship to attend the Sewanee Writers' Conference and study playwriting with Horton Foote and Wendy Hammond. As part of my prize I got to do a public reading from my work, and I chose to read "White Light," an excerpt from the novel that had been published in *Christopher Street* magazine and in which my character Dale, sick with AIDS in the hospital, regales his friend Eric with tales of the St. Mark's Baths, his vision of what heaven must be like. It was fairly sexually graphic and brought the house down at the University of the South, in a room that was packed because the next speaker on the bill was none other than Arthur Miller, who stared daggers at me as the applause went on and on and was said to ask the person next to him, "Who *is* that young man?"

This all kept me thinking I'd written something of merit, even as no publisher came knocking on my door. Many, many friends also fulfilled that need over the years, giving the manuscript a read and me notes, as well as generously telling me how much it had meant to them. A few of my favorite reactions were one from a straight woman who surprised me by telling me in tears that she absolutely identified with my hero, Eric, and his long journey to fulfillment; an HIV-positive gay man who told me that he admired the novel greatly but had experienced it as "radioactive," feeling the need to leave it in another room when he took a break from reading; and another friend who compared Eric's "Yes!" at the end to Molly Bloom's, and thus, if only indirectly and perhaps inadvertently, compared me to one the greatest of all writers.

A lot has changed since I wrote *A Friend of Dorothy's*. HIV is now a manageable infection, gay men can marry, and we carry computers in our pockets (I wrote the first draft of the novel on a typewriter). And we've seen more and more dramatic challenges come along, in the form of 9/11, the political division surrounding the election of Donald Trump, the Covid pandemic, to name a few. But I can still so vividly remember that first time a catastrophe of this measure visited the life around me. "Gosh, it seems like we just got over polio," my mother said when I first talked to her about AIDS, and I realized even then that this would be my generation's polio, its Vietnam, and perhaps its World War II and Depression rolled into one. But one thing I believe remains the same all these years later in our history, and that I tried to write about in these pages at the time, is that the greatest calamities often call out the better angels of our nature. Much as we may resent it, our character is frequently forged in challenge.

In my play *Triptych*, Heather, mourning the death of her teenage son, says, "The weight of time is suddenly clearer to me. It's not day-to-day anymore. I see the future of things. One day, the clothes we're wearing will be out of fashion, and our furniture, our haircuts. The photographs of Keith we treasure now will fade; the technology behind them will seem antiquated. Dust will blow through these rooms. And his life will be a footnote." Like most people, I eventually came to have a number of friends with HIV and AIDS, and to lose too many of them. One of my goals in publishing this book now is to see that they never become footnotes.

—RICHARD WILLETT
West Hollywood, California, November 2024

about the author

RICHARD WILLETT's short stories have been published in *Christopher Street*, *Hawaii Review*, *American Writing*, *Karamu*, and *Oxalis*, among others, as well as short-listed for New American Library's *Men on Men: Best New Gay Fiction*, edited by David Bergman. His short play about AIDS *Boys Will Be Boys* was included in the anthology *Art & Understanding: Literature from the First Twenty Years of A&U*, and he is also the author of the plays *Triptych*, *Random Harvest*, *The Flid Show*, *Tiny Bubbles*, *9/10*, *A Terminal Event*, and *Grief at High Tide*, presented off-off-Broadway and at theaters across the country. Honors include an Edward F. Albee Foundation Fellowship and a Tennessee Williams Scholarship, designation as a finalist for the Dramatists Guild National Fellows Program and the Sundance Labs, and listing twice in the Academy of Motion Picture Arts and Sciences' Nicholl Top 50. He lives in West Hollywood, California. Visit richardwillettwriter.com.

www.ingramcontent.com/pod-product-compliance
Lightning Source LLC
Chambersburg PA
CBHW020134120726
47903CB00007B/2258